Beyond the Horizon

Beyond the Horizon

Elena Goudelias

Spring Creek Publishing

First Printing, 2021

To Brooklyn, who will always be my Bluebell.

One

As I crossed the soft pasture, I still felt the ghost of cool concrete below my feet. I stepped carefully between overgrown blades of grass, noticing how they sprung up with new life after being baptized by last night's rain. The lingering droplets that kissed the tips of the grass were the only sign that it had rained at all. Now, the sun hung lazily in the sky, nudging the peaceful countryside awake with its soft, golden glow.

This kind of serene beauty had no place in the restless city I'd called home for the first twenty years of my life. The continuous rhythm of sirens and car horns was etched into the fabric of the city, leaving no room for silence that lasted more than a fleeting moment.

I dug the toe of my boot into the dewy soil, trying to ground myself in the vast stretch of sky above me, in the russet barn beside the farmhouse, and in the undulating hills in the distance. That other life didn't matter anymore. I'd left it behind fifteen years ago to embrace everything I was looking at now. To remind myself I was still alive.

A gentle hand rested on my shoulder, exposing its tenseness. I turned to find my husband standing behind me. His sandy-brown hair was lightly tousled by the wind, and his light-brown eyes took on a hazel tint in the sunlight. As my eyes rested on his placid face, the weight of my past melted away, if only for a moment.

"Turned out to be a beautiful morning, Nora," he said in his gentle way of prying me free from the past. "It's not every day that it hits the fifties in January. We should take the cows out so they can enjoy it too."

Tyler and I had shared the same life for twelve years, but we came from two different worlds. A fourth-generation dairy farmer, Tyler had grown up on the same Iowa farm where we lived now. I was the native New Yorker who had traded concrete and skyscrapers for cows and rolling pastures. I always marveled at how different our lives had been when we first met: his, a steady rhythm of milking cows and hauling hay; and mine, a permanent ride on the expressway, weaving in and out of lanes as I tried to find a place where I belonged.

As I started to follow him into the barn, the farmhouse door swung open. I turned and saw our eight-year-old daughter leap in my direction, a bundle of boundless energy. Bridget's second semester of third grade was just beginning, and she was determined to finish off the year strong.

"What do you think of this, Mommy?" She gestured to her mint-green T-shirt, which was emblazoned with a glittery star.

I smiled. Even though it had been years since I'd picked up a fashion magazine, Bridget still sought out my fashion advice whenever she could. "It's perfect, honey. It looks great with your new sneakers."

Her face lit up at my approval. "I can't wait to show them to everyone at school." The herd of cows that Tyler had just released onto the pasture stole her attention, and she darted toward the animals without another word.

Bridget had made the farm her home from the moment she was born. The gentleness in her demeanor when caring for the cattle convinced me she was destined to become a veterinarian, if not a farmer herself. "She got that from you," I always said to Tyler. We both knew farm life had been an adjustment for me. In the beginning, the cows showed resistance to my untrained touch, as if they suspected I was an outsider. Even now, I sensed that I lacked the natural connection Tyler and Bridget had with them.

My gaze drifted up to my son's bedroom window. I didn't even have to step inside his room to know he was still buried under the covers. At ten, Caleb had already skipped ahead to full-on teenagerhood. He did his chores and farmwork in a way that suggested he would rather be doing anything else—probably hanging out with his friends, playing video games, or not being confined to this forgotten town on the fringes of Iowa.

A sigh escaped me as I plodded toward the house. Before I could take another step, he burst through the door, his bag fully packed and his clothes fresh and crisp. "I'm ready," he said, just as I opened my mouth to ask.

I blinked to clear away my confusion like a dense fog. Not a second later, it dissipated. Before winter break, several boys older than Caleb had deemed him cool enough to gain entry into their group. Now that he was one of them, he was embarrassed by anything that suggested he was still a young, dependent child—like his mother having to traipse into his room and force him out of bed.

As I watched him, still a child in my thirty-five-year-old eyes, loss welled up inside me. I wasn't prepared to mourn the death of his innocence until he turned thirteen, at least. Now I felt as if I should've cherished his easy, agreeable nature while it was still there.

I pushed aside the thoughts and gave Caleb an encouraging nudge. "Go help Dad feed the calves if you're ready. We'll leave in a few minutes."

I headed to the outside of the barn, where Tyler was refilling the water troughs with fresh water for the calves. "Need anything from Daryl's?" I asked. We were due for our monthly grocery store visit, and I couldn't leave anything out. The two-hour round trip already swallowed up enough time without having to do it all over again.

"Good thing you asked. We're running low on coffee." Tyler needed coffee like most people needed oxygen.

"Enough said." I updated the shopping list on my phone just as Bridget finished greeting her cow friends. She rushed over to me, her blond pigtails bouncing along with each step. "Can we leave now?"

I laughed. "You're an eager one, aren't you?" Turning to Tyler, I said, "I'd better get going now."

He leaned over to give me a quick kiss. "Drive safe."

My attention shifted to Caleb, whose gaze was locked on the tablet the school had given him, just like all the other fifth graders. "Come on, Caleb. We don't want to be late."

He tore his eyes away from the screen with the same look he used to give the vegetables on his plate when he was little. Wordlessly, he jumped into the pickup truck and shut the door. Bridget followed him into the backseat of the cab as I settled into the driver's seat.

"Are we all set?" I asked. When Bridget nodded her head vigorously, I started the engine and set off toward the school.

As the farmland morphed into an indistinct blur, I began to ease back into my school year routine. Life on a dairy farm was always unpredictable, but something as simple as driving the kids to school and running errands added some much-needed structure to my day. I let myself fall into the rhythm of the familiar while the quiet road carried me to my destination.

Twenty minutes later, the weathered brick building came into view. Bridget unclicked her seatbelt before I even came to a full stop. "Finally! I can't wait to tell everyone what I did over break."

I stopped in front of the main entrance of Fairlane Public School and turned to face both kids. "Enjoy your day, guys."

"We will, Mommy." Bridget leaned over and kissed me on the cheek before leaping out of the truck.

"See you later." The words were barely out of Caleb's mouth before he rushed to join the cluster of kids outside the double doors. As I watched him, I couldn't help but think back to the first time I dropped him off in this exact spot when he started kindergarten. It never failed to amaze me how the kids seemed to have grown up in the blink of an eye.

Once they were safely inside the school, I pulled out of the drop-off lane and headed toward Daryl's Deli & Mini-Mart. The road stretched out lavishly in front of me as I flipped on the radio and turned up the volume. Even though I'd lived in Fairlane for over a decade, I still relished the feeling of driving underneath such a sweeping expanse of sky. Car rides in New York were limited to cramped taxi trips in stop-and-go traffic that made my stomach churn. Here, having the boundless, open road almost entirely to myself was the closest I could come to flying.

I'd wanted my kids to have the idyllic upbringing I'd missed out on growing up in the city. Watching them roam freely across the fields was like gifting the child I used to be with the freedom I'd never been able to enjoy. I knew that every day, they felt the same way I'd felt when I first saw the farm at twenty years old: filled with wonder at the endless beauty waiting outside their doorstep.

After finally passing the sign outside Daryl's, I pulled into the parking lot and shut off the engine. As I entered, I said hi to Kathleen, Daryl's daughter who worked as the cashier. I'd spent the past fifteen years getting to know store owners and their families in Fairlane and the surrounding towns, and each of them had welcomed me as if I were one of their own. It was as if I belonged to an extended family that only existed within the borders of Green Ridge County.

I snaked through the aisles and started to make a dent in my shopping list. I filled my cart with snacks for school, dinner ingredients, and Tyler's coffee. I'd just picked up a canister of White Mountain Morning Brew when the bell on the door jingled. I glanced up, only able to see a few rebellious curls of dark-brown hair from my vantage point. I didn't think anything of it until Kathleen said, "Nice to meet you, ma'am."

My head snapped up. *A newcomer.* For people living in a place as desolate as Green Ridge County, newcomers might as well have been exhibits at the zoo. My curiosity piqued, I slunk over to the cash register, where the mystery woman was chatting up Kathleen. As she turned around to face me, my heart stalled.

"Nora!" she exclaimed, her voice a ringing soprano in the

empty shop. "Well, this is quite the coincidence, don't you think?"

"Jeanette," I managed. Her name felt foreign in my mouth, like I'd tried on an old pair of shoes that no longer fit me. "What brings you here?"

"Oh, I just came for a visit," she said offhandedly, waving a set of manicured nails that matched her black leather jacket.

I struggled to find words. Nobody "came to visit" The Middle of Nowhere, Iowa. They only ended up here if they were lost on the way to some other, more important place. Yet here she was: Jeanette Peterson, in all her leather-clad glory.

"Uh, that's ni — "

"Here, I'll pay for that," she said, without asking if I was finished shopping. She gathered the few items I'd managed to find before her arrival and set them down on the counter.

I opened my mouth to protest, but nothing came out. My system was still trying to process the shock. After a bewildered Kathleen scanned the items, Jeanette paid and swiped the plastic bags from the counter. She flashed a smile at the cashier and made a beeline for the exit while I trailed behind her, in a dreamlike state.

"Which one is yours?" she asked, gesturing to the three trucks parked in front of the store.

I pointed to the rust-red Ford, then she stuffed my groceries into the bed of the truck. Once she'd released her load, she leaned against the truck and turned to face me. For a pregnant moment, Jeanette studied my face while the wind caressed her dark curls. Inevitably, my old high school friend looked older than the teenager I'd known in New York, but the age she showed went deeper than her appearance. There was a wisdom in her eyes, an awareness that cut straight to the bone. She knew something. Something that I'd buried under my consciousness for the last fifteen years. Whatever it was, I knew I wasn't ready to bring it to the surface yet.

She gave me a once-over, her probing blue eyes scanning my flannel top and faded denim jeans. "Your fashion choices have definitely... relaxed since high school."

I tensed up. I knew too well where this was going.

"Do you even want any of this?" Her hand swept across the miles of crops that surrounded us. "Or is this just your idea of running as far as you can from the past?"

I swallowed, refusing to let the sharp edges of her words leave even the slightest trickle of blood in their wake. If my friend was anything like the girl I'd known all those years ago, she was wielding a weapon to protect herself from something else. Something that was hurting her.

As I studied Jeanette, the past fifteen years flashed by me at a dizzying speed. Fifteen years punctuated by one-word texts wedged between endless stretches of silence. Fifteen years of watching our iron bond devolve into a thread that would unravel at a single snip. Fifteen years, and now we were standing face-to-face for the first time since high school. I'd never known what our reunion would look like if it happened, but I hadn't pictured it quite like this.

"You know we haven't seen each other since high school, right?" I said calmly, trying to find my old friend inside her. "And I know you didn't leave your glamorous life in New York just to come for a visit." I searched her eyes to hear what she wasn't telling me. "What's really going on, Jeanette?"

She flashed me her trademark smile, that chillingly perceptive look returning to her eyes. She wasn't about to let her guard down just yet.

"If you went to Grant, you would know exactly why I'm here. There's no telling where the fashion world can take you sometimes." She glanced back at Daryl's, wrinkling her nose as if some putrid scent were emanating from it. "But considering the most fashionable thing in that store was an outdated copy of *Cosmo,* I don't know how much longer I can last in this town."

The mention of Grant had been unavoidable, but that didn't mean I was ready for it. I never would be. Alarm bells went off in some distant part of my mind, warning me to get out of here while I still had the chance. But I knew it was too late. Jeanette only went somewhere when she had a job to do, and she didn't leave until it was finished.

Her question from a moment earlier slunk back into my thoughts: *Do you even want any of this?* I crossed my arms against the chill of her words and looked her in the eye. "You can believe whatever you want, but I'm happy with my choices. Maybe things didn't turn out as planned, but they turned out pretty great." My eyes landed on the winding road outside the store and the acres of farmland that hugged either side of the highway. "This is my town. This is my *home.*"

She gave me a pitiful smile that told me she'd picked up on the quiver in my voice. The confidence I'd tried to grasp had slid right through my fingers like sand.

"Oh, Nora," she said, crossing the parking lot to unlock her car. "We both know it never was."

Two

⚓

Later that afternoon, I drove in complete silence on my way to the school. Of all the people who could have shown up in this one-horse town, the last person I would've predicted was Jeanette. Jeanette, with her larger-than-life personality, New York–bred attitude, and sense of style that would make a top fashion designer jealous.

But the rift between us went deeper than shoes or dresses. Jeanette had something that I couldn't buy from her, that she couldn't even loan me temporarily. She had an entire life. A life that I'd willingly given up while fear had me in its suffocating grasp. A life I hadn't realized I'd missed out on until I watched it unfold perfectly for my friend, without a single crease or seam.

I gripped the steering wheel until my knuckles turned white. The street signs blurred as I blinked back tears. I'd done so well. I'd gotten out of that city as fast as I could. I'd created a new life for myself without anyone's help. Yet as soon as Jeanette stepped foot into that life, she'd made it seem like one big fraud.

Do you even want any of this?

I clicked on the radio and flipped through the stations, only to be met with incoherent static. "Dammit," I muttered. I clicked off the radio and stared at the back of the truck in front of me. There was no escaping my thoughts today.

As I hit a red light, my phone vibrated next to me. I pulled it out of the glove compartment and read the display. My breath caught in my throat. After all these years, could it really be him?

With a hesitant finger, I put the phone on speaker. "Luke?"

"Hey, Nora." Even from a thousand miles away, my older brother's voice transported me back to my childhood. "I hope this isn't a bad time."

"Not at all. How've you been?"

"I was calling to ask about you, actually. How's life on the farm?"

The question caught me off guard. He'd asked it with the closest thing to genuine interest that I'd heard in fifteen years. "The usual," I said, trying to match his casual tone. "The cows need to be milked, no matter what."

He laughed. "No vacation time over there, huh?"

"Nope. Well, it does feel a little more like vacation when the kids go back to school." I paused as I turned onto Oak Hill. "So... how's the city?" I ventured.

"Pretty calm for now. Things always quiet down after the holidays."

"That's true. I haven't forgotten about the holiday madness." I hesitated before wading in a little deeper. "What about Mom and Dad?"

Luke wavered, and that was when I knew he understood. "They're fine."

"Have they asked about me at all?"

After another pause, he answered, "Not directly, but..."

"They hate me, don't they?" I felt childish for saying it, but that didn't make it any less true.

"Come on, Nora. They don't hate you." He struggled to find the right words. "They're just..."

"Disappointed in me."

He took a breath, steadying his tone. "You made a choice. And you know it wasn't what Mom and Dad wanted for you. You can't expect everything to be all sunshine and roses after what you did."

I tried to swallow the lump in my throat, but that only betrayed its presence when I spoke. "I couldn't stay there anymore. You knew that."

"But they didn't. They had no idea until you picked up and left in the middle of your sophomore year of college."

His words pierced right through me. "So that's it, huh? That's the family consensus. That I'm some kind of pariah."

"I didn't—"

"This is the first time we've had a real conversation in—what? Three years? Just admit it. You only called to remind me that I'm still an outsider in my own family."

"You can't blame us for the choices you made. Besides, isn't that what you wanted? If you didn't want us out of your life, why did you leave without warning?"

A small part of me was rooted in the conversation we were having, but the rest of me had drifted off to the life I'd left behind in that small Upper West Side apartment. The life that had stifled me until I had no choice but to fill my lungs with the fresh air of the world beyond it. That was what Luke and my parents would never understand. I hadn't run away from them. I'd run away from everything they'd forced me to become.

I wasn't even thinking straight when I hung up. The cab of the truck suddenly felt too small to hold the baggage I'd been lugging around with me for over a decade. As I shoved my phone back into the glove compartment, I released a weighted breath and focused on the road ahead of me. All that mattered was where I was going. The pavement behind me didn't deserve another second of my attention.

Fairlane Public School emerged a few minutes later, the lively campus dotted with kids in brightly colored backpacks and shiny new sneakers. I pulled into the pickup lane and caught sight of Bridget immediately. She waved and hurried over to my truck, the feather keychain on her backpack flapping in the wind.

"How was your day?" I asked as my daughter slid into the backseat.

While she fed me all the details of her day, it struck me how refreshing it was to hear an eight-year-old ramble on about her routine. Every moment was important to her, from the compliment she received in class to the cookie she was surprised with at lunch. It was saddening to think about how many details had passed me by that day that Bridget would've marveled at.

A moment later, Caleb strode out of the school with his hands stuffed in his pockets. Each step was deliberately drawn out as he approached my truck. He didn't look up from the ground a single time, his attention focused entirely on the stone path that snaked up toward the pickup lane.

I took a deep breath as he opened the door to the backseat. "How did your day go?" I asked, trying to sound as neutral as possible.

He shrugged. "Fine."

I pursed my lips, conflicted. I didn't want to push too hard, but at the same time, I had a right to know what was going on. As a compromise, I changed course. "Do you like your new classes?"

"They're fine."

This was turning out to be a long day. I turned and smiled at him, even though he was staring out the window absently. "Well, let me know if you need help with schoolwork or anything else."

"Fine."

Turning back to the steering wheel, I told myself I'd done what I could. There was no use in pushing him. I remembered the way my mom and dad had tried to squeeze every last drop of information out of me when I started skipping classes in college. I'd had my reasons, just like Caleb did, but I'd only become more reluctant to share them the more my parents demanded to know them.

When I reached the farm, Tyler was already making his way toward the barn for the second milking of the day. Bridget leapt out of the truck like she couldn't get there fast enough. Caleb followed soon after, but not without making a show of dragging his feet toward the barn.

I was the last to shut the truck door behind me. While the kids milked the cows near the front of the barn, I waded deeper into the room and helped Tyler out with the rest of the cattle.

"Hey," he said as I approached. "Did you find everything at the store?"

I tensed up, hoping he didn't notice. "Yeah. I got there pretty quickly too. The roads were quiet today."

He nodded as he hooked up the milking machine to Pearl,

one of our older cows. "Good thing you came back in time. The nutritionist's supposed to swing by any minute now." Every week, a dairy nutritionist visited the farm to analyze the cows' nutrient intake and make sure they were staying healthy.

My mind drifted as I milked Primrose. Part of me wanted to speak up, to tell him what had happened at the grocery store. But a bigger part of me knew it was easier to fall into the rhythm of our daily routine, where the shadows of my past didn't belong.

When they were finished milking, Caleb and Bridget left the barn—Caleb more eagerly than his sister. I watched him disappear into the farmhouse with his eyes glued to his tablet, sending an invisible message to an unknown recipient.

"Have you noticed anything weird about Caleb lately?" I asked Tyler. "He seems upset about something."

He shrugged. "You know how kids are, Nora. Whatever it is, he'll probably be over it by tomorrow."

My gaze lingered on my son as the worry burrowed deeper inside me. "I don't know. This seems different."

Tyler glanced at me. "Are you sure you're not the one who's upset about something?"

My breath hitched in my throat. He'd noticed the whole time. "I'm fine," I insisted.

"Come on, Nora. 'The roads were quiet today'? You know the roads are always quiet around here." His eyes were knowing as they locked with mine. "Something's gotta be up if you're talking about traffic patterns."

I sighed and sat on a bale of hay. "I saw Jeanette at Daryl's."

Tyler sat down next to me, his eyes mirroring the shock I'd

experienced that morning. "Your old high school friend? What has it been? Fifteen years?"

"Since we last saw each other, yeah. And seventeen years since she accepted the offer from Grant."

That day was stored in my mind with as much vivid detail as my most recent memories. As I reflected on it, the woman I'd grown to become stepped back to make room for the girl I used to be. The girl who'd read her acceptance letter from the Grant School of Fashion and Design, one of the country's most prestigious fashion schools, and realized she couldn't do it. The girl who saw phrases like "creative energy" and "exceptional talent" jump out from the laminated paper and saw everything she wasn't. The girl who imagined herself in a room full of visionaries and trendsetters and knew they would find out she was an imposter sooner or later.

I'd been that girl for an excruciating two months while College Decision Day loomed in the distance. Once it arrived, turning down my dream school wasn't the only decision I made. That day, I'd also grabbed fear by the hand while doubt followed closely behind, and together, we'd walked away from the life I'd been working toward since sixth grade.

Looking back, I knew I should've known better. I should've known that Jeanette couldn't bear to see anyone give up such a massive opportunity. That she couldn't help herself when she tossed her own Grant application into the pile, only to hold the same acceptance letter in her hands a week later.

Now, I knew what she'd seen in my mistake. She'd seen all the places that Grant could have taken me, and she'd gone down those roads herself. And as I'd watched her get A's across the board and secure an internship at *Couture* magazine during her junior year, it'd become painfully clear that she was living the life I'd never had the courage to live.

A stretch of silence filled the barn until I said, "I just don't know why she came all the way out here. I mean, we've barely spoken to each other in over ten years."

"Maybe she wants to start over. Try to be a friend to you again."

I paused, amazed by how much weight a single word could hold. In some distant past, we'd definitely been friends. Not just friends, but the secret-swapping, jewelry-sharing, practically-sisters type of friends. What had happened between then and now had blurred the definition of the word, making me question if we could ever return to the way we used to be.

"I wish it weren't so complicated," I said, giving him a sad smile. "But after our senior year, nothing was ever the same between us."

My heart sank as I saw that his eyes didn't hold the understanding I desperately wanted them to. Sometimes I forgot that Tyler had grown up on this land, had done the same job since he'd learned to walk, and still held on to the same group of friends who'd shared his childhood. There were certain things about my past he would never understand, just like there were certain things I wouldn't understand about his.

That reality had always trailed closely behind me like an early-morning shadow, an ever-present echo of my mother's warning to me. "You'll never fit in there, Nora," she'd told me after I moved to Fairlane. "People there live differently than you. You weren't raised to be a farmer like them."

I got up and dusted myself off before I became submerged in my insecurities. I'd managed to keep them tightly wrapped in an unseen part of me for years, and I wasn't about to let them tumble out now. "We should get going. The nutritionist will be here soon."

Tyler followed me out of the barn to meet the specialist. I hardly registered what she told us, my thoughts still in limbo between the past and present. Seeing Jeanette had reminded me that my younger years were never far behind me, despite everything that had changed since then. Trying to outrun them was a futile effort, because they would always catch up to me eventually.

After the nutritionist left, I ducked into my bedroom to have a moment to myself. Realizing I hadn't checked my phone in a while, I whipped it out of my pocket and scrolled through my messages. I had a text from our neighbor confirming Bridget's playdate with her daughter and two voicemails.

I pressed the phone to my ear. The first voicemail had come from a number I vaguely recognized, like it belonged to a memory that I'd stored away for years. My finger hovered over the screen for a moment before I pressed Play.

"Hey! It's me. I think I'm starting to get the hang of this town of yours, but it isn't New York—that's for sure. Maybe you can give me a tour or something? While we're at it, I was hoping we could meet for coffee so I can tell you about the new *Couture* issue I'm working on. I thought of you as soon as my boss gave me the assignment. I know you're busy with farming, but I'm sure we could fit in a quick chat over some mocha Frappuccinos. Those were your favorite in high school, remember? Anyway, let me know what time works for you. See ya!"

While Jeanette's chipper voice bubbled out of the speaker, I stared out the window, knowing I'd been right all along. She'd read me like an open book while we spoke outside of Daryl's, just like she'd seen right through my lie when I told her Grant wasn't right for me anymore. She knew that my ambitious dreams hadn't died in this sleepy town. That in the still of the night, I often lay awake, fantasizing about what could have been.

I sat up straight and held the phone firmly in my hand. She might have been right about my dream, but there was plenty that she was wrong about. I loved the life I'd created in Fairlane, despite her insistence that I'd only settled for it. Everything I had—my loving family, my beautiful home, and the hard work I did to keep the farm alive—was my own achievement. And I wore it proudly like a badge that no one could take away from me.

I called Jeanette's number and waited for her to pick up. While the ringing filled the silence in the room, I thought I detected a shard of hope inside me. So much time had passed between our senior year of high school and the moment we were living in now. Enough time, maybe, for us to find our way back to what we'd once had. Back to a time when we each had our own goals that never competed with each other. Back when we were both on the same side.

Before I could decide what I wanted to say, my thoughts were interrupted by her voicemail greeting. "You've reached Jeanette Peterson, fashion director at *Couture*. I have places to go and people to see, so make it snappy."

After the beep, I drew in a breath. "You wanted snappy, so here goes. I'd love to help you out with your project. Actually, I already have a few ideas in mind. But I can't get too invested in this, okay? I already left Armani and Chanel in

New York, where they belong." My attempt at sounding light-hearted backfired spectacularly, making it sound like I'd forgotten how to breathe. I cleared my throat. "Anyway, Saturday at three is fine for me. Let me know if you're free."

When I ended the message, I lay back on my bed and stared up at the ceiling. The past was smothering me when I hadn't even opened the door to let it in. And I had the feeling it would continue to force its way inside until it had claimed not only my present, but the future as well.

Three

꒰⁓꒱

The bell on the door of the Bluebird Café greeted me with a cheerful jingle. I stepped inside and gave a cursory glance at the tables, which were already filled with patrons sipping coffees and nibbling at Bluebird's renowned cornbread.

This cozy nook just outside Fairlane was the first place that had come to my mind when Jeanette suggested meeting for coffee. The Bluebird Café had the charming atmosphere of an intimate European bistro, and all Green Ridge residents were in agreement that it served the best pastries and coffee in the county. It was nowhere near the upscale cafés that Jeanette was used to frequenting in New York, but this was the best it was going to get.

I found an empty table next to the window and sat down before glancing at the menu. As I scanned the options, I wondered if Jeanette had gotten lost on her way here. When I'd been fresh out of New York like her, I'd directed quite a few profanities at the GPS when it failed to locate this out-of-the-way, small-town gem.

The waitress came over to my table and took my order. I rattled off my go-to combination—a cinnamon latte and blueberry muffin—and shot another glance at the door. I reached into my bag, took out my phone, and searched for Jeanette's name in my recent conversations. I was just about to ask her where she was when the door jangled open.

She rushed over to my table, looking slightly out of breath. "This is why I live in the city," she said as she set her Chloé bag on the table. "You need me to go to Sixtieth and Eighth? No problem, just follow the numbers. But here? It's anyone's guess where Fawn Lane is."

I couldn't help but laugh. "You haven't changed one bit since high school."

"Can't say the same for you." She looked around and frowned at the décor. "Since when do you get your coffee from tacky places like this?"

"Since I moved to a town where the closest Starbucks is eighty miles away. You won't find any mocha Frappuccinos here. But Daryl's has a mocha blend that almost tastes like the real thing, depending on how good your imagination is."

"I don't know how you survive here." She grimaced at the menu on the wall. "Where do I order?"

"The waitress should be back soon." I crossed my legs as she settled into her chair. "So, what's this *Couture* assignment about? Because it must be quite the project if it brought you all the way out here."

Jeanette flashed me her signature grin. "I'm glad you asked." She zipped open her bag and retrieved a small tablet. After tapping a few times on the screen, she turned it toward me. "We've already started planning out the September issue. These are some of the ideas the editorial team came up with."

I studied the screen, which displayed a rough outline of ideas for the most anticipated issue of *Couture*. Words like *innovation* and *transformation* jumped out at me from between the bullet points, parts of a puzzle I was starting to piece together. It wasn't until I read the working title of the main feature—*Breaking the Mold: How to Make a Fearless Life Change*—that it all came together.

I looked up at Jeanette, who was patiently awaiting my reaction. "You thought of me because of the way I left home and changed my life?"

She nodded. "Exactly. I don't know anyone else who's taken such a big risk in life and with no safety net. You're basically a walking inspiration for this issue. As soon as I thought of you, I asked my boss if I could arrange to meet you in person." She gestured to the tables around us. "And here we are."

For a moment, I was at a loss for words. After I'd watched Jeanette achieve every definition of success at her *Couture* internship, I'd run off to Fairlane to create a life that was the farthest thing possible from the life I'd given up. Now, somehow, those two lives were bleeding together until they were almost indistinguishable.

"A walking inspiration?" I forced out a laugh. "It's been a while since I read *Couture,* but I'm pretty sure there's nothing fashionable about getting up before dawn to milk the cows."

"That's where you're wrong. *Couture* has always been more than just a fashion magazine. Our readers pick up a copy every month to be inspired. To connect with new ideas. And it's those ideas that leave our readers better than they were."

A smile tugged at the corners of my mouth. "You sound exactly like Mrs. Shapiro."

She flipped her hair over her shoulder with theatrical exaggeration. "Go forth and change lives, my loves," she said in a spot-on impression of our former art teacher. "The world is your oyster."

I laughed for real this time, and it was like time had erased the fifteen years of tension between us. We could've been sitting in the school cafeteria again, swapping stories and making each other laugh. I saw in her face that she, too, was remembering the way things were back then, when our uncomplicated friendship was all we had and when that was more than enough.

Before I could hold on to the feeling for a second longer, the waitress returned to our table with my drink and pastry. "Here you go," she said, gingerly setting the items down. She turned to Jeanette with a warm smile. "And what can I get for you today?"

My friend took her time scanning the options on the menu. I knew how hard she was working to find something halfway decent, and I fought back an amused smile.

"I'll take a green tea, please." She handed the menu to the waitress with a polite smile.

"Nothing to eat, dear?"

"No, thanks. I'm fine."

After the woman left, I raised an eyebrow at Jeanette. "You never drink tea."

"Well, I refuse to call that sugary slop coffee," she said, glaring pointedly at my cinnamon latte.

"Suit yourself."

She laid her palms on the table and looked directly at me. "Anyway, enough about me. Let's get back to the reason I came here." She had that searching look in her eyes again, the one that had dissected my every thought outside of Daryl's. "You're twenty years old again. You're about to set off on your big escape, and your future is wide open." She rested her chin in her hand. "Tell me what that was like."

It took me a second to return to that place in my mind. I'd forgotten about Jeanette's directness, the way she got someone to bare their soul with a few words. They were the same words that had gotten her a *Couture* internship, the same ones that fed her success as a fashion director. Jeanette would stop at nothing to get what she wanted. And what she wanted this time was to exhume a part of my past that I'd kept buried for fifteen years.

I took a breath and found my way back to that day. Spring break had just started at my college, and everyone in my dorm apartment was lying on a beach somewhere, their problems a thousand miles away. But mine had never been closer.

Two days before I arrived home, my parents were greeted coldly by a warning letter in the mail. I was two bad grades away from being put on academic probation and not that much farther from saying goodbye to the Hallford University campus. Facing my parents was the most difficult part of it all. The way my mom and dad saw it, earning my college degree was as much of a given as taking my first steps. If I failed out of school, my life was over as far as they knew.

The day I came home for spring break, my parents sat me down in the living room of our apartment and did all they could to talk some sense into me. They told me I was wasting my potential, that I would regret not trying harder. What they didn't understand was that my life had already ended the moment I chose my safety school and declared a major in accounting. Once I gave up my dream school, choosing the practical path was the only option I had left. But my choices turned me into a zombie, drifting aimlessly through the days, watching Jeanette live the life that was supposed to be mine while I lived a life that belonged to a stranger.

Early the next morning, I decided it was time. I packed a single suitcase, got into my dusty gray Civic, and set off toward an unknown destination. My hands trembled on the steering wheel as the skyscrapers receded into the distance. I hadn't said a word to my parents before leaving. The meager note I'd scratched out and left on the kitchen table was the only explanation I'd given them. The thought of escaping without a single glance back made my stomach knot up with excitement and terror. But I knew that if I hesitated, if I tried to reason with my parents first, I would never find the courage to fulfill the mission that was calling out to me.

The farther I drove, the more the knot loosened. The landscape morphed from the jagged city skyline into flat, lush plains as far as the eye could see. Once I was a good forty miles away from home, a simple truth dawned on me: I was free. My entire future was as wide open as the road ahead of me, and no one was around to write it out for me.

With the sun beating down on my face, I let the road signs guide me along the highway. I drove below the mountains of West Virginia, snaked through the rolling hills of the Carolinas, and wandered through the dense forests of Illinois. Somewhere beyond the Mississippi River, I stumbled upon the faded Welcome to Fairlane sign just before the Iowa-Wisconsin border. The second I laid eyes on it, I had a gut feeling that this beautiful place in the middle of nowhere was exactly where I needed to be. Everything about the small town was different from anything I'd ever known, from the infinite stretches of verdant land to the ready kindness of the locals, who always had a story and a smile to share. Later, I understood that everything that made Fairlane different from the city was everything that made it feel like home.

I paused for the first time since I'd started speaking, the story I'd kept locked inside for years finally stealing a glimpse of light. As I met Jeanette's eyes, I saw that she'd stopped taking notes a long time ago. She studied me with a fascinated look that had a calculating edge to it, as if she were struggling to figure out how I'd pulled off such a big risk.

Before I could say anything, an impish smile crept onto her face. "Oh, Nora. You did such a good job of playing the shrinking violet back in school, and boy, did you fool all of us. Props given." She paused and gave a short laugh. "Although I'm about fifteen years late. Sorry."

I offered a weak smile in response, but my friend radar was going off. If I didn't know any better, I would've thought that Jeanette was threatened by me. Threatened by the person I'd become as opposed to the person she thought I was. Because, according to her, I was the same girl who'd dropped an armful of books on the first day of middle school and frozen in fear when the entire hall fell silent. That was the girl she remembered—not the one who'd left home without anyone's help to change her life for the better.

But I did know better, and I knew the only thing that intimidated Jeanette was the idea of falling short of her own goals. Her ambition had always outshined everything around her. I'd learned that the hard way when she claimed the empty spot at Grant before I finished saying no. She had no reason to compare herself to me when she had a life that exceeded her wildest dreams.

"Anyway, that was quite the story. But we're not done yet." She took a sip of her green tea before meeting my gaze. "What do you think about the new Valentino collection? You're the only person I know outside the office who still stays current with fashion trends, so I figured you could give me some insight."

I was about to ask how she knew that about me, but then I remembered who I was talking to. This was the same person who'd caught me poring over a fresh issue of *Couture* during one of Mr. Martin's mind-numbing history lessons. The same person who'd blocked the principal's view of me so she wouldn't see that I'd sassed up my school uniform with knee-high boots from Versace's fall collection. Of course she knew that I still snuck the occasional peek at the latest runway fashions while Tyler was fast asleep. That I'd never really abandoned the life I thought I'd left behind.

I pushed the thoughts away and shifted my focus to Jeanette's question. As I thought back to the collection and its highlights, I shared my thoughts on it with the ease of someone who had been working at *Couture* her whole life. Fashion was a language I still spoke fluently, no matter how many years I'd kept it to myself.

Jeanette nodded along as she took diligent notes on her tablet. She asked me questions about the trends I still kept up with, about the future of some of the biggest designer brands. The words came out of me like they'd been waiting for an outlet for the past fifteen years. It hadn't occurred to me until now that my passion had been lying dormant inside me since I silenced my inner designer on College Decision Day.

After she'd gone through several questions, Jeanette set down her device and looked at me head-on. "One last thing before we call it a day. I know you said you haven't picked up a copy of *Couture* in a while, but try to remember this." She paused for a moment, and I saw her trying to find the girl I once was somewhere inside my eyes. "What was your favorite part about reading the magazine?"

The question took me by surprise, even though it fit right into the other questions she'd asked. Once I absorbed her words, the answer came to me as effortlessly as the rest of them. "*Couture* has always been an outlet for me. I used to feel like I could just be myself when I read it." I thought about how I'd always been the first one in my family to check the mail, eager to see the glossy cover of a new issue wink at me from atop the catalogs and envelopes. "I remember how they always had such innovative ideas. It made me feel like it was okay not to fit in, and that gave me hope."

Jeanette's intense gaze made me feel oddly self-conscious. I shifted in my seat. "Why do you ask?"

"Just wondering," she said, as if she'd asked me what kind of music I enjoyed listening to. "We're always looking for ways to improve the magazine, so it helps to hear what our loyal readers think."

I was about to remind her that I wasn't a loyal reader anymore when her phone buzzed. She glanced at the screen and frowned. "Shit, that's my assistant. We have a code red in the fashion closet." She sighed. "My work is never really done."

"Well, I won't keep you any longer. You have to keep the readers happy, right?"

"Exactly. I knew you would understand." With a knowing look, she added, "It's like you never stopped aspiring to work in fashion."

I held my gaze on her as she flagged down our waitress for the check. "Jeanette," I began carefully. "I meant what I said in that voicemail. I've moved on from wanting to work in the fashion industry. This has been fun and all, but I can't keep acting like I'm still fifteen."

Her expression was unreadable as she tucked her tablet back into her bag. She set the bag on the table and looked at me levelly. "You can tell me you've moved on if it makes you feel better. But you heard me say on the phone that I needed your help with a *Couture* assignment." She was quiet for a moment, her eyes searching. "And you still agreed to come."

With her words heavy in the air, I absentmindedly watched the waitress hand over our check. Something had changed in the air around me, something invisible but palpable. It clung to me long after I'd left the café, weighing down my bones like an omen that only I could sense.

Four

Bridget glanced up at me, her eyes wide. "Forty-six?" Her voice was saturated with so much hope that I considered bending the rules of mathematics just for her.

"So close. Forty-eight." I wrote down the two digits next to the problem on her math worksheet: *What is the product of 6 and 8?*

"This is too hard," she said, letting her pencil slide across the kitchen table in defeat.

"Just keep practicing. Once you learn your multiplication tables, you'll never forget them," I said, thinking back to my own days in my third-grade classroom. "I still remember mine."

"Can we do this later?" She pushed back her chair and jumped to her feet. "Daddy said it's time to feed the cows."

I checked the time: 4:32. We'd already been at this for an hour and a half. The poor girl deserved a break.

"All right. Go ahead." She turned and rushed out of the house as I called after her, "Make sure you finish your worksheet before Monday!"

I watched her disappear into the barn before rising from my chair to join her. After I helped Tyler feed the cows, I checked my phone for updates from Caleb. Lately, he'd been spending his weekends with his friends, conveniently arranging to meet with them during milking or feeding times. He was supposed to have called by now—then again, I wasn't surprised he was putting off coming back home for as long as possible.

"I'm gonna go pick up Caleb," I called out to Tyler before heading to the truck.

I backed out of the gravel driveway and made my way toward the neighboring farm. Dave, Tyler's close friend from childhood and the father of Caleb's friend, owned a dairy that had once been like ours. But a couple of years ago, Dave had made the difficult choice of raising hundreds of more cows and installing robotic milking equipment in his barn. Now, his land more closely resembled a factory than the small family farm it once was.

Dave's story was one that every farmer was all too familiar with. The pressure to expand was always weighing on our shoulders, reminding us that we were never safe. As milk prices continued to drop and the cost of feed rose higher and higher, the only option most farmers had was to produce more.

I pulled into the field and saw Dave walking out of the farmhouse. As I jumped out of the truck, he waved at me. "Hey, Nora. How are ya?"

"I'm doing all right." I smiled. "How's Caleb?"

"Last I checked, he and Brian were glued to one of those video games. Seems to be keeping them pretty busy." He turned back toward the farmhouse. "I'll let Caleb know you're here."

After he disappeared into the house, my eyes swept across the expanse of grass that hugged the farmhouse and barn. The land had a cold feeling to it, as if it had been untouched by cow hooves for months. I held my gaze on the barn at the far end of the pasture, thinking about all the cattle cooped up in there with hardly any room to move, and fought back a shudder.

Dave returned with a sulking Caleb shuffling beside him. "Hi, Mom," he muttered without raising his eyes to me.

"Hey, honey. I heard you had a lot of fun." I smiled at Dave. "Thanks for looking after him."

"Anytime." He glanced down at his watch as a frown creased his forehead. "I better get going. If I don't get more milk over to the plant than last month, my poor Julia won't have her sweet sixteen."

The hard truth sent a pang of anxiety through my chest. With the way he'd sped up milk production over the last couple years, it was hard to believe he was still struggling. "But how can that be?"

He gave me a sad smile that held every truth I was too afraid to admit. "You know how tough this business is, Nora. We can't afford to slow down. Just when you think you're producing enough, you need to do more."

"You're right," I said quietly, trying to ignore the dread that had settled in the pit of my stomach. With a weak smile, I looked up at him. "Well, thanks again."

He gave a quick wave as I started up the truck and drove back to the farm. I gave Caleb a sidelong glance, wondering what was going through his mind. Decoding his thoughts was like trying to solve a puzzle with a missing piece. Lately, I hadn't been able to shake the feeling that I was destined to never find it.

When I reached the clearing, Caleb hopped out and ducked into the farmhouse without another word. I was just about to follow him inside when I spotted Tyler walking back from the barn. Even from my vantage point, I could see the deep creases carved into his forehead.

I frowned as he approached. "What's wrong?"

He pursed his lips. "She's back."

"She...?"

"Your friend. Jeanette, right?"

I looked at him, trying to put all the pieces together. "Here? But... How did she even...?" I stopped and shook my head. "Never mind. Do you know why she's here?"

"She wouldn't tell me. I think she wants to talk to you privately."

"I guess I'll be right back, then." I plodded over to the front of the barn, where Jeanette was leaning against the side of the building like she was on a random street corner in Manhattan. When she saw me, she waved me over with a frantic look in her eyes.

I caught up to her and crossed my arms. "What are you doing here? And how did you figure out where my farm is?"

She waved a dismissive hand. "Details now, questions later. Anywho, I've been doing tons of research for the September issue, but there's only so much you can learn when you're stuck in the middle of nowhere. Then I thought, what am I still doing here? And, more importantly, what are *you* still doing here?" She looked at me expectantly. "So I decided. We're going back."

"Going back where?"

She threw me an impatient look. "To New York. Where else?"

I met her eyes, trying to figure out if she was serious. "You want me to just pick up and leave everything behind? My home? My family? I know you only have yourself to worry about, but I have children to take care of. Not to mention my husband needs me on the farm."

"Of course you wouldn't leave your family here. You'd take them with you." She said it matter-of-factly, like we were discussing a party we planned to attend.

Convinced it was pointless to talk any sense into her, I played along. "And do what in New York, exactly?"

"That's easy. I'll go back to living my life, and you'll start living yours."

"This *is* my life. And I'm pretty happy with it."

"Stop lying to yourself, Nora. You won't get anywhere by doing that."

"I'm serious."

She peered into the barn. "If you can't see that there's more to life than milking and feeding cows, then I can't help you."

Whatever bond we'd formed at the Bluebird had dissolved entirely, leaving us to stumble back into the strained relationship that had haunted us since college. I looked her dead in the eye. "You know what? Maybe you shouldn't."

She flinched. It was barely perceptible, but I saw it. Just as swiftly as she lost her composure, she reclaimed it. "Do you remember what you said to me when we met? 'I'm going to Grant and starting a career in fashion.' And you meant it. You meant it all the way up to our senior year, when you got your acceptance letter." Her eyes softened, and for a fraction of a second, I saw the best friend I used to have. "What happened? You had everything going for you, and you're the one who stopped it from happening."

Her words were too raw, the wound still too fresh inside

me. "I was eighteen then," I said, keeping my voice even. "I was barely an adult."

"You still want it, though. I know you do."

"Why do you care?" My voice cracked on the last word, my composed front finally unraveling. "Why do you care so much that I lost out on my dream? And don't say it's because you care about me. I know you do, in your own way, but that's not why you're here." I searched her face, trying to unveil what she was guarding so carefully inside her. "I'm tired of this, Jeanette. We're too old for this. Can't you tell me what's going on?"

She looked away from me, and that was when I knew I'd peeled away her protective layer. She was exposed. Vulnerable. When she turned to me again, she cast her eyes downward, like a child in the principal's office. "I'm pregnant."

The words didn't belong to her. They were an imposter, a fraud. "You're *what*?"

She glared at me, but her lip was quivering. "You heard me."

"I'm sorry, I just don't..." The questions darted through my mind like ping-pong balls. I managed to grasp one of them and carefully verbalize it. "When did this happen?"

"About a week ago."

I studied my friend, unable to see her the same way as before. I'd known Jeanette since sixth grade, and it would've been less of a shock if she'd announced that she planned to join a circus.

"I... I need to process this." I found a soft patch of grass beside the barn and sat down, my head resting against the side of the building. Jeanette joined me soon after. It wasn't until she was sitting right next to me that I glimpsed the fear in her eyes. It was unnerving to see her like this, the same girl who'd abolished the social hierarchy in the middle school cafeteria by deciding she could sit wherever she wanted. And in the world of middle school, that wasn't much different from slaying a dragon with her bare hands.

I watched a crow slice through the cloudless sky. "You didn't want this to happen, did you?"

She paused. "At first, no. But things have gotten serious with Derek and me." Derek, her fiancé, had taken their relationship to the next level a month ago, when he surprised her with a ring—sapphire, to match her birthstone. "And when I look at him now, I see someone who would be such an amazing father." She glanced at me. "Isn't that crazy? That I'd want to be a mom someday?"

Crazier than me becoming a farmer's wife, I thought. "But you know what you're getting into, right? I mean, we're talking about raising a living, breathing child. Are you sure you're ready for that?"

"Really? I thought I was going to give birth to a Barbie doll." She averted her gaze, her attention now devoted to her Vince cashmere sweater.

That was when it hit me. Jeanette was so used to being in control, to creating a blueprint for every single step in her life. Now that life had thrown her a curveball, she was at a loss. Of course she wouldn't get rid of the baby. If she did that, she would be admitting that she'd messed up.

"But isn't it perfect now?" she asked, doubt melting away from the crevices of her face. "I can focus on starting a family, and you can finally see what you've been missing out on all these years. You know I don't believe in fate, but even I can see that this is meant to be."

I faltered. "So now that you're pregnant, you want me to go back to New York and..." The thought was there, but for some reason, I couldn't put it into words.

"Exactly," she said, even though I hadn't finished my sentence. "I need time to prepare for the baby, but my job is way too important for me to just abandon it. Plus, I can tell you're a perfect fit from the ideas you gave me at the café." She was practically glowing with excitement. "Can you believe it? You're going to be the new fashion director. At *Couture,* no less."

It took me a second to figure it out, but when I did, I couldn't believe how clueless I'd been. "That's why you arranged our coffee meeting, right? You didn't want me to help you with your project. You were pre-screening me to see if I was a good fit for the job."

She didn't try to hold back the smile that spread across her face. "See? This is why my job is perfect for you. You've always been so clever."

"And you knew I would say no if you asked me out of the blue. So you reeled me in slowly."

"Like I said. Clever, clever girl."

"This isn't okay, Jeanette. You tricked me."

She sighed. "You might be right, but you know what? You had so much *passion* in your eyes when you answered my questions. It was like your vision for the magazine was written on your face." Her lips curled up into a grin. "It would kill me to let that vision go to waste, so I had no choice but to choose you for the job."

The farm was still there, but it seemed to belong to a separate universe. Just like that, I'd stepped back into the shoes of my younger self, haunted by the decision I'd made to attend a different college. All these years, I was only vaguely aware of the grip my past had on me. But now that I was face-to-face with the choices I'd made, I saw how I'd buried the regret to the point it had become a part of me.

"Now, don't get me wrong," Jeanette said, tearing me away from my thoughts. "I know you and your family do a lot of hard work on this farm. I mean, I don't even know how you get up at four a.m. every freaking morning. So I'll give you some time to think it through. But remember," she added, her eyes boring a hole through the deepest part of me. "You're lucky enough to have this opportunity again."

With that, she rose from the grass and headed to her car. I watched in a cloud of bewilderment as she unlocked the vehicle, slid into the driver's seat, and turned onto the road without another look. My eyes stayed glued to the spot where her car had been long after she left.

I'd imagined this moment for my entire adult life. I'd nursed the what-ifs like a newborn. But I didn't think it would happen like this. I didn't think it would happen, period. And now that it was happening, I realized I hadn't prepared for it at all.

I stood up and made my way toward the farmhouse, feeling a bit unsteady on my feet. I climbed up the stairs and closed my bedroom door before collapsing on my bed. As the silence enveloped me, I became entangled in the web of thoughts that was all too familiar between these four walls.

I didn't know how many times I'd revisited the moment I turned down Grant. The only thought that had passed through my mind as I checked the "decline" box was Accepted Students Day. I remembered crossing the quad among a crowd of budding designers clad in runway-worthy clothing and professional makeup, feeling like my steps had a different rhythm than everyone else's. I remembered waiting for someone to find out that I wasn't one of them. That I was just playing the part. That underneath the clothes Jeanette had helped me pick out at Bloomingdale's, I was just a woefully unprepared student who'd bitten off more than she could chew.

Whenever I replayed the scene in my mind, I told myself I had years of preparation now. That I'd grown into someone far more capable and confident than that timid eighteen-year-old. Above all, I told myself that with the gift of a new opportunity, I would see everything with clearer eyes. I would recognize everything I was about to lose. But the voice of my doubts was never far behind, and I always found myself wondering: *Would I?*

Or am I hopelessly myself, doomed to repeat the same mistakes no matter how many do-overs I get?

As Jeanette had rightly pointed out, I was lucky enough to have a second chance. And while I could blame my first mistake on a lack of confidence, there was no excuse for missing the same train twice. This time, I was waiting on the platform, ticket in hand. If I let the train reach its destination without me, it would no longer be a mistake. It would be a choice.

I walked over to the window and looked out at our homestead. The difference between making the decision now and making it when I was eighteen was that now, I had an entire life of my own. Besides the fact that the farm would suffer without my help, I would miss it all. I would miss starting my day with Tyler every morning as we welcomed another breathtaking sunrise. I would miss seeing Bridget pop out of school every afternoon at three o'clock, bursting at the seams with all the stories she wanted to share with me. I would even miss the way Caleb tuned us all out during the ride back home, his face pointed toward the window and his eyes somewhere far away. Somewhere I imagined was similar to the place I went when I used to fantasize about escaping home.

In spite of how hard it was to leave, I couldn't deny that turning down this opportunity was like slapping the universe in the face. The reason for so many sleepless nights, the burden that had strained my relationship with my parents, and the way my life always felt inexplicably unfinished lay in that single opportunity. Surely there were some risks attached to Jeanette's offer, but the bigger risk was walking away from it. Again.

I grabbed my phone from the nightstand and called Jeanette. I knew what to do. My heart thumped as I waited for her to pick up.

When she did, I didn't even wait for her to speak. "You're going to have to find someone else."

I could practically see her rolling her eyes. "Seriously? You're so predictable, Nora."

"But you'll need someone there while you find a full-time replacement, right?"

She hesitated. "I guess so. Why?"

I couldn't hold back my smile. "I'll be there."

"Now you're confusing me."

I sat back down on the bed. "You said it yourself. I have a busy life. I can't commit to filling your position for your entire maternity leave, but I can do it temporarily. No more than a couple of weeks."

There was silence as she processed my offer. "You're quite the negotiator."

"Is that a yes?"

"Not the exact plan I had in mind, but it'll work. Just make sure you stay until I find someone."

"You have my word. But if I need to come back for any reason, I'm getting on the next flight to Des Moines. No questions."

"I don't remember you becoming so demanding."

"You're having a baby now, Jeanette. You should know better."

Because that silenced her for a moment, I went on with my stipulations. "And if you haven't figured it out yet, I can't bring my family with me. Someone needs to take care of the animals while I'm gone. So I'll also need to head back home if there are any emergencies on the farm."

"Anything else?"

"Yes, actually." I looked out the window at the invisible skyline that lay somewhere beyond the horizon. The buzz of excitement that sprouted inside me made me feel young again. "When should I start packing?"

* * *

His expression gave nothing away, making it impossible to decode his thoughts. I fed my suitcase another sweater as silence settled like dust over the room.

"Are you sure?" I asked for what might've been the fourth time that night.

"I told you, the kids and I will have it all covered. And if we do need help, I'll just give Dave a call."

"But he's already so busy with his own farm. If this place

falls apart because of me, I won't be able to live with myself." I studied the contents of my suitcase, trying to think of anything important that I'd forgotten. The thrill of the two weeks ahead of me had worn off long ago, leaving me with all the reasons why my plan would backfire. I knew I was lucky to have Tyler, though, who had been more understanding than I'd expected. He was one of the few people who knew the entire story of what had happened during my senior year. Now I knew that every time I'd shrugged it off and assured him it was in the past, he'd seen beyond my façade.

"Relax, Nora." He knelt beside my stuffed suitcase so that we were at eye level. "I'm not saying it won't be hard without you, but I know filling in for Jeanette is a huge opportunity for you. Besides, you'll be back before February."

I knew just what he meant. For three years in a row, February had unleashed its wrath of below-freezing temperatures and torrential snowstorms, causing the milking machines to shut down. It had taken months to make up for all the precious time we'd lost during those treacherous few weeks. While we'd been blessed with relatively calm conditions over the past year, there was no telling what the coming month had in store for us.

"I guess you're right." My shoulders were still tense as I said it.

He brushed a stray hair from my face. "Sometimes you just have to do it. If you look for reasons not to, you'll always find one."

"What about the kids?"

"They'll be fine. It's only a couple of weeks, remember?"

As I looked at him, I blocked out all the worries competing for my attention. I leaned forward and pressed my lips to his, trying to tattoo the taste of him in my mind. The sample I'd gotten made me hunger for every part of him, like my body was already anticipating what it would lose for the next two weeks.

I wasn't the only one. There was an urgency in the way he held me, like he was terrified he would lose me. The feeling dampened the thrill that was running through me at his touch, and I came up for air, whispering, "I'm right here."

"I know," he whispered back. Before I could take another breath, we'd found our way between the sheets, making love like it was the first time. And, in a way, it was. I was shedding my old skin so the new layer could shine through, so I could unveil the person I was meant to be. So I could freely be everything I longed to be without the chains of my doubts holding me back.

Still me, but better. Better than I'd ever been.

Five

≈

When my alarm blared at three thirty in the morning, I was already wide awake. I reached for my phone to switch off the alarm and sat up in bed, my eyes slowly adjusting to the darkness.

I pulled my knees to my chest, my heart slamming against my ribs. I'd woken up filled with equal parts exhilaration and terror, like the split second before hitting the big drop on a rollercoaster. My conversation with Jeanette outside the barn was blurred around the edges in my memory, as if I'd dreamed the whole thing. A part of me still expected her to call and tell me she'd changed her mind, that she'd already found someone else to take her place.

I took a deep breath, telling myself that I needed time. I needed to see the city skyline again, to see the streets come alive with its flow of commuters and tourists. I needed to jolt myself awake after being lulled by the sedate countryside for too long. Once I threw myself into the center of the action, it would all start to feel real again.

On the other side of the bed, Tyler turned over and stroked my cheek. "Hey," he said, his voice still thick with sleep. "You ready?"

I looked at him, letting the calm in his eyes quell my anxiety. "Now or never."

He leaned over to kiss me, then he pulled back the covers and got out of bed. As he changed into his work clothes, he said, "Might as well get a head start on the cows. I need to see how the new calves are doing."

His words cast a shadow over me as I grew painfully aware of what I was about to miss. I hadn't realized how dependent I'd become on my daily routine until it was pulled out from under me. Now that I thought about it, I couldn't remember how I'd started my day before greeting the cows and milking them.

With a sigh, I got up and started getting dressed. It was an adjustment—that was all. Years ago, this farm had been just as unfamiliar as the inside of *Couture*'s headquarters, and it had eventually become my home. Besides, I would be coming back to Fairlane before I grew too accustomed to city life.

Once I'd dressed and brushed my teeth, I tiptoed down the hall, careful not to wake the kids. I'd gotten up a half hour earlier than usual so I would have time to milk the cows before heading to the airport at five thirty. I knew Caleb and Bridget would still be sleeping at that time, so I'd said my goodbyes the night before.

Caleb had taken the news with his usual nonchalance, but Bridget was the one who nearly made me change my plans. "If it's a vacation, why isn't Daddy going with you?" she'd asked, her eyes wide with concern. It had taken a herculean effort not to break down into tears while I assured her it was just an important trip for work. Now, as I passed by my children's closed bedroom doors, my throat tightened again.

I padded down the stairs with my luggage and headed for

the door. As I turned the knob, a small voice came from behind me. "Mom?"

I whirled around and saw Caleb standing in the hall. "What is it, honey?"

For a moment, he just stood there with his hands stuffed in the pockets of his Star Wars pajama pants. As I looked down at my son, I caught a rare glimpse of the little kid he used to be. The one who would come racing down the stairs on Saturday mornings when Tyler made pancakes for everyone. The one who would run barefoot around the pasture with Bridget before he decided he was too old to play with his sister.

He looked up at me with his brow furrowed, the same expression he wore when he was figuring out a tough math problem. Then he abruptly looked away and said, "Never mind." He started to walk away but stole another glance at me. "Have a good trip."

I opened my mouth to ask what he wanted to tell me, but he was already rushing up the stairs two at a time. As I watched him go, my mind flashed back to him escaping into the house after milking the cows on the first day of school. His head had been bowed in the same way, his shoulders slumped like he'd been the victim of some great defeat. Now, I watched him retreat to his room and wondered how I was supposed to leave him like this.

I pulled open the front door and marched straight to the barn, where Tyler was starting the first round of milking. "He's not okay," I said.

"Who?"

"Caleb. He looked like he wanted to tell me something just now, but then he changed his mind and ran back to his room.

Something's going on with him. I know it." I bit down on my lip, willing myself to hold back tears. The timing of this situation couldn't have been any worse.

"You're overthinking it. I'm sure he's fine."

"No. He isn't. He's going through something, and someone needs to help him." I glanced back at the house, descending into panic. "I can't do this. I can't leave." I started to go, but Tyler's voice stopped me before I took another step.

"Don't do this, Nora. You're coming up with excuses. That's what got you into trouble when you turned down Grant, remember?"

I stood there with one foot facing the road and the other facing the farmhouse, like I was trapped between two different worlds. "But..."

"Do you remember when we first met? After you'd been here a couple of months?"

I remembered. I'd been working at Swift Shop, the major supermarket that was wedged between Fairlane and Dubuque, trying to save up for my own place. I was busy stocking shelves one day when I overheard my manager on the phone, demanding to know what had happened to the most recent milk delivery. From what I heard, the milk had never made it to the processing plant.

As a New Yorker who knew nothing about milk distribution, I knew it wasn't my place to intervene. But I was poising myself for a raise, and I would seize any opportunity to show my boss I was willing to go the extra mile.

After she hung up, I asked for the address of the farm and drove to the place that would one day become my home. One of Tyler's farmhands greeted me, and I explained the problem to him with such single-minded determination that I almost didn't see my future husband strolling up from behind him. My cheeks grew hot as I noticed he'd heard everything I said, his eyes smiling as they rested on mine.

"There must've been a mix-up at the plant," he told me after the farmhand had left. Then, with the confidence of someone who'd known me all his life, he said, "Come on. Let's straighten things out."

Later, I realized there was nothing to straighten out. He'd already sent out the milk delivery, and my manager was just two steps behind. When he brought me into his pickup, with the windows rolled down and the Eagles' "Take it Easy" floating out of the speakers, it was because he saw something in us that I was only beginning to see. As I glimpsed his broad shoulders out of the corner of my eye, his strong, calloused farmer's hands taking the wheel, something stirred inside me that I'd never felt before. There was a rawness about him that the boys in my school and even the young men on my college campus lacked. Something *real*.

He smiled at me now, just as he had that first day on the farm. "I remember seeing you for the first time and thinking, 'That girl is on a mission.' You had this fire in your eyes, like you'd do anything to get what you wanted. And as soon as you saw the farm, I could tell you were ready to start your new life here."

A smile came to me as naturally as the air in my lungs. "I was." It hadn't taken me long to understand that farming was a job without shortcuts. No matter the weather or how he felt, Tyler went out to the fields every morning to care for the animals that depended on him. It was that steadfast loyalty, that unwavering commitment, that had drawn me to him. And as I followed him every step of the way, I'd discovered a purpose in farming that filled the empty space I'd tried to seal by leaving home.

His smile faltered as his tone grew solemn. "But sometimes, I catch you deep in thought, or just looking sad. You're always thinking. And it seems like... I don't know, like you missed out on something."

Hearing Tyler speak the truths I'd buried in my heart made them feel more real. I studied him, wondering if he meant everything he said. "You don't think I'm happy here?"

"I know you're happy. I know you found everything you wanted when you came here. But you never finished what you had to do." A hint of the smile he had earlier returned to his face. "I know you, Nora, and you're a go-getter. You won't ever be satisfied until you do what you have to do."

His words untethered a weight that I hadn't known was inside me. "How do you know me so well?"

"You do too. That's why you're going to New York." He motioned to the cows. "Now let's get this done so you can head to the airport."

As I helped him give the cows one last milking, the air around me took on a heavy stillness. It was like the entire town was preparing for my departure by ceasing its usual activity. Even the bed of grass outside the barn stood still against the roaring January wind, as if it were holding its breath in anticipation of what was to come.

When we were done, Tyler turned to me. "Well, I guess this is it."

The finality of the sentence unsettled me, but I didn't show it. I was the one who'd decided to take this risk, and it was my job to reassure everyone that I could handle it.

"Yeah. This is it." I glanced down at my phone, rereading the message Jeanette had sent me. "Jeanette should be here any minute now."

He nodded, his eyes still fixed on mine. I tried to find the right words to say to him, something other than a trite goodbye, but my throat was too full for me to speak. When he pulled me into his arms and kissed me, I knew I didn't have to say a single word. We stayed like that for longer than we should have, delaying the inevitable as much as we could.

A honk sliced through the air, startling both of us. "Time to break it up, lovebirds."

Jeanette waved at us from the open window of a shiny black Mercedes. The whole "when in Rome" thing clearly went right over her head.

I said one last goodbye to Tyler and hopped into the passenger seat of the rental car. The sound of the door closing rang in my ears, carrying an undeniable permanence. Even though I could still see the farm through the window, it seemed miles away.

Not one for sappy goodbyes, Jeanette pressed on the gas and tore me away from my town before I could blink. "Let's get out of here," she said.

I checked the time on my phone. "Relax. We're early."

"In New York, you're already late." She hurtled down local roads, either not noticing the speed limit or blatantly ignoring it.

I turned my attention to the view out the window, taking in the peaceful countryside before it became nothing but a memory. I knew I would be dreaming of sprawling fields and fresh, unsullied air after my first week in the concrete jungle.

"So," Jeanette began, "I know you were going to stay at the Marriott, but I upgraded you to a suite at the Four Seasons downtown. It's a five-minute walk from the office."

I winced. "Jeanette, you didn't have to do that."

"Of course I did. If you're going to stay in New York, you're going to do it right."

The kind gesture reminded me of when my friend had paid for all my items at Daryl's without question. For someone like Jeanette, who spent her days picking out designer clothes for models and sampling Manhattan's five-star restaurants, booking this suite was her way of saying she wanted the best for me.

I turned to her with a smile. "Thanks. I can't wait to see it."

As we turned onto the expressway, the GPS on Jeanette's phone chirped, "Follow Interstate 80 east for approximately one hundred ten miles."

"One hundred ten miles?" She glared at her device as if it were to blame for the long drive. "Well, I can't stare at this road in silence for another hour and a half." With that, she turned on the radio and flipped through the stations. A schizophrenic medley of country, pop, rock, and classical assaulted my eardrums as she looked for something that suited her. Finally settling on "White Wedding" by Billy Idol, she turned up the volume and continued to act like she was the only driver on the road.

I watched the scenery blur outside my window as the electric guitars reverberated through the car. The lyrics reached deep inside me, pulling me away from everything I knew and dropping me into the unfamiliar life I was about to enter.

It really *was* a nice day to start again.

Six

❦

Jeanette sat in the taxi with her arms crossed over her chest. We'd left JFK about thirty minutes ago and were still caught in bumper-to-bumper traffic. Every so often, Jeanette would make a show of checking her watch and sighing obnoxiously. It was amazing that she'd gotten this far in life without any semblance of patience.

Meanwhile, I hadn't torn my eyes from the window. The continuous rush of people made me feel like I was part of something big again. Professionals clad in suits and heels strode purposefully toward their destinations, many of them tapping away on their phones while they fielded calls on their wireless earbuds. Scattered across the streets were clusters of brightly dressed tourists, who stared up and pointed at the towering buildings while the locals walked around them, visibly inconvenienced. It was just like I remembered it.

"We're never gonna get out of here," Jeanette muttered as she fished through her bag.

"It's a Friday afternoon in Midtown. What did you expect?"

"I know you're back in New York, but you can spare me the attitude." She whipped out a tube of MAC lipstick and held up a compact mirror as she applied it to her lips. I had to admit, her ability to stay inside the lines while the cab weaved in and out of traffic was impressive.

"Practice," she said, reading my mind. She capped the lipstick and tossed it back into her bag. "Once you get the hang of my job, you'll see what I mean. Multitasking is vital in the editorial world."

I squelched the urge to tell her how many times I'd talked on the phone with the vet while putting out the feed for the cows with at least one of the kids on my heels. Instead, I smiled and said, "I can't wait."

I turned back to the scene outside my window as we inched down the FDR Drive. After what seemed like an eternity of moving at a snail's pace, we finally reached Lower Manhattan, where One World Trade Center dutifully kept its watch over all of New York. I looked up in awe at the structure that towered over its stout companions, a type of metaphor for New York itself. The thought of working in that building every day sent a surge of excitement through me like an electric current. It felt surreal, like this was just a rehearsal that preceded the real thing.

Jeanette laughed. "You look like such a tourist right now."

"I haven't been here in years," I reminded her. In reality, though, her words didn't bother me in the slightest. I *was* a tourist, in a strange sort of way. In a place as dynamic as New York, the streets were never the same from one day to the next.

For so long, I'd seen the world beyond the city as my only ticket to freedom. But now, for the first time in my life, I saw New York open its doors to me, along with all the opportunity it had to offer. The thought of unlocking a new side of my potential during the next two weeks filled me with hope.

After a couple of minutes, the taxi driver pulled up to our

destination, where a doorman in a hat and white gloves kept watch by the hotel entrance. He sprang into action, hurrying to open the taxi door for us. After he escorted Jeanette and me to the entrance of the Four Seasons, we spilled out into a spacious, well-lit lobby. I surveyed the room, which was punctuated by modern décor and generously illuminated by floor-to-ceiling windows. As I stood beneath the room's high ceilings, I couldn't help but notice how everything about the city made me feel so small.

The concierge handed over my key card, and Jeanette hurried to the elevator before I could take a step forward. "You are going to love your suite," she said as she hit the call button.

The second I opened the door to my hotel room, I knew she was right. In front of me was a living room bigger than the one I had back home, furnished with a couch, matching chairs, and a coffee table. In the corner of the room was a desk that would give me plenty of room to work on assignments when I wasn't in the office. As I looked a little off to the side, I caught a glimpse of a bedroom and bathroom that complemented the décor in the lobby.

The room itself was enough to leave me speechless, but that wasn't the main showstopper. Once I'd granted myself enough time to take in the suite, I walked straight to the floor-to-ceiling window behind the couch and pressed my hand to the glass, as if touching it would convince me that the view was real. From my vantage point on the twenty-third floor, it looked like I was suspended in the middle of the sky.

I'd lived in New York before, but not like this. This was how celebrities experienced the city from their luxury high-rise condos. Not people like me.

"I'll go ahead and assume you love it," Jeanette said, breaking me out of my reverie. Even though I wasn't facing her, the satisfied half-smile that was undoubtedly perched on her face was crystal clear in my mind.

"How could you not?" I turned away from the view and faced her. "Jeanette, this is perfect. Really." I started to thank her, but her phone beeped to announce an incoming text.

"That's Derek," she said, glancing down at the screen. "I'd better head back to the apartment." She grabbed her bag and turned back to me. "Oh, I almost forgot. Derek and I made a reservation for three at L'Artusi tonight. Seven o'clock. Be there." With that, she slipped her bag onto her shoulder and clopped toward the door. "Enjoy your room."

After she closed the door behind her, I made myself comfortable on the couch, soaking in the suite and the view behind me again. Part of me felt like this was all too good to be true, like I would wake up the next morning and discover that time had rewound to before Jeanette showed up at Daryl's. But the rest of me was too enmeshed in the fantasy to care how transient it was.

Unable to keep the excitement to myself, I grabbed my phone and aimed it toward the window behind me. After I'd snapped a picture that did the view justice, I sent it to Tyler. His reply came only a minute later: *Hey, just don't get too comfortable there, okay?*

He'd punctuated his text with a smiley emoji, but the light-hearted emoticon failed to soften the edge in his words. I tried to quell my anxiety by reminding myself that he'd supported my decision to come. The first few days would be an adjustment for both of us, but we would eventually fall into a routine.

I closed the messaging app and checked the time on my phone. Dinner was in a little over an hour, and I was still dressed in my faded denim jeans and fleece vest jacket. It was going to take a lot of work to undo everything I'd learned on the farm, starting with my wardrobe. I'd been in New York for barely two hours, and I felt like I belonged in an L.L. Bean catalog rather than a *Couture* byline.

I unzipped my suitcase and rummaged through it, praying I'd had the foresight to pack a black dress. When I saw the fabric peeking out from underneath my pile of work attire, I pulled it out victoriously. The dress would look perfect with the stilettos I'd dug out of a dust-coated corner of my closet back home.

I changed out of my regular clothes and slipped on the LBD, just to make sure it looked okay for dinner. After I'd done my makeup and added some jewelry, I walked over to the full-length mirror by the bathroom. The woman who appeared in the reflection startled me. It was as if a stranger had slipped into the room when I wasn't looking.

After I'd adjusted to the image in the mirror, I recognized the person I was looking at. It was my past self, the girl who saw her outfit as her canvas and expressed herself through the art she created. The girl who longed to give her trendsetting ideas a home between the pages of *Couture*. I could almost hear her voice again, coaching me as I tried to make a name for myself in the city I'd left behind so long ago.

I'd abandoned that girl all this time, but now I saw her waiting patiently in the wings, ready to have her moment. *I won't let you down,* I told her silently. *I'm here to make you proud. We both deserve it.*

***

I stepped into the restaurant, feeling like an A-lister who'd been invited to the hottest party of the year. The dining room was buzzing with sound and activity as sharply dressed New Yorkers discussed work and life over expensive wine and fruity cocktails. Compared to eating at run-of-the-mill restaurants with Tyler and the kids back home, being here was like attending the VMAs. I felt important. Wanted. Something I hadn't felt in a long time.

I scanned the room for Jeanette or Derek and saw Jeanette wave me over. I sauntered over to the table and set my bag down as I greeted the two of them.

"Long time, no see," Jeanette said.

Her fiancé smiled and extended a hand toward me. "Derek. You must be Nora."

I shook his hand. "I am. Nice to meet you."

"Nora's here to fill in for me while I prepare for our baby," Jeanette said as she lovingly placed a hand over her stomach.

"So I heard." Turning to me, he said, "Jeanette also told me you're quite the budding designer."

"You have no idea," Jeanette said before I could respond. "You should see some of the sketches she did in our high school art class."

I waved a hand dismissively, desperate to turn the spotlight away from me. "That wasn't anything."

"Are you kidding? Girl, now is not the time to be modest.

You need to think big. You need to *live* big. Otherwise, everyone at the office will drop you faster than last season's shoes."

I laughed, trying to go along with her lighthearted tone, but I couldn't ignore the anxiety blooming in my stomach. During my trip back to the city, I'd clung to the belief that I'd overcome the fears that had held me back when I was a teenager. But now, as I pictured myself trying to blend in with professionals who knew the industry inside and out, I didn't feel any more confident than I had all those years ago.

As I clutched the stem of my empty wineglass, I told myself it was too late now. I had to go through with it, whether I liked it or not. The thought made me feel like someone had deflated my parachute just as I summoned enough courage to jump.

"Can I start you off with some drinks?"

I was so engrossed in my thoughts that I hadn't seen the waiter arrive at our table. Jeanette took charge, rattling off the names of fancy drinks I'd never heard of. "Nothing for me, though. Have to keep the baby healthy," she told him. *As if he cares about what's going on in her womb*, I thought.

As the man left our table, I gave Jeanette a questioning look. "I didn't even get to decide what I wanted."

"Don't worry. You'll love what I ordered for you."

Derek nodded, as if this were a common occurrence whenever they went out together. "It's true." He looked at his fiancée with admiration. "She knows her stuff."

As they shared a cloying moment together, I seized the opportunity to turn the spotlight toward them. "So, are you guys planning on staying in New York? You know, now that you're having a baby and all."

They exchanged a knowing glance that made me feel like I'd

accidentally walked in on an intimate moment. Derek turned his attention back to me. "Actually, Jeanette and I decided that it's time to move on. We both love living here, but it isn't conducive to starting a family."

"We were thinking about moving to the suburbs," Jeanette said. "Somewhere quiet, with plenty of grass and open space where the kids can play."

It was a good thing our drinks hadn't arrived yet, because if they had, I would've had the alcohol to blame for the hallucination I was surely having. The thought of Jeanette settling down in a suburban home, complete with a yard and white picket fence, belonged in an alternate universe. I looked around me, half convinced that a cameraman would jump out from behind a table and declare that I'd been punked.

"It's wild, isn't it?" Jeanette said, decoding my thoughts. "Years ago, I wouldn't have given any thought to it. But there's no telling where life can take you sometimes."

The waiter came over with our drinks, and I'd never been so grateful for the diversion. If Jeanette started talking about how she planned to buy a minivan and take her future kids to soccer practice, I would have to get drunker than I planned to.

Once Derek and I had our drinks, Jeanette raised her glass of water. "Cheers to this new beginning in our lives. Derek and me with our future family, and Nora with her first day at *Couture*. Let's all kick ass in the next couple weeks."

We all clinked our glasses and took the first sip of our drinks. Jeanette had been right about me loving the drink she'd picked out for me, just like she'd been right that I would fall in love with my hotel room. I couldn't help but wonder if she knew more about my stint as a fashion director than she was letting on.

"So," Derek said as he set down his glass. "Jeanette told me you moved to Iowa and live on a farm now. Can't say I know any other New Yorker who's done that before."

I nodded. "I've lived there about fifteen years now. I love it there, but it's nice to be back in my hometown for a little while."

"Where do you like it better?" he asked point-blank.

The question took me by surprise. It was an innocent question, a completely natural one, given the conversation we were having, yet it left me defenseless. "Well, New York will always have a special place in my heart, because I spent most of my life here. But I couldn't stay here forever. You have to move on when the time is right."

Jeanette took a sip of her water. "Amen to that." But as she drank, her eyes landed on me with a look that took me back to the Daryl's parking lot. A look that said she'd heard something in my words that I hadn't said aloud.

I averted my gaze a little too quickly, eyeing the waiter as if to summon my meal. When my entrée finally appeared in front of me, it was like a godsend. I disappeared into an exquisite mound of spaghetti Bolognese, savoring every bite like it was my last meal on Earth. I couldn't remember the last time I genuinely enjoyed food like this. Back at home, I had little time to eat, and when I did, I usually threw together something quick that hardly registered on my taste buds.

Derek smiled in amusement as he watched my embarrassingly public food orgasm. "You don't seem too eager to go back home right now," he joked.

The mix of the food and alcohol softened the edges around his words, and I found myself at the mercy of the energy that permeated through the dining room and the city lights that bled through the windows. I thought about what Tyler had said about seizing this opportunity while I still could. *I can see how much you want this. Sometimes you just have to do it.*

I would never be eating a meal like this again, with my dream job waiting for me that coming Monday. If I didn't enjoy it, what would be the point?

"Until I get on the plane back home," I said, tilting the glass to my lips, "you can assume there's nowhere else I'd rather be."

Seven

～

I stood in front of the bathroom mirror, using my makeup to disguise any evidence of the restless night I'd had. But there was only so much that concealer could do for the dark circles under my eyes, and my blush hardly succeeded at brightening my skin's pallor. I could only hope that my carefully selected outfit made up for my lack of beauty sleep.

When I was done getting ready, I threw one final glance at the mirror. Despite all the time that had passed since Accepted Students Day, I still saw myself through the critical eyes of the women who would be openly assessing me at the office. I took a breath and reminded myself it was all in my head, that Jeanette had chosen me to take her place for a reason. If I'd made it all the way here, I was already ahead of the eighteen-year-old who lacked the courage to take the first step.

I took the elevator down to the lobby before stepping out into the crisp morning. After a relatively quiet weekend, I was reminded that New York came to life once the work week began. Harried professionals took over the streets, most of them hailing taxi cabs or ducking into subway entrances. Even the streets seemed livelier than they had over the past two days, with an endless stream of yellow cabs and black Ubers making up most of the traffic flow.

Five minutes later, I found myself in front of One World Trade Center, just as Jeanette had promised. I stopped walking and paused in front of the entrance to soak in the feeling. I was here. Maybe the situation wasn't exactly how I'd expected it to be, but I was here. That was all that mattered.

I took in one last breath of the January air and strolled into the building. After checking in at the front desk, I made my way toward the elevators, where a small cluster of workers had congregated. I shifted my gaze to my phone as I waited, pretending to be engrossed by my old messages. The nerves that stirred inside me reminded me of the way I used to feel on my first day at a new school. This time, though, everyone but me knew their way around.

The elevator doors opened on the twenty-fifth floor, revealing a long fluorescent-lit hallway. I took slow, cautious steps across the marble floor, as if a ticking time bomb would explode in my face at any moment. After reaching the end of the hallway, I turned right toward the offices.

The space was set up as an open office plan, with rows of chairs occupied by workers who typed away diligently at computers or answered phones. At the far left of the office was a large window similar to the one in my hotel room that boasted a breathtaking view of the city. As I scanned the room, I fought back a stab of disappointment. If it weren't for the larger-than-life sights or the chicly dressed employees, I would've believed I'd walked into any random office building in the country.

I moved swiftly down the hall in an effort to hide my lack of direction. Jeanette had given me directions to her office, but navigating the space on my own was a different story. The entire floor looked more and more like a maze as I bumbled my way around it.

"Can I help you with something?"

I looked around me, searching for the owner of the friendly but firm voice. Standing behind me was a tall, rail-thin woman with the sleek brown bob of someone who meant business. I recognized her charcoal-gray sweater as a Proenza Schouler and enjoyed a brief moment of victory for remembering my fashion brands. Of course, I still had a lot to learn before I could fill Jeanette's shoes.

She threw me an impatient look, and I realized I hadn't answered her question. I was barely three minutes into my first day on the job, and I'd already made quite the impression.

"I'm here to fill in for Jeanette Peterson," I said. "She's on maternity leave. I was looking for her office."

The woman raised an eyebrow as if to say, "You?" I suddenly felt ridiculous for being here, for playing the role of someone I wasn't. Maybe relinquishing this opportunity hadn't been a careless mistake. Maybe, at eighteen, I'd been more in tune with what I wanted. Maybe—

"Right this way." The woman led me toward a separate wing of the office before I could meditate on another *maybe*. She stopped in front of a large, glass-walled room and turned to face me. "Here we are."

I stared dumbly at the closed door before remembering the key in my pocket. As I fished it out and unlocked the door, I felt her eyes boring a hole into me. I might have proven that I was Jeanette's substitute, but the test didn't end there. For the next two weeks, everyone on this floor would be watching me more closely than an insect under a microscope. The glass walls and door of Jeanette's office would give them a front row seat the entire time.

After the mystery woman left me alone, I sat down at Jeanette's desk and absorbed the setting. Every square inch of the office was sparkling clean, and the modern furniture and wood paneling looked like it belonged in a museum. I gazed out at her slice of the city view, taking in the cluster of tall buildings that grasped at a deep-blue sky. It was mindboggling to think this was how she lived while I stayed within the confines of the farm, blissfully unaware that a life like this could exist.

I turned to the computer and noticed a sheet of printer paper taped to the monitor. Even after all these years, I recognized Jeanette's handwriting tattooed across it. I peeled off the sheet and read it:

Hey, girl! I know you're still settling in, but you have plenty of work to catch up on. I told my assistant, Liz, that you were coming, so she should be there to welcome you. My planner's in the top drawer of my desk. That'll tell you what you need to do for the next 2 weeks. Shoot me an email or text if you need anything, but I can't guarantee that I'll be available. In that case, direct your questions to Liz. Good luck!!

-Jeanette

The woman with the brown bob flashed into my mind as I read Liz's name. That must have been Jeanette's assistant. Either Jeanette was wrong, and she hadn't been expecting me, or Liz had pictured someone very different than the woman who'd strode into the office.

I pulled open the top desk drawer, and sure enough, there was Jeanette's planner. I took it out and flipped through the pages until I reached the week of January fourteenth. I was looking over my to-do list for the day, wondering why she'd crammed a week's worth of tasks into a single space, when it hit me. This was everything she had to do in one workday.

I hit the home button on my phone and checked the time: 8:25. I'd already wasted twenty-five precious minutes finding my way around the building and settling into my new office. How would I find the time to even make a dent in Jeanette's to-do list?

I heard a knock at my door and looked up, flustered. A guy dressed in full hipster gear stood in the doorway, eyeing me closely. "Are you filling in for Jeanette?"

I nodded. "I'm Nora. I'll be here for the next two weeks." I offered him a warm smile. "What can I help you with?"

"I came by to pick up Bianca's draft on winter hairstyles."

In a flash of panic, I revisited the stack of folders on my desk and searched for any indication of hair or winter. Somewhere in the pile was a folder entitled *Winter 2019 Feat.,* which seemed like the closest match. I silently commended myself for my quick thinking as I handed him the file.

I turned on Jeanette's desktop and took another peek at her planner. From what it looked like, she had a slew of emails waiting for her every morning that I hadn't gotten to yet.

"Excuse me?"

I turned away from the computer to find another visitor waiting at the door. This time, it was a bright-eyed, petite woman who looked like she'd just finished flinging her graduation cap into the air.

"Yes. I'm Nora, Jeanette's temporary substitute," I said before she could ask if I was filling in for her. I had a feeling that question would be coming up a lot over the next few days.

"I'm Kristen," she said. "I report to Jacob, who's in charge of social media. He was wondering if you could look over these posts and make sure they're SEO-friendly."

I tried to remember where I'd heard the acronym before. Jeanette's lime-green folder jumped out at me in response: *SEO Strategies.* Before I could look up its meaning, I caught sight of another visitor standing in the doorway behind Kristen.

I took another panicked glance at the time and saw that it wasn't even nine o'clock yet. Would this go on all day? My eyes traveled to my untouched checklist. The empty boxes almost seemed to mock me.

I took care of the last visitor and immediately dialed Jeanette's number. After the third ring, her voice came on the other line. "Hey, how's it going? Living the dream?"

"Do you always have this many people coming into your office?"

"Pretty much. That's only half the crowd, though. Liz takes care of the other half for me."

"I haven't even gotten to my checklist yet."

"Remember what I said about multitasking? This is the time to take that advice."

I sighed, ashamed of how naïve I'd been in the past. Even dream jobs had their downsides, and if I'd planned for them earlier, I would've handled this more professionally.

"Hey, listen." Jeanette's voice softened, as if she could sense my dwindling self-confidence. "You know how many people would kill to be where you are right now? I had plenty of options when I looked for someone to take my place, but I chose you. And you know I wouldn't trust anyone with this job. I would put the whole company in jeopardy." She paused for a moment. "What I'm trying to say is, you're fully capable of this. And until I find a full-time replacement, I know you'll prove me right."

Her encouragement relieved some of the weight pressing down on my shoulders, and I let myself indulge in the possibility that she was right. I had, after all, made it far enough to earn an acceptance letter from Grant. That had to count for something.

"Thanks for the pep talk. I needed that." The bright-green folder caught my eye again. "Quick question. What does SEO stand for?"

"Search engine optimization."

"Oh, that explains everything."

"It's just a fancy term for helping content rank better on search engines. More viewers leads to more clicks, which leads to more revenue, and so on. Don't get too hung up on the jargon, anyway. You'll figure it out as you go along."

"Here's hoping." I glanced back at my stuffed to-do list. "Well, I'd better go. No rest for the wicked."

"Now you got it." I faintly heard Derek's voice in the background as Jeanette said, "I have to go too, actually. Keep me updated."

"I will."

I hazarded a look at the doorway, and miraculously, it was empty. I seized the opportunity to comb through the stack of PR emails in my inbox. As I clicked through the messages, it struck me how many people depended on Jeanette—not just within the editorial team, but across other departments too. The editor in chief must have been the only person who carried a load heavier than hers.

For the next three hours, I waded through a sea of assignments with no discernable end. I didn't tear my eyes away from my work, not even when my stomach started growling obnoxiously at around noon. Taking a lunch break was out of the question at the rate I was going.

I peeked into my bag and whipped out the granola bar I'd packed that morning. I unwrapped it and took a bite while I used my other hand to type away at the computer.

"Hey," a voice at the door said. It belonged to a dark-skinned, statuesque woman who had a Chanel clutch tucked under her arm. "We're heading out to grab lunch. Wanna come with?"

I glanced behind her and recognized a familiar face that had stopped by my office that morning. They both seemed friendly, and the thought of eating a decent meal was nothing short of tempting, but I had to turn down the offer. Jeanette's words rang through my mind, a threat that kept me glued to my seat: *I would put the whole company in jeopardy.*

"Sorry, guys." I flashed them a regretful smile. "I'd love to, but I'm swamped right now."

"Oh, come on," the woman with the Chanel said. "No one should work *that* hard. Get some air. Everything will still be here when you come back."

I took one last look at my cluttered desk and, with a reluctance that I tried to stifle, got up from my chair. "I guess a quick break couldn't hurt."

"That's the spirit."

After I left the office, the leader of the group headed toward the elevators and hit the call button. She turned to me while we waited. "I'm Vanessa, the features editor here. I don't know if Jeanette told you, but we'll be working together a lot for the September issue." She turned to her friend. "And this is Chloe. She's one of the news editors."

"I'm Nora. I'm the new fashion director." I added quickly, "But only temporarily."

Vanessa smiled. "Nice to meet you." She touched my arm and revealed a set of artistic rings adorning her fingers. "You're gonna love it here, trust me."

"I already do," I said, relieved to be warmly welcomed to the *Couture* team. I'd been so fixated on doing my job well that I hadn't considered the possibility of meeting like-minded people who shared my passion.

The elevator arrived, and we squeezed into it, making room beside a couple of unshaven IT guys from the lower floors. As if the *Couture* office itself weren't exciting enough, the entire Trade Center was constantly buzzing with activity, and it seemed that I met someone new every time I stepped into the elevator.

We poured out into the lobby before emerging into the bright afternoon, which was turning out to be more pleasant than the morning had suggested. People took to the streets in droves to savor the unseasonable warmth before the earth woke from its slumber and remembered it was wintertime.

"Love your shoes, by the way," Chloe said to me. She had porcelain skin that made her look like one of my treasured dolls from childhood, and her cascading white-blonde hair completed the image.

"Thanks." I glanced down at my shoes, glad I'd gone with them after all. I returned my attention to the street, where dozens of eateries popped up every ten feet or so. My mouth watered at the sight of customers strolling out with their to-go cartons. "Where are we going?"

"Only the best sandwich place in all of Manhattan," Vanessa said. "I gained, like, ten pounds from their food when I first started."

Chloe nodded. "It's true. She completely boycotted it for a while."

"And now I'm back." Vanessa flashed a smile as she approached the entrance of The Bread Bistro.

Judging from the line that snaked across the dining room, my coworker wasn't the only one with an addiction to its food. We stood at the back of the line while I surveyed the options behind the glass case. Deciding between a caprese sandwich and balsamic chicken wrap was no easy task.

Since indoor seating was out of the question, I followed the two women to a bench overlooking a circular fountain. We sat down and started devouring our sandwiches, which lived up to Vanessa's praise, to say the least. Between this and the meal at L'Artusi, I couldn't see the justice in the fact that people ate like this every day.

Chloe stole a curious glance at me. "What's the verdict, new girl?"

"Just as good as you promised. Actually, this place reminds me of a little café I used to visit in high school. I grew up on the Upper West Side."

"Do you still live there now?" Vanessa asked.

"Not anymore. I moved to a small town in Iowa when I was twenty. Now I live on a dairy farm with my husband and kids."

"Wow. That must've been so different from what you were

used to." She looked at me with genuine awe as a surge of pride flowed through me.

"It was. But now that I'm used to it, I'm glad I made such a big change."

"I have so much respect for that. Just going out there and taking control of your life," Chloe said. "I've thought about starting over like you did, but I've never had the guts to pull it off."

"It wasn't easy, but I never regret taking a chance," I said, reflecting on my decision to accept Jeanette's offer. "Even if it's the wrong choice, it's better than not knowing what could've happened."

Both women nodded in agreement. As I took the next glorious bite of my sandwich, a ding tore through the air. Vanessa shot a look at her Apple watch and sighed. "Celeste needs us back in the office ASAP. We can't keep the queen waiting."

I stared at her in disbelief. "You're on a first name basis with Celeste Moore?"

"Of course. Just one of the many perks of what we do."

Meeting Celeste Moore, the editor in chief of *Couture,* wasn't a far cry from seeing a Hollywood celebrity in the flesh. In a starstruck daze, I gathered my things, wondering if my job could possibly get any more exciting.

As I followed my coworkers back to the office, Chloe caught up to me. "Hey," she said. "I just wanted to say I'm glad you're here. It's been a while since we've had a new face in the office."

I smiled. "I'm excited to be here. It still feels like I'm in a dream, though."

"I know what you mean. My arms were sore from all the times I pinched myself the first week."

We laughed for a moment before Chloe went on. "I know it can be hard to be the newest person here. I remember how frustrating it was to figure everything out on my own while everyone else already knew what they were doing. So if you ever need anything, I'm here to help."

"Thanks. That means a lot."

As I followed Chloe into the building, I wondered what I'd been so worried about as a teen. It was only my first day, and I was fitting into the company like I'd been working here for years. Aside from Liz, the women I'd met so far hardly resembled the standoffish, judgmental caricature I'd conjured up in my mind during my Grant visit. They were here because they shared the same passion that I did, and they recognized me as one of them because they saw that passion too.

I settled into my chair to look over the blog posts that Kristen had given me earlier. Speaking of passion, it was time to put it to work. No more distractions. Aside from the inevitable afternoon visitors, I had to keep my nose down and focus.

I toiled into the evening, my back stiff from the hours I'd spent glued to my desk chair. I watched my computer screen announce that it was five o'clock, six, then seven. At seven forty-five, I sent my last email and looked around me. The entire office was empty.

With a sigh, I gathered my things and locked up for the night. The walk to the elevators was long and lonely, and a cold, eerie vibe had replaced the energy of the workplace. When I stepped into the elevator, a janitor greeted me. I must have been one of the last workers to leave the building.

The minute I crossed the threshold of my hotel room, I changed into my pajamas and accepted the tempting invitation from my bed. I buried myself under the covers and went straight to my phone to call home. When Tyler's voice came on, it unwound the knot I'd tied myself into over the past twelve hours. He was always the steady rhythm of ocean waves when I was the fraught winds of a hurricane.

"I have so much to tell you," I said as I lay back in bed, the day coming back to me in short snippets. I relayed him every detail I could remember, from my run-in with Liz to the new friends I'd made during lunch. At some point in my anecdote, I sat up as the reality of the past twenty-four hours soaked in.

I'd made it through my first day at *Couture*. It might not have been a walk in the park, but it was an accomplishment that had seemed out of reach until now. I was one step closer to fulfilling the purpose I'd left open-ended for so long, and I had the pen poised in my hand, ready to fill in the blanks.

I rested my head on the pillow, a small smile forming on my lips. Jeanette might have done me the biggest favor yet, and she didn't even know it.

Eight

✎

Two days later, I opened my planner to find a note high-lighted in neon pink: *EDITORIAL MEETING @ 9 AM.*

The first hour of my day was filled to the brim with admin work, so a meeting would be a welcome reprieve from the monotony of answering calls and planning out the rest of the week. I got to work right away, inching my way down the to-do list before I had to head to the conference room.

I'd just booked the next photo shoot when there was a knock at my door. I turned and saw Vanessa standing there with her face twisted into a mischievous smile.

"You busy?" she said.

"Busy and hopelessly bored." I rested my chin on my hand and leaned toward her. "What's up?"

"I have the perfect remedy for that." She motioned for me to follow her, and I got up and met her in the hall. "You haven't had the full *Couture* experience yet. Trust me, this beats sitting at your computer by a mile."

I trailed behind her as she led me to a room at the far end of the hallway. She stopped at the entrance. "Ready?"

"As ready as I'll ever be."

She stepped back to make space for me as I gingerly entered

the room. As soon as I caught a glimpse of what lay inside, a tiny gasp escaped me.

In front of me were shelves upon shelves of shoes in every hue imaginable, surrounded by racks of designer clothes that looked too perfect to wear. The small, white-walled space seemed to glimmer with an aura of beauty that emanated from each corner. As I soaked up every last detail, it occurred to me that this was what I'd been waiting to see since my first day at *Couture*.

"When did I die and go to heaven?"

Vanessa laughed. "You should see your face right now. It's priceless."

"Is this it? *The* fashion closet?"

"Yes, the world-famous fashion closet. You're standing in it right now."

I wandered around like a kid on her first trip to Disney World, reaching out toward the crisp garments without daring to touch them. "Imagine this was my office. I would never want to go home."

"That's why I brought you here. Well, mostly so I could witness your reaction, but also because this is where you'll be taking charge of all the orders. You know, for photo shoots, fashion shows, and so on."

"It feels like I'm trespassing. This is seriously where I'll get to work?" My eyes singled out the unmistakable red underside of a pair of Louboutins as my heart beat a little faster.

"Seems too good to be true, right?" Vanessa crossed the room until she was standing right next to me. "Well, believe it. This is your life now."

In the back of my mind, I was thinking about the farm and

the life I would soon return to after this one was over. But the rest of me was focused on the life I was living in that moment. A life where brands I could only dream of wearing were close enough to touch. A life where I didn't have to stick out like a sore thumb in a town that was ruled by flannel and faded denim.

"Anyway, we have our meeting soon." Vanessa checked her watch. "Scratch that. We have our meeting now."

As we headed back out, I turned around and allowed myself one more longing look at the paradise behind me. *We will meet again,* I told it silently.

I entered the conference room to find a group of bored-looking workers gathered around the circular table. After surveying the empty seats, I plopped down next to Chloe and Vanessa, who were killing time by scrolling through social media. The novelty of my job still hadn't worn off, so I kept busy by observing the room and my colleagues' outfits while I waited for the meeting to begin.

If I hadn't been paying such close attention to my surroundings, I would have missed the one and only Celeste Moore swoop into the room. I held back my second gasp of the morning as she set her things down on the edge of the table and examined the group. It was hard to ignore the shift in the atmosphere that had accompanied her arrival, as if her mere presence reminded everyone that their jobs were as fragile as the glass doors of the conference room.

She sat down and sifted through her tower of folders and papers. The air grew thick as I waited for her to offer a greeting, even if it was a simple "good morning." Instead, she maintained a razor-sharp focus on the files she was handling. I itched to say something to Vanessa to melt away the tension, but the only thing more unnatural than sitting in this uncomfortable silence was breaking it.

"Is there a Nora here?" Celeste asked, eyes still glued to her papers. "Nora Evans?"

My heard jerked up to see a roomful of people staring at me. I nodded. "That's me."

"Great." Celeste's silver eyes landed on me as she pushed away a tuft of short raven-black hair. "Tell us what you came up with."

My eyes flitted over to Vanessa, whose expectant look matched everyone else's. For a flash of a moment, I was back in my English lit class in high school, being singled out by the teacher during a group discussion. Except this time, it seemed that everyone but me had done the reading assignment.

I bought time by rummaging through the few papers I had with me, much like Celeste had done herself. While I carried out my act, a piece of notebook paper materialized on my lap. It read: *She wants to hear your ideas for the Sep. issue.*

I met Chloe's eyes and saw that she was nodding encouragingly at me. I mouthed "Thank you" to her before turning to face my audience. Now that I'd relaxed a bit, all the ideas I'd come up with after my coffee meeting with Jeanette floated back up to the surface, ready to see the light of day.

"I've been thinking about how the September issue focuses on big life changes, and it would be great if we could inspire our readers to change their lives for the better," I began. "We could include makeover tips, major wardrobe changes, stuff like that. I was also thinking about featuring inspiring success stories in the lifestyle section. People need real-life examples to follow so they can improve their own lives."

The words poured out of me like they'd been trapped inside for years. And in a way, they had.

Celeste's expression was unreadable as she processed my idea. "I need an example."

I tried to swallow, but it was like my throat was coated with sandpaper. "We could profile some of the biggest trendsetters in the fashion industry, because they've taken major risks to get to where they are now. As far as the success stories go, our readers would be inspired by people who have made huge changes in their lives. It could be anything, really. Changing careers, starting a new family, or even a journey of personal development." Afraid I was rambling, I shut up and placed my hands in my lap. My palms were damp with sweat.

Celeste was eyeing me with interest, as opposed to the professional detachment she'd displayed moments ago. "You have a unique way of thinking, Nora. Unfortunately, I don't see how it can fit into our publication."

Part of me had seen it coming, but that didn't mean it hurt any less. In a desperate attempt to redeem myself, I struggled to come up with something to say. But Celeste had already moved on to the next victim.

The rest of the meeting was a blur. I half listened to what my coworkers said while the other half of me dwelled on my defeat. I knew it could've gone worse, but that didn't stop my face from burning every time I replayed my failed presentation in my head.

Once the meeting was over, I headed straight to my office without being too obvious. I wasn't in the mood to talk to anyone, and I had the feeling Vanessa would approach me about what had happened. When I was halfway there, though, I heard a familiar voice coming from behind me. "Slow down there, cowgirl."

I turned around and saw Vanessa giving me a sympathetic smile, which only made me feel worse. "Don't take it too hard, okay? We've all been shot down by Celeste at some point. Some publicly, others not."

I ignored the sting of her last sentence. "It's fine. There will be other meetings, anyway."

"That's the right attitude." She leaned closer like she was about to let me in on a secret. "By the way, you handled that pretty well. The first time Celeste did that to me, I had to force myself not to burst into tears."

I hadn't been too far from that myself, but I chose to act as cool and collected as she believed I was. "I mean, rejection is inevitable, right? You just have to move on from it."

"Easier said than done, my friend. But I admire your optimism."

After Vanessa had returned to her desk, I made my way back to mine and tried to refocus on all the work I had to do. Thankfully, the meeting had ended earlier than expected, so I had a little extra time to make some progress in my to-do list.

I opened the file that one of the writers had sent me and entered editing mode. I hadn't even finished reading the first sentence when snippets of the meeting and my conversation with Vanessa invaded my thoughts.

I don't see how it can fit into our publication.
Don't take it too hard, okay?
There will be other meetings, anyway.

The final sentence gnawed at me until I could no longer ignore it. I'd said it to Vanessa offhandedly, in the same way someone might say, "There's always next year!" after a snowstorm ruined their holiday travel plans. But in my case, there would be no other meeting. Liz had told me that the editorial team held biweekly meetings, which meant the next one would take place once I was back on the farm.

I stopped what I was doing and opened a new tab on my browser. I started scouring the internet for any information that would back up my idea. Celeste might have dismissed me in the conference room, but it was hard to ignore someone who had cold, hard facts.

I told myself that if she turned down my pitch a second time, I would accept it and move on. But I couldn't do that without knowing I'd made an effort.

The printer spit out page after page of statistics and figures, and I organized each sheet into a neat packet. After stapling it all together, I headed down the hall.

I was standing two inches from Celeste's office door when I froze in place. What did I think I was doing? I still hadn't learned all the rules of the *Couture* workplace, but strolling up to the editor in chief's office uninvited seemed like an overt infringement of them.

My mouth was drying up like it had in the conference room, and my heart had broken into a sprint inside my chest. Just before I turned back to my office, I realized what doing that would mean. It would mean I hadn't changed since turning down this opportunity at eighteen. It would mean I hadn't conquered the self-doubt that fed over fifteen years of regret.

I'd come here to prove to myself that I *had* changed, and I couldn't forget that. Before I could think twice, I knocked on her door and waited. There was no going back now.

"Come in," she called.

I turned the knob and took a tentative step inside. Celeste was sitting behind a large mahogany desk, her face pointed toward a shiny new Mac. The wall behind her was lined with framed covers of past *Couture* issues that boasted fashion icons from Madonna to Taylor Swift. Right in the center, like an island in a sea of glamour, was a glossy diploma from Grant. I ignored the pang in my chest and cleared my throat.

"Sorry to bother you. I'm Nora Evans. I was in the editorial meeting just now. I understand you didn't approve of my idea, but I've done some research on it that might change your mind. I was hoping I could show you, if it isn't too much trouble."

She eyed the stack of papers under my arm. "Go on."

I handed her each sheet of paper as I explained it. "These are the search engine rankings for the keywords I proposed. *Self-improvement* has been steadily rising in popularity over the last few months. On Twitter, hashtags like #MondayMotivation and #Hustle are taking over the platform. Plus, if you look at website traffic for these top online publications, you'll see that articles on success and personal growth have been getting the most views."

She studied each graph while I stood patiently in front of her desk. To my genuine surprise, she seemed to be carefully evaluating each piece of data instead of glossing over it like I'd expected her to.

Once she'd digested everything, Celeste peered up at me from behind her reading glasses. "I can tell you care about this a lot."

"I do." I hoped my conviction shone through in my voice.

She studied me for another moment then set her glasses down on the stack of papers. "I'll tell you what. You find a way to make your idea work, and I'll let you do what you want with it. Needless to say, I'll have the final word once we get to the publication stage."

"Of course," I said, relief washing over me. "You won't be disappointed."

"I hope not." She shot me a questioning glance. "You're only here temporarily, correct?"

"That's right. Jeanette's still looking for someone to take up a long-term position. But I'm taking care of everything for her in the meantime."

"Well, I'll have you know that you have big shoes to fill." Her unblinking eyes fixed themselves on me, holding an unspoken warning. "Jeanette was a smart and passionate worker, and she did many great things for this magazine. I expect you to live up to her reputation."

My heart tumbled, but I smothered the feeling with a bright smile that made me feel more capable than I was. "I'm up to the challenge. I've wanted to work in fashion for as long as I can remember, so this is a huge opportunity for me."

"I can tell. You have an eye for it." While I registered the fact that Celeste Moore had just complimented my fashion taste, she said, "Get the rough draft of the feature article to me by the twenty-fifth."

"Definitely." I smiled. "Thank you for your time. It means a lot."

As I turned to leave, Celeste spoke again. "Nora?"

"Yes?"

"You have potential. I can see it. And if there's one thing I hate more than the athleisure trend, it's seeing perfectly good potential go to waste." I thought a saw a hint of a smile adorn her face. "You might have a big job ahead of you, but I see how dedicated you are. Just be sure to put that dedication to work."

My smile came naturally this time. "Don't worry. I will."

As I left the room, I felt like I was walking on air. The feeling was so pure, so perfect, that it seemed wrong to keep it to myself. I paced the hall and scanned the rows of faces to find someone to share the news with. Vanessa's head of wavy black hair stuck out from the back of the room, and I strode over to her desk.

"You won't believe this," I said as I edged in next to her.

"This better be good. I'm making some serious editing magic over here."

"You know how Celeste turned down my idea earlier? Well, I think I just talked her into it."

She laughed. "Right, and I'm going to quit my job tomorrow and become a stripper."

"I'm serious. I did a ton of research on user intent to prove why readers would love my idea, and she decided to give me another chance. Looks like all those SEO assignments paid off."

A shadow passed over her face for just a moment, but she recovered quickly. "That's great, Nora. Really. It takes guts to do that."

"I know. I'm glad I didn't back down." I glanced over at my office. "Well, I'd better get back to work."

"Yup. You have a lot to do." She smiled, but the warm gesture didn't soften the edge in her voice.

As I walked back to my office, I tried to dismiss the entire exchange. Just as I turned the knob, though, my curiosity won over. I looked back at Vanessa's desk and found her leaning toward another colleague. Both of them seemed to be exchanging words under their breath. For a split second, the other woman's eyes landed on mine.

I turned around and went straight to my desk before I had the chance to become an exhibit. As I sat down, I stole a final glance at Vanessa and her friend. That was when it hit me.

I wasn't supposed to be getting approval from the editor in chief. I was supposed to be quietly blending into the background, staying inside the lines until Jeanette returned. At most, I was permitted a barely noticeable ripple in the ocean that was this company. But I'd been here for three days, and I was already creating waves that hurtled onto the sand, swallowing everything in their wake until they could no longer be ignored.

Vanessa might have been my friend, but she wasn't like me. I'd come here to get a taste of the life I'd missed out on for so many years, and I wasn't about to let an obstacle in my path stop me. Not even if that obstacle was the enormous pressure of living up to Jeanette's reputation.

My newfound confidence supplied me with a fresh surge of energy, and I got back to work right away. It was time for Vanessa to get used to the way I operated. After all, I was just getting started.

Nine

〜

My phone stared up at me from atop the papers scattered across my hotel room desk. I'd gotten up early to get a head start on the feature story that Celeste had assigned to me, and my mind was buzzing with ideas. But my blank phone screen was a stark reminder that my hunger for success was a lonely feeling. There was a gaping hole where the ones I'd left behind at home were supposed to be, and it was up to me to fill it.

I unlocked my phone and tapped on the FaceTime app. While I waited for Tyler to pick up, longing swelled inside me. It had only been a few days since the last time I'd seen my family, but it felt like we belonged to separate worlds now.

When their faces filled the screen, I failed to find the words I needed. The feeling of longing ballooned deep inside me until it was all I could focus on. "Hey, guys. I miss you so much."

"We miss you too, Mommy!" Bridget said. Her eyes widened as she took in my background. "Ooh, can I see your hotel room?"

"Sure." I held up my phone and tilted it toward the room so everyone could see it. When I glanced back at my family, I noticed that Caleb looked the most enthralled. The glimmer in his eyes reminded me of the thrill I'd felt when I first returned to the city.

"You get to look at that every day? That's so cool." My son's eyes were fixated on the tips of the skyscrapers outside my window, and his mouth hung open in captivation.

"I know. I still can't believe it myself." Smiling at Bridget and Caleb, I said, "So, how's school going?"

"Great! I'm in the same class as Andrea and Kyler, so we get to see each other all day. Plus, my music teacher is really nice." Bridget's features twisted into a grimace. "But math class stinks. I hate multiplication."

"You're learning," I told her. "As long as you keep practicing, you'll get it. Just don't give up."

She still looked unconvinced until a new thought stole her attention. "Oh, and I saw Caleb in the hall yesterday with a bunch of older kids. One of them pushed a third grader into the lockers. They don't seem very nice." She shot her brother a disapproving look.

My heart sank with dread as Caleb looked at Bridget sharply, as if to stop her from saying anything more. All I could think about was the way he'd approached me before I left for the airport, his eyebrows knitted in a silent plea for help. I'd let that plea go unanswered, and now he was getting in trouble with a crowd he didn't belong to.

Tyler turned to the kids before I could respond. "It's almost time to leave for school. Say goodbye to Mom so you can finish getting ready."

There was so much more I wanted to ask my kids about, but I knew Tyler was trying to give us the chance to talk alone. I returned Bridget's and Caleb's goodbyes and offered them a smile that I hoped was enough to conceal the worry planted in my heart.

After they'd both left to get ready, I frowned at Tyler. "Is Caleb really hanging out with those kids?"

"You know Bridget doesn't lie. I saw Caleb's new friends myself when I picked him up. They're not the types of kids he normally hangs out with at all."

"This has been going on for a while," I said quietly, remembering the way Caleb couldn't get out of my truck fast enough to join his posse on the first day of the new semester. They'd looked innocent enough back then, but I must have only seen what I wanted to see. "I just don't understand. This isn't like him."

Tyler shifted his eyes away from the screen, and I knew there was something he wasn't telling me.

"What is it?" I asked.

A wave of disappointment passed over his eyes as he met my gaze. "Caleb told me he doesn't want the farm anymore."

The phone suddenly felt too heavy in my hand. "What?" I scrambled to dig up a feasible explanation, something that would tamp down the worry that was rising inside me. "Maybe he's just going through something. He is only ten, you know. You can't expect a ten-year-old to know what they want to do for the rest of their life."

"This is how it all started with Dylan," he said. As soon as the words were out of his mouth, I regretted making light of the situation.

Tyler's older brother, Dylan, had strayed from farming when he was a teenager. After going on a class trip to Chicago, he'd been drawn to the energy of the city like sparks clinging to hot coals. He'd secured a finance internship during his junior year of college and worked his way up the corporate ladder without so much as a fleeting glance backward.

Then, when Dylan was twenty-two and Tyler was twenty, their dad died suddenly of heart failure. In the wake of the immense tragedy was an all-encompassing sense of uncertainty about the future of the farm. The tradition with family-owned farms was that the eldest child inherited the land, which meant that Dylan should have been the one to look after the cattle. But it was clear he'd made his decision the minute his feet touched Chicago concrete.

Now I knew what Tyler saw in Caleb's announcement. He saw the beginnings of a lifelong rejection of farming. He saw the end of a tradition that had been in his family for four generations. He used to tell me how he'd found solace in the farm after his dad died, how it had grounded him and given him purpose. Now, it pained me to see the sadness in his eyes, as if he'd already lost something that meant the world to him.

"What about Bridget?" I said gently. "She's a total natural with the animals. She'd be great as a farmer."

"I know she would. But if she changes her mind like Caleb, there will be no one to take over the farm." His voice took on a somber note. "My dad dedicated his whole life to farming. This is his legacy. If I hand down the farm to one of the kids, I need to know it'll be in good hands."

"It will," I said, trying to help him see that all wasn't lost. "We've given both of them a great work ethic, and they know how important this is to you."

"I know." I could see in his face that he wanted to believe me. Before I could say anything else, I heard Bridget's voice in the distance. He turned and said something to her before facing me again. "I have to get going. School's starting soon."

"Perfect timing, because I have to head to work now."

He smiled. "Hey, thanks for checking in. You must be really busy over there."

"It is pretty crazy. Then again, getting up at six is sleeping in compared to my old schedule."

He laughed. "Well, good luck with everything. And remember, you can always call me whenever you need to."

"I know." The reminder made me feel anchored to home, and a soft smile spread across my face. "Love you."

"Love you too."

When we hung up, the warmth of our exchange dissolved just as quickly as it had embraced me. All I was left with were the words I'd uttered about Caleb—words that I knew were cold comfort. I was still haunted by the look on my son's face when he'd caught a glimpse of my hotel room view. That wasn't the look of a child enjoying a temporary pleasure that he would soon move on from. That was the look of pure hunger. It was the kind of hunger I'd recognized in Jeanette when she chased down her *Couture* internship and in myself when I marched into Celeste's office after the meeting, refusing to take no for an answer.

As I walked toward the Trade Center and settled into my office, I couldn't help but worry that Caleb was becoming someone he wasn't meant to be. He'd never been as close to the animals as Bridget, but he would never abandon the farm. Whatever those kids were doing to him, it was robbing us of the Caleb we all knew.

A light knock on my door pulled me out of my rumination.

I turned around, making a sincere effort to swallow my pain and be the professional I was expected to be. Chloe stood there with a knowing look on her face, like she was waiting for me to quit my act.

"Trouble in paradise?" she asked.

I smiled. "I wish I could talk about it, but I'm crazy busy right now." I pulled a file out of a random folder to make my point.

She raised an eyebrow. "You're busy editing a story from eight years ago?"

I looked down at the file, which was emblazoned with the title *2011 Spring Feature.* "I was looking for inspiration."

She sat down on the chair opposite me. "Look, I get it if you don't want to talk about it. But just in case you change your mind, I'm here."

"Thanks," I said with a weak smile.

"Anyway, the real reason I'm here is to finally get you started on the September issue. Vanessa works closely with Megan, one of our visual editors, and she said Megan has a ton of ideas to go with your pitch. She was thinking of focusing on a relaxed country vibe and contrasting that with the high energy of the city. I told her it was perfect. Not only does it encourage people to dream big, but it also echoes the change you made in your own life."

I wanted her to keep talking, because it was the only thing that reminded me of why I'd come here in the first place. Why I'd finally taken such a big risk after spending years doubting myself.

"That sounds great. I'll talk to Vanessa right away."

"Awesome." Chloe stood up to leave then turned back toward me. "I know I haven't said anything since you got here, but you're doing a great job so far. You should've seen how everyone reacted when Jeanette announced she was leaving. As demanding as she could be sometimes, she held this place together." She smiled. "But now that you're here, it's clear we have nothing to worry about."

Her words simultaneously lifted my spirits and pressed down on me with a crushing weight. The entire staff was depending on me. If I messed up, there would be no coming back from it.

I forced a smile that held the confidence I wished I had. "Thanks, Chloe."

Once my office was empty again, I turned to my computer and typed out a quick message to Vanessa. Picturing my creation coming to fruition for all the world to see made me feel more alive than I'd felt in a while. For a fleeting moment, my worries about Caleb fizzled into the background as my goals for the magazine took center stage. I wasn't going anywhere until I saw my work grace the pages of the biggest *Couture* issue of the year—no matter how long it took to make it happen.

Five minutes later, Vanessa appeared in my doorway with a stack of papers tucked under her arm. "As a former marketing manager, I can tell you that Megan's photo layout has a lot of selling potential." She strode up to me and dropped the papers onto my desk. "But as someone who hoofed it all the way from the subway in these painful Jimmy Choos, I say we need to give these pictures a more fashion-focused angle."

"I agree." I glanced at the notes I'd brought with me from the hotel room. "Actually, I have some ideas to go along with the photo spread."

"Well, what are you waiting for? I'm desperate for material here."

Seeing the eager look on her face sent a rush of power through me. The fashion pages were one of the most important parts of the magazine, and I'd been given the role of breathing life into them. It felt good to know that what I did mattered and that it would still matter after I was back in my small town, my stint as a fashion director long forgotten.

I glanced up at Vanessa and let my ideas flow out of me. "I want to put together a story on how to dress boldly at work. I went to private school, and I remember how restricting it was to wear the same uniform every single day. I was always looking for edgy ways to add my own touch to that bland outfit. Anyway, I think workers who are forced to hide their true style in the office should find creative ways to be themselves, while staying professional, of course."

She pointed her pen at me. "I like the way you think." Her eyes grew wider. "Maybe we could do the shoot on a crowded city street and have the model dress in something totally different from standard work clothing. You know, like a dreamy boho vibe or something with a rock and roll feel to it."

"That's perfect," I said.

Vanessa watched me intently as I gave my own take on her idea, even nodding with genuine interest. It occurred to me for the first time that I was treated like an adult here. People heard me out and took my ideas seriously when I needed them to. Somewhere between all the diaper changing and PTA meetings, I'd missed out on the opportunity to know what that felt like.

"I'm going to talk to Celeste. I'm sure she can't wait to hear your idea."

"Sounds great," I said, hardly containing my enthusiasm.

"We'll keep in touch, okay?" She turned to the door. "Let me know if any more inspiration strikes."

"I will."

After she left, I turned my attention back to my planner and started to tackle the next item on my to-do list. As I worked, I realized the tasks that had once seemed mundane now excited me. Every little thing I did fit into the bigger picture of *Couture,* and I had an active role in all of it. I was here for a reason—a reason I was just starting to fully comprehend.

I held on to the thought fervently, like it was the only hope I had left. Ever since I started my job here, a part of me had been afraid of being trapped in a world that wasn't meant for me anymore. But now I knew that it was up to me to make my time here mean something. Through the next week I'd spend here. Through all the challenges I would have to encounter during that time. Through becoming who I was supposed to be all along, no matter how hard I had to work to get there.

Ten

~~~

I stood in front of the bathroom mirror and admired the haircut I'd gotten over the weekend. My stylist, an eccentric New York native with an entire display of awards at her station, had effortlessly transformed my uninspired, monochromatic blonde bob into an asymmetrically layered cut with caramel highlights.

It hadn't occurred to me all these years that I'd been settling for averageness. I'd been trying to blend in with the Fairlane status quo by letting my individuality wither away in some forgotten part of me. Most importantly, though, I hadn't realized until now that it didn't have to be that way. The person I really was and the style that defined me was silently waiting to emerge, just as long as I granted it permission.

A toilet flushed behind me, and the stall door opened. I recognized the woman who walked out as Kristen, one of my visitors from my first day at the office. She eyed me as she turned on the water. "I love what you did with your hair."

I smiled. "Thanks."

"One time, when I was fourteen or something, I cut about eight inches off my hair until it was as short as yours. Then I bought this hair dye kit at the drugstore and dyed my hair electric blue." She chuckled at the memory. "I think I almost gave my mom a heart attack."

"I can't imagine how my mom would've reacted if I did something like that."

As soon as the words were out of my mouth, they thickened the air around me. I hadn't seen my mom and dad for over four years, since Thanksgiving of 2015. Before then, we'd stuck to our agreement to alternate between spending the holidays in New York and Fairlane. But that Thanksgiving, which had been a Fairlane year, my mom had griped over her untouched food about how much of a hassle it was to come all the way out there. If I'd chosen to stay in New York, she said, she wouldn't have to hop on a plane just to see her daughter. And if she was going to fly out to the middle of nowhere, could she at least enjoy her meal in a house that wasn't attached to a barn?

Any time she brought up my past and the scars I'd left behind, I had to steel myself. But that time was different. That time, I wasn't the only one who bore the brunt of her bitterness. As I watched Tyler's mouth form a thin line and Bridget's eyes widen with confusion and hurt, the betrayal I felt was amplified by the weight of my family's pain. That was the last time the six of us had eaten Thanksgiving dinner together.

The way my mom had treated my family that day left a dull ache in my heart. But a part of me still longed to have a normal relationship with my parents. I knew how close Tyler had been to his father and how close he still was to his mother. Maybe my parents and I would never reach that level, but the stubborn optimism inside me wanted to believe that there was hope of mending our fractured bond.

I finished drying my hands and swung open the door of the

ladies' room. The voice in my head was telling me it was useless to call. A single conversation couldn't resolve fifteen years of tension. Luke's words from our last phone call rang through my mind: *You can't expect everything to be all sunshine and roses after what you did.* I knew I should have taken the hint and left everything where it had always been. But if I gave in that easily, would I be in New York now, working my dream job? The answer rang through my ears, telling me it was now or never.

I sat down at my desk and scrolled through my contacts. With a shaky breath, I tapped my mom's number and held the phone to my ear.

When her voice came on, it was noticeably guarded, as if she were trying to conceal her surprise. "Nora?"

"Hi, Mom. I hope it's not a bad time."

"No, of course not. Is everything all right?"

I tried to ignore how strained her voice sounded, which seemed to underscore how long it'd been since we'd last spoken. "Everything's fine." I took a deep breath. "I'm in New York."

"You're in New York?" She said it like I'd told her I was hiking through the Amazon.

"I got here last Friday. I'm filling in for my friend at *Couture.* You remember Jeanette, right?"

"Oh yes, your friend from high school. What happened? Did she get fired?"

"No, she's on maternity leave. She needs someone to take her place, so I offered to help out for a couple weeks while she looks for a replacement."

There was a pause, as if my mother needed time to digest everything I'd told her. "So you're in the city now? Working at *Couture*?" She was silent again, and I braced myself for what was to come. "I don't understand. If you wanted that job, why did you turn down Grant?"

There it was, sooner than I'd expected it to come. "I told you, Mom, I messed up. I was young, and I... I didn't feel ready to take such a big step." I swallowed, trying to place myself back in the present. "But that doesn't matter now. I'm lucky enough to have a second chance, so I'm making the best of it."

"Well, then. I take it you've finally come to your senses. Of course, if you'd done so before you decided to leave mid-semester, things would have gone more smoothly." She was picking up steam now, and I had no chance of stopping her. "So, is that it, now? Are you staying in New York? Perhaps it isn't too late for you to find someone else. I have to say, I never thought Tyler was good enough for you. He didn't even go to college."

I tightened my grip on the phone. "He was too busy running an entire farm on his own. And I told you, I'm only staying here for two weeks."

"You can't leave," she said matter-of-factly, like we were discussing the weather forecast. "There's no future for you back in Iowa. If you want to make something of yourself, New York is your only chance."

I'd heard that before. I instinctively tensed up as I remembered sitting in the living room of my old apartment while she lectured me about throwing my life away. "Mom, I have a family at home. A family who misses me a lot. I can't just start a new life here."

"It's a shame, Nora. I never saw you as the farmer type. Of all the things you could have become." After sighing for dramatic effect, she said, "Anyway, moving on. What brought you to call in the middle of the day like this? I imagine you have plenty to do at work."

I'd had a preface in mind earlier, but I decided it was better to dive right in. "I was wondering if we could meet sometime for lunch or coffee. You, me, and Dad. There's this amazing sandwich place near my office. Or I can meet you guys on the West Side. Whatever works best."

I could only imagine what was going through her head. After a beat, she said, "I'll have to speak with your father, but we should have time for a quick bite. What's the name of the restaurant you mentioned?"

"The Bread Bistro."

"Hold on." I heard muffled voices in the background. "How does Wednesday at one p.m. sound?" She spoke like she was making an appointment with a client, not discussing lunch plans with her daughter.

"Perfect."

"Great. I'll see you then."

"Bye, Mom."

When the call was over, I rested my head against my desk chair and stared up at the ceiling. Revisiting this corner of my past hadn't been part of the plan, but there was no telling the next time I would be in New York. This might be the only chance I had to tie up all the loose ends that dangled in anticipation before my eyes.

I owed it to my mom. I owed it to my dad and brother. And, most of all, I owed it to the person in the mirror—the person I'd been trying to pay back since I came here.

***

Celeste called an emergency editorial meeting the next afternoon. According to Liz, this had only happened twice before: once, when an editor accidentally sent out an unfinished article, and again when a pair of Aquazzura shoes went missing. I subtly observed my coworkers through the glass walls of my office, trying to spot someone who looked on edge. I couldn't help but wonder who had messed up badly enough to warrant such a rare meeting.

At two o'clock, I turned off my monitor and headed to the conference room. I could tell I wasn't the only one who'd let the suspense get the best of her. Some people spoke under their breath to one another, while others darted furtive glances at their coworkers. By the time we reached the circular table, the air was thick with everything we weren't saying.

I took a seat next to Chloe, remembering how she'd thrown me a lifeline during our first meeting. If Celeste started interrogating me again, I needed to be next to someone I could trust. Just as the thought passed through my head, the queen herself entered the room, her heels clicking purposefully on the marble tile. She dropped her papers onto the desk and set her unblinking eyes on us like a hawk. She didn't sit down.

"Before we begin, I want to say that I recognize the hard work you've all been doing. We've made some great progress over the past few weeks." The tone she used was markedly different than what we were all expecting—I saw it in the way people's shoulders relaxed as soon as she began speaking. Still, when it came to Celeste, I could never be too sure.

"I know you're all doing your part here. However, I'm a firm believer in giving credit where credit is due." She turned toward me, and my heart seized up with anxiety. "Vanessa, can you tell us about what you've been working on?"

I turned to my left and saw Vanessa sitting right next to me, perfectly poised and smiling, as if she were waiting for Celeste to ask the question.

"Of course," she said brightly then cleared her throat. "I've been thinking about the theme of change and risk-taking that we're focusing on for the September issue, which led me to brainstorm some ideas. That's when I started thinking about how the way we dress for work is such an important part of our everyday style. But let's face it—it can be hard to let our true style shine through when we're confined to a professional environment. And that's exactly what I want the focus of my article to be."

Her words sounded familiar. Too familiar. It wasn't until she was halfway through her pitch that I remembered where I'd heard it before. She wouldn't stoop that low—or would she?

"It's our job to help readers come up with creative ways to give their work outfits a personal touch. Whether they're into an edgy rocker look or a folksy, free-spirit style, it's important for everyone to feel like they can express themselves in the office. As long as they stay professional, they shouldn't be forced to hide their individuality."

"Beautiful. Thank you, Vanessa." Celeste spoke with the closest thing to a smile that I'd seen since I got here.

My eyes darted back and forth between Vanessa and Celeste like I was watching a tennis match. The whole time, I was waiting for someone to call her out on what she'd done. But that was impossible, because I was the only one who knew what had just happened.

"I hope you were all taking notes, because this is a prime example of the type of content I'm looking for. Fresh. Current. Exciting. Vanessa's idea is all of those things and more."

But it's not her idea. It's mine. I shouted the words in my head, as if that would make everyone hear them somehow. It was like someone was holding my head underwater, rendering everything I said incoherent.

"I know I don't call emergency meetings often, but this seemed necessary. I need all of you to start thinking like Vanessa from now on. In the meantime, we need to get started on the photo shoot for this story. I'm confident it'll reach a much wider audience than we're used to." She clapped her hands. "Meeting adjourned. I expect you all to be very busy during the next few hours."

As everyone gathered their things, Vanessa exchanged a few words with Celeste. My coworker then turned around and strode up to me. "Hey, Nora. We did a great job during our chat last week. It's amazing what we can do when we put our heads together."

I blinked, wondering if we'd just attended the same meeting. "That's not the way you made it look. Because what I witnessed was you passing off my idea as your own."

She dismissed my comment with a flick of her wrist. "Ideas are ideas, Nora. They bounce from one person to another. It's impossible to know where they come from." Placing a reassuring hand on my arm, she added, "But that doesn't matter. What matters is that we're about to make *Couture* history."

Before I could say anything else, she turned to the door and left in a cloud of Clive Christian perfume. I stared blankly at the exit as everyone filed out of the room. Everyone, that was, except me.

While Celeste gathered her belongings, I tried to hatch a game plan. The thought of Vanessa taking credit for my idea made me want to march up to my boss and tell her what her star employee had done. At the same time, where would that take me? She had no reason to believe I was telling the truth. I knew deep down that it was safer to keep quiet and work privately on my next idea.

As I struggled to make a decision, I caught myself thinking back to the time I'd approached Celeste on my own. The reason she'd given me her attention and approved my idea was because I'd presented her with concrete evidence. I was still new here, but I was beginning to see that Celeste preferred cold, hard facts over nebulous feelings and ideas.

I headed straight for the door and marched over to the fashion closet. I may have lost this battle, but I wasn't about to lose the war. I lowered myself onto the stool in the corner of the closet and studied the newly supplied clothes and shoes. The answer lay somewhere in the array of colors and textures, and it was up to me to find it.

I stood and wandered through the racks, which exuded the same air of magic that I'd felt the first time I stepped into the room. I could almost see all the ideas that had been born in this closet. I could feel the inspiration blossoming inside me. This was where miracles happened. And I needed a miracle to come up with an idea that put Vanessa's to shame.

While I paced in front of the shoe rack, it hit me. I straightened, feeling the gentle tap of my muse rouse me from my mental fog. *That's it. How did I not see it all this time?*

Before the idea eluded me, I hurried back to my office and got to work, scribbling down notes like my life depended on it. Every now and then, I pretended to look bored or stopped to check in with one of my office visitors, just in case someone suspected that I was up to something.

By five o'clock, I'd checked off every item on my planner for that day and had a new idea safely tucked away in my work bag. I'd learned my lesson this time. From now on, my sketches would stay between Celeste and me.

When I left the building, the streets glowed faintly in the waning daylight. I clutched my denim jacket against the biting wind, already mourning the unseasonably nice weather that had graced the city a couple days ago. Now that winter was finally here, I felt it in the air that it was here to stay.

I watched the last rays of sun disappear behind the buildings, reflecting on the week that had passed since I started working at *Couture*. In those seven days, I'd already bounced back from obstacles that would have knocked me down when I was eighteen. From Vanessa taking credit for my idea to the blunt way Celeste had turned down my initial pitch, I'd handled everything life had thrown at me with the self-assuredness I'd longed for as a young adult.

The thought struck me as I approached my hotel room. Was this how things would have turned out if I'd accepted the opportunity the first time? Or was my success a result of being older and more experienced? There was a good chance that twenty-two-year-old me would have busied herself with taking coffee orders or doing inventory before she reached my current position. *If she ever made it this far at all...*

It was impossible to know who I could've been when I was

only allowed to be who I was. Imagining my unactualized self was like piecing together the hazy details of a dream after waking up. But maybe missing out on my first chance had been a blessing in disguise. Maybe I'd needed to say no the first time so I could say yes to everything I had now. Maybe I'd needed to wait until I was ready to be the person I had become. And I'd never felt more ready in my life.

Eleven

One o'clock on Wednesday afternoon arrived, along with a pit of dread in my stomach. I should've known from the wary tone of voice my mom used on the phone that it wasn't the real Nora who'd arranged our lunch plans. It someone else—someone who'd deceived herself into thinking that a lunch meeting would be enough to patch up the past. Now the real me was stuck staring at my office door, trying to get my brain to agree with my body that it was time to face reality.

I plucked my bag from my chair and trudged over to the door. I almost hoped that Chloe or even Vanessa would offer to take me out to lunch so I would have a legitimate excuse to skip the meeting with my parents. Of course, both women chose today of all days to keep their noses to the grindstone. Even my not-so-subtle lingering by their desks did nothing to interrupt their frantic typing.

Accepting my fate, I took the elevator down to the lobby and made my way toward The Bread Bistro. I'd barely stepped inside when I spotted my mom and dad standing in line, looking bored and a bit uncomfortable. I couldn't help noticing how they looked like fish out of water among a sea of young people. Back when I was a kid, they would have fit right into the scene.

As I waded through the crowd, I had a flashback to my high school graduation ceremony. Once I'd collected my diploma and flung my cap into the air, I'd searched a sea of people similar to this one to find my parents. I remembered seeing the pride on their faces, how it'd made me feel like I'd genuinely pleased them for the first time in my life.

Now I knew why they'd been so happy. To my parents, that sunny day in mid-June was the peak of everything I would become. Everything after that was just an embarrassing mistake they preferred to cover up.

"Nora?" My mom said my name like she'd made an unusual discovery and wasn't sure what to think of it.

"Yup. In the flesh." I turned to my dad, who was standing beside my mom in line. "Hey, Dad."

My father looked at me like it was the first time he'd ever seen me, which was true in a sense. The last time I'd seen my parents, I'd long ago shed the designer wardrobe and New York swagger that I'd picked up again over the past week. I must have looked as unfamiliar to them as the plain country girl they'd met when I first moved to Fairlane.

"There's nowhere to sit," my mom said as she glanced pointedly around the room.

"There never is. I was thinking we could sit on a bench outside. I know it's a little chilly, but at least the sun is out." Even after all this time, I still felt the need to justify my every decision for them.

"Fine with me," my dad said. He was fine with anything as long as it didn't involve disease or economic turmoil. I was more worried about my mom.

"Well, if you insist. I was hoping we could sit at a table like civilized people." The complaint reminded me of her jab at the farm on Thanksgiving, and my body stiffened.

As I waited for my turn to order, I studied my parents for the first time in more than four years. Seeing them again was a stark reminder of how quickly the time had passed. My father's dark-brown hair was now speckled with gray, and my mother's creamy complexion had been fractured by hair-like lines and wrinkles. I couldn't help but wonder what they thought of me. Were they relieved to see the New Yorker I used to be? Or was the sight of me a bitter reminder of where I'd gone wrong over the past fifteen years? I longed to find the answers I needed in the words they weren't saying.

Once we all had our food, I led the way toward the bench where I'd sat with Vanessa and Chloe the week earlier. My dad took a seat beside me while my mom checked for crumbs or pigeon droppings. Even after she failed to find any offenders, she perched on the edge of the bench as if she were ready to bolt at any moment.

"So, when did you get here?" my dad asked.

"Last Friday. I needed a couple of days to settle in before I started working."

"I see." He paused to wipe his mouth. "Where are you staying?"

"The Four Seasons. It's only a five-minute walk from here."

"May I ask how you're paying for that?" my mom asked.

"I'm not," I faltered. "Jeanette paid for it. I was going to stay at the Marriott, but she told me at the last minute that she booked a suite for me."

"That was very nice of her. I never understood why you two drifted apart after high school."

"Things change," I said noncommittedly. "We're not the same as we were at eighteen." I took another bite of my sandwich, hoping my cover-up was enough to distract them from the truth. I couldn't imagine what they would think if they knew Jeanette had snatched the Grant offer that I'd willingly surrendered.

We ate in silence for a minute or so before a wailing siren filled the lull in our conversation. I'd thought of a dozen things to say since we'd sat down, but they all seemed trivial or irrelevant. The weight of everything that had caused us to drift apart seemed too heavy to put into words.

"So, how do you like it?"

I turned to my mom. "How do I like what?"

"Your job. I know you just started, but you must have some thoughts on it so far."

It wasn't the question that caught me off guard. It was the way she said it. For the first time since my graduation ceremony, I could've sworn I saw a glimmer of pride in her eyes. I hated that it happened, but my heart lifted as I realized I hadn't completely failed her.

"It's pretty amazing. It's definitely hard work, but I love knowing that I'm bringing the magazine to life every day. Oh, and I met Celeste Moore for the first time last week."

"You *met* her?" my mom asked, sounding like a starstruck fangirl.

"I sure did. Not only that, but she even approved an idea I had for the September issue."

"That's incredible, Nora."

"Yeah." I smiled. "I guess it is."

"See what happens when you apply yourself?" my dad asked.

My mom nodded sagely. "Your father's right. Of course, we always knew you were capable of all this. We were just waiting for you to see it."

As I looked at her, I asked myself the question that had been rustling in my head for the past twenty minutes. Was this what it all boiled down to? Had my mom and dad been sitting there with bated breath since I left home, waiting for me to wake up and live the life I was meant to live? I'd always known that my choices were to blame for the way we'd grown apart, but I hadn't known it would be this easy to patch things up again. I'd accepted a temporary position, and my parents were suddenly showering me with the praise that they'd withheld for fifteen years.

"We're just happy you found your place," my dad said in his diplomatic way. "It's good to try new things every once in a while. Helps build character."

We all seemed to be in agreement with that. As I polished off the remnants of my sandwich, I turned to both of them. "What about you guys? How's the city been treating you?"

"Well, you know how New York is. Always something exciting going on." My mom's eyes were sparkling, and she looked more excited than she had all afternoon. "You know, I signed up for a class the other day."

"Really? What kind of class?"

She waved a hand, as if the question were irrelevant. "Nothing special. Just an opportunity to keep me sharp in my old age."

I was debating whether to prod her for more details or refute her comment about being old when her eyes lit up. "Oh, I almost forgot! I brought a sign-up sheet with me, just in case you were interested in joining." She produced a small white envelope seemingly out of thin air and handed it to me. While the obvious question of why a flyer required its own envelope ran through my mind, I hesitantly accepted the gift.

"Open it when you get back to the office," she said, a little too forcefully.

"Okay." I searched her face for some explanation for her behavior, but came up empty-handed, as usual.

My dad sat back and folded his hands in his lap. "That was one hell of a sandwich."

"I'm glad you liked it, Dad." I hit the home button on my phone and took a quick peek at the time. It was already ten minutes to two. "I should get back to work now. It was great seeing you guys again."

"Likewise, sweetie." My mom smiled as she slid her bag onto her shoulder. She leaned in to give me a hug, a gesture that seemed to take both of us by surprise. While the subtle scent of her perfume filled the air around us, I thought of being a little kid again, sitting up in bed as she read stories to me in her soothing voice. I swallowed the lump in my throat and pushed the memory away. Things had changed too much for us to ever return to that place.

When I broke away, my dad smiled at me. "Good luck with everything, Nora. And if you need anything, just give us a call."

"I will." An uneasy feeling wormed its way into my gut. I couldn't help but wonder why he hadn't told me that when I moved away at the tender age of twenty—when I actually needed to hear it.

A minute later, my parents were nothing more than an indistinct shape in the distance. I followed the path back to the Trade Center, the cryptic white envelope still in my hand. *Why couldn't I just open it while she was there?* I turned around to make sure she couldn't see me anymore and sat down on the closest bench.

I tore open the envelope, not bothering to keep the crisp white paper intact. Inside was a folded sheet of paper that boasted pictures of tall, upscale buildings, not too different from the ones that surrounded my office. I unfolded it to reveal shots of pristine living rooms and spotless bathrooms dotting the rest of the flyer. Overlooking the glossy pictures was a bold heading at the top of the paper:

OPEN HOUSE: 351 W 57th St. Enjoy the best that New York has to offer! Dazzling views, luxury rooms, and only a 10-minute walk from the World Trade Center. Stop by on Saturday, January 26th between 1-4 pm to take a tour.

Anger flared inside me as I realized my mom had never joined a class or intended to share a sign-up sheet with me. I stared at the words until my vision started to blur. She knew. She knew I had an entire life back at home, that this was only temporary. But to her, my temporary life was the only one that counted.

I shoved the flyer into my bag and sprang up from the bench, suddenly desperate to get back to work. I pushed past the lines of tourists posing in front of the Trade Center until I was encased in the safety of my office. I grabbed my phone and went straight to my mom's number. As I waited for her to pick up, I paced restlessly around the room, trying to decide what I could possibly say to her.

That was a decision I never had to make, because the phone went to voicemail. Either she was still on the subway, or she'd chosen to avoid confronting my reaction altogether. If I had to place a bet on one of those scenarios, my money would go toward the latter.

I tossed my phone into my bag and sat down at my desk, turning my focus to the coworkers who were waiting outside my door. I spent the rest of the afternoon knee-deep in my fashion zone, wrapping myself in my work until I was insulated from the world around me. During my walk back to the hotel that evening, I was sharply aware of the flyer's presence at the bottom of my bag. It sat there like a curse, reminding me that I was only bringing myself closer and closer to the life I'd separated myself from for all these years.

When I was back in my room, I collapsed on the couch and whipped out my phone. Wondering how her pregnancy was going, I waited for Jeanette to pick up. Besides the obvious changes that came with expecting a baby, this was the longest she'd gone without bustling around the city and meeting with top models while putting the finishing touches on her latest article. Her new life was probably unnervingly quiet in the same way that mine felt a little too loud sometimes.

"Hey," she said in a raspy voice. "Getting the hang of everything yet?"

"Yeah. I think I've adapted pretty quickly to office life, considering I've never worked in an office before." I paused. "Are you okay? You don't sound so great."

"Well, you just undid all of Derek's efforts to make me feel sexy again. So thanks for that."

"Sorry." I had to smile, though, because Jeanette couldn't help being her sarcastic self even in her less-than-ideal state.

"But since you asked, no, I'm not okay. I don't know what asshat decided to call it morning sickness, because it's not just morning sickness. It's afternoon, night, and hey-I-just-decided-to-pop-in-because-why-the-fuck-not sickness. But I guess that's too wordy for all the stupid pregnancy guides I'm reading."

"Sorry, Jeanette. I hope you feel better."

"My mom had the same thing when she was pregnant with me, so I kind of knew I was in for it." She let out an exasperated breath. "Anyway, enough about me. What's up?"

I lay back on the couch and sighed. "I had lunch with my parents today."

"After your last meal with them, I can't imagine that went well."

"The lunch itself was fine, actually. A little awkward, but nothing inflammatory from them this time." My eyes landed on my bag on the corner of the coffee table. "But then my mom gave me this flyer for an open house downtown. The building is only a ten-minute walk from my office. I might be reading too much into it, but it seems like she thinks my job is a long-term thing."

"Whoa. First of all, you're definitely not reading too much into it. The only way she could've made it more obvious was by saying it to your face."

I let out a deflated breath. "I know. I was just hoping I was wrong."

"Second of all…" She was quiet for a moment, and the pit in my stomach told me I knew what was coming next. "Have you thought about it at all? What it would be like to stay in the city for a while?"

I bristled at the question. "That's not even an option, Jeanette. You know that. That's why I told you I was staying for two weeks."

"Trust me, I get it. I was just..." She paused for a thoughtful moment. "I guess starting a family made me realize that life is full of possibilities. You shouldn't have to limit yourself to one path just because that's all you've ever known."

"Those are some serious hormones you're dealing with right now. That line was straight out of a Bob Ross video."

She laughed. The airy, lilting sound reminded me of the old Jeanette. "God, I've been so uptight lately. You always know when I need a laugh."

"No problem." I smiled.

"But I mean what I said. You're in New York now. If there's a time to try something new, this is it."

Her voice had a note of urgency, as if there were an hour-glass sitting between us that only she could see. A crease settled over my forehead. "Okay. I'll try."

"That's the spirit." After a brief pause, she said, "Speaking of which, how's everything going at work?"

"So much better than I expected. Celeste loved the idea I suggested to her. Basically, I decided that I wanted to focus on—"

"Hold up. Did you just say Celeste Moore *loved* your idea?"

"Yeah. It took her a little while to warm up to it, but she eventually came around."

"Girl, you struck gold without even realizing it. Celeste

turns down all the newbies' ideas as a rule. How did you pull that off?"

"Well, she did say no to me at the editorial meeting, which makes complete sense now. But I wasn't going down without a fight, so I went into her office and changed her mind."

"I have to say, I'm impressed." With a sigh, she said, "You know, it's too bad you're figuring everything out now. If you hadn't taken that fifteen-year detour in Fairlane, who knows where you would've been?"

"Detour?" The word came out more sharply than I'd intended. "Is that what you think the last fifteen years were?"

"That's not what I meant," she backpedaled, but she'd already swerved into the wrong lane. And she knew it.

"I think that is what you meant. Otherwise you wouldn't have said it."

"Come on, Nora. Your parents were thinking like me when they gave you that flyer. You know why? Because they remember the girl who got top marks in every art class for her fashion sketches. Not the one who settled for a life she happened to find off I-80."

Settled. That single word slashed deeper into me than any hurtful remark could have. "I have to go."

"But—"

"Good luck with everything, Jeanette."

Without another word, I ended the call and dropped my phone onto the couch. As I stared at the ceiling, the fragments of the day pieced themselves together one by one. The look of undiluted pride on my parents' faces. The contents of the envelope my mom had given me. Jeanette telling me to stay open to the possibilities.

Hey, just don't get too comfortable there, okay? Tyler had said to me.

I'd tried. Hell, I was still trying. But to everyone around me, I'd already settled into my New York life like it was an over-stuffed chair at the end of a long day. And the longer I let the plush, velvety fabric encase me, the more I convinced myself it was okay to stay there a while.

Twelve

I sat at my computer, staring at the list of available flights back home. I'd spent the last twenty minutes talking myself into jumping on the next plane to Iowa before I got too attached to my life here. Before I couldn't tear myself away from my success. Before I proved Jeanette and my parents right.

But the longer I stared at the screen, the more I realized I was already in too deep. I searched for the next flight to Des Moines and felt the electricity of New York. I scrolled through the available seats and thought of the vision I had for the September issue. And just as I placed my cursor on the Book Flight button, I heard an echo of my parents telling me I was more capable than I thought. There were whispers of my new life in everything I did, an ever-present reminder that there was no turning back now.

I closed out of the window and pulled up my inbox. Just because I couldn't get myself to book a flight now didn't mean I would never do it. I was repeating that in my head, trying to engrave it in my brain like initials on the inside of a locket, when I saw the outline for my feature article peeking out of my desk drawer.

I pulled out the file that I was supposed to deliver to Celeste by the end of the week. I looked it over, making sure it was exactly what I wanted. This was the first assignment I'd completed since taking Jeanette's place, and I had to make sure it was material that I was proud of. This was the mark that I was about to leave on *Couture*. It was my own voice translated into the season's most cutting-edge fashion. If there was a time to make that voice count, it was now.

I read through the pitch, already feeling the impact it would have on our readers. It was just the way I'd envisioned it:

Fashion shouldn't just be for the fashionable. Too many people see living a life of style as a chore, whether they're too busy to spend time on their appearance or simply don't know how to begin defining their own look. But the problem isn't ignorance: it's misguidedness. With a few simple changes to their wardrobe, those who never thought twice about their personal style can recognize that staying on trend is easier than it seems.

Below the description, I'd included a selection of simple accessories and clothing items that helped create an effortless look. I saw more of myself in this idea than the one I'd shared with Vanessa. If there was a story worthy of Celeste's attention, this was it.

I picked up the sheet of paper and tucked it into a folder to deliver to the editor. When I stood up from my chair and headed to the door, I hesitated for only a moment. As much faith as I had in my idea, it was still Celeste. Giving her anything that wasn't my best work would be a sort of death sentence. But the moment of doubt was fleeting, and I strode up to the editor's office with the confidence that she would see everything I saw in it.

I knocked on her door and entered after she gave me permission. I walked inside with more confidence than I'd had the first time. I was no longer the new kid trying to fit in. I belonged here just as much as everyone else.

"I have my outline for the feature story," I said, handing her the paper.

She looked it over, her probing gaze dissecting the words I'd sewn together ever so carefully. The more time that passed without her speaking, the more aware I became of every movement on her face. But trying to decipher what was going through her mind was a game that I was destined to lose.

After what felt like a lifetime, Celeste gave me an inquisitive look. "Do you have any experience working in fashion?"

A pang of dread wormed its way through me. I knew all along that this was too good to be true. Jeanette had chosen me to take her place because of our history as best friends and because she saw my passion for what I did. But the editor in chief of one of the country's leading fashion magazines saw me for who I really was: an unqualified college dropout.

"I don't," I said carefully. "But I'm really excited to be here. I have a lot of great ideas that I have planned." I didn't realize how inadequate the words sounded until they left my mouth.

"That's why you're perfect for this job."

I hesitated, unsure if I'd heard her correctly. "I'm sorry?"

She sat back in her chair and gazed out the window, a wistful look on her face. "I've been running this magazine for almost thirty years now. I've seen it all: writers with ideas they copied from *Cosmo* or *Glamour*, stylists who acted like they knew the fashion industry better than they actually did, editors who were so worried about fitting in that they didn't bring anything new to the table. The one thing they all had in common was that they were focused on doing what fashion magazines have always done: appeal to the savvy, fashion-minded consumer." She turned to me, and I almost thought I saw a sparkle in her eye. "But you're different. I can't quite put my finger on it, but there's something inside you that sees past all the noise. It's not just about the trends with you. You seem like you care about something bigger." She paused as she tried to grasp the right words. "You have a *purpose*, Nora. That's what roots you to what you do."

Purpose. The word was heavy with meaning, just as it'd been on that hot July day twelve years ago. I could still feel the sun's generous rays wrap themselves around me as the memory floated to the front of my mind.

It was the summer of 2007, just two months after Tyler and I had gotten married. We were lying beside each other on the pasture at the end of a long afternoon of farming. For a peaceful moment, all I heard was his breathing, still labored from the hard work he'd just finished. He turned to me and ran a hand through my hair. "What's on your mind?"

I rested my head on the crook of his arm, letting the late afternoon sunlight soothe my tired bones. "Well, first of all, I already want to call it a night at five o'clock. Farming is turning me into a twenty-three-year-old grandma."

He laughed, a sound I never grew tired of hearing. His laugh reminded me of long, carefree summer nights, where the star-studded sky and the embrace of lingering warmth in the air made my worries feel a little lighter.

I glanced at him, thinking about the life we'd built so far and how we still had so much life ahead of us, stretching out before our eyes like the emerald pasture surrounding us. "But I was also thinking about how I finally found something I want to do for the rest of my life. This farm, this job... It makes me feel like I have a purpose. That's something I never felt the entire time I was in college."

His eyes were deep with understanding, and I knew we felt the same connection to our work when we went out to the fields every morning. But I saw something else there. Something so real I could reach out and touch it. Just like I'd taken a chance by leaving behind everything I knew and making this unfamiliar life my own, Tyler had taken his own risk by marrying a city girl who didn't have this lifestyle ingrained in her from birth like everyone else in Fairlane. And by some beautiful twist of fate, each blind leap we'd taken had landed us right where we were in that moment.

"Your idea is a perfect example of that deeper purpose inside you," Celeste said, tearing me away from my thoughts. "You're giving a voice to those who normally wouldn't think to pick up a copy of *Couture*. It's brilliant. We'll reach a much wider audience thanks to your innovative thinking." She stopped at once, her expression laced with concern. "Is everything all right?"

I hadn't noticed the misty layer over my eyes until she asked the question. "What? I mean, yes, I'm fine. Sorry." I cleared my throat. "So, where do I go from here?"

"I'll need the final proofs from the photo shoot by February twelfth, the latest." She pulled up the calendar app on her computer, all business again at the drop of a hat. "Once you've picked out all the outfits and prepared the models, reach out to Megan. She'll choose the photographers for the shoot."

My heart flipped over in my chest. "February twelfth?"

"Yes. Is there a problem?"

I tried to respond, but my eyes were glued to the numbers

on her screen. There it was, just four days from now: January twenty-eighth. Exactly two weeks after my first day at *Couture*.

The date had crept up on me, blindsiding me before I had the chance to form a plan. Somewhere between the surrealness of the *Couture* office and the empowering praise from my boss, I'd lost track of when I was supposed to go back home. But now that the date was closer than ever, I knew I wasn't in a place to leave my new life behind.

"No. I mean, yes," I stammered. "I only agreed to stay here for two weeks while Jeanette looks for a replacement."

She eyed me for a moment, not saying a word. "So you did." She methodically rearranged the papers on her desk, dedicating her full attention to the task until I was convinced she'd forgotten I was there. "Well, I suppose you could leave if that's what you want to do. But it would be a shame, Nora. Especially after what you just put together here."

I swallowed, feeling like my heart was being pulled in two different directions. This was the mission I'd come all the way here to fulfill, and I was closer than ever to reaching that goal. But I had another mission too—the one I'd left behind on that sun-soaked pasture. I knew with every fiber of my being that my life would be a gaping void if I left the farm behind. But I knew with the same fierce certainty that cutting this job short would be a different kind of pain. Before I came here, there was a hole inside me where my unlived life was supposed to be. But if I left now, after the editor in chief had told me I had the power to change *Couture,* that hole would become a crater.

"I guess I could stay a little bit longer." The words seemed to escape me before I gave them permission to. Before I decided that they were the right words to say.

"Good choice." She looked at me head-on, her penetrating stare burning through her glasses like a laser beam. "Just make sure you give this idea the unique flavor I know only you can offer. You're different, and our readers will notice that about you. But if you try too hard to fit in, they'll notice that too. Think hard about the type of mark you want to leave on this magazine."

I nodded, feeling like my head weighed a hundred pounds. "I will."

"Well, then, there's no sense in delaying. You'd better start getting busy."

As I made my way back to my desk, I tried to dissect my impulsive answer like it was a math formula scrawled out on a blackboard. It was easy to tell myself that I hadn't been thinking clearly when I said it, but I knew better. If I was truly ready to give up on my goal, I would've packed up my things and said goodbye to everyone at the office. But I wasn't ready. I'd known it from the crushing feeling in my chest when I realized it was almost time to leave.

I sank into my chair, wanting nothing more than to close my eyes and make this all feel like a fever dream that would inevitably burn out, leaving a feeble trail of ashes in its wake. But I'd made my decision. Wrong or right, it was time to own that choice.

I'd just shifted my eyes to my open planner when my phone vibrated next to me. I glanced at the name on the display, feeling my heart sink down to the pit of my stomach. My fingers trembled as I held the phone to my ear.

"Hey. I've been meaning to call you."

"Caleb never went to school today," Tyler said.

My breath caught in my throat. "What?"

"I got a call from Dave a few hours after I dropped him off at school. He went to pick up something at the store and saw Caleb and his friends coming out of the movie theater. Looked like one of his friends' older brothers drove them there. I don't know when they snuck out of school, but they couldn't have been there long."

For once, I was eternally grateful that no one could hide anything in our small town. "He would never do something like that on his own. Those kids must have talked him into it." As soon as the words escaped my lips, I knew they were true. Caleb might have been moody at times, but he was a good kid. He would never play hooky unless he had a good reason to. And in a preteen's eyes, few reasons were more compelling than peer pressure.

"I know." The pause that followed was so heavy, I could feel it weighing on my shoulders. I knew what he was going to say next, and I wasn't ready to hear it. He drew in a breath. "Nora, I think you should come home."

My heart was in my throat now, barring any chance of me speaking. Maybe it was better that way. I could tell from the strain in his normally easygoing tone that he was struggling, and anything I said would only make it worse.

"It's been getting tough," Tyler went on. "And it's not just the kids. Milk prices are dropping again, and it's only getting harder to pay for the feed. I don't know if we'll get approved for our next loan if things keep going at this rate."

"Why didn't you tell me this?" I said, my breathing unsteady.

"I'm telling you now. Everything is—"

"I mean, why didn't you tell me before?" My voice was shaking now. "Before I flew all the way over here? You told me you'd have it all under control. I was the one who kept doubting myself, and you said it'd be fine, over and over again."

"Things are different now. If I'm being honest, this is a lot harder than I thought it would be." His tone softened a little. "But I know you're busy, too, so I get it if you need to stay until the two weeks are up. You're still scheduled to come home this Monday, right?"

I bit down hard on my lip to stop the tears from spilling over, but it was too late. A salty drop landed on my planner, saturating today's date.

"Nora? Say something."

"I... This is my fault, okay? I shouldn't have come here. I knew I shouldn't have done it, because now I can't leave."

"Don't tell me you can't. We both know you can. It's not like the company would fall apart without you."

My sadness ignited into anger, so quickly I couldn't see straight. "How would you know? You never ask me what I do at work every day. And since you don't, I guess I'll tell you. Almost everyone relies on me here. The only person who's above me is the editor in chief. There's a reason Jeanette had to find someone so quickly."

I didn't realize what I sounded like until I heard myself speak. I'd become the person I'd tried to escape all these years. I'd become the haughty college student who showed me around Grant back in high school, with her glossy hair and designer jeans. She'd barely made eye contact with me during the entire tour, like it was her job to make sure I knew my place.

"Nora, do you hear yourself? That's not the woman I married."

He'd noticed it too. I knew he would. I swallowed, still determined to maintain the little dignity I had left. "Do you know how many times I've thought about coming home? You have no idea how much I want to be back. It's just that... I can't give all this up when I spent a lifetime waiting for this."

"I have a hard time believing you want to come home when you're not here."

"Please, Tyler." My cry for help was just as pathetic as it sounded. When it was met with dead air, I knew it was exactly what I deserved.

I set down the phone and held my head in my hands. His every word was a shard that pierced my skin, exposing everything I'd tried to forget about. And the worst part of what he said was that all of it was true.

As I stared blankly at my unread emails, Jeanette's question from our last phone call echoed through my mind: *Have you thought about it at all? What it would be like to stay in the city for a while?*

I knew the answer now. I *had* thought about it, in the same way that a student walled into a classroom stared longingly out the window at the world she couldn't be a part of. And I hated every second that I let myself indulge in the fantasy.

I shut off my monitor and stared at the rugged skyline outside my window until my vision blurred. *At what point do I give up? At what point do I tell myself I've had my moment in the spotlight, that I've done the best I could, and that it's time to move on?*

My gaze remained fixed on the skyscrapers, as if the answer

lay somewhere in the spaces between the peaks. But all I received in return was a silence that exposed the truth: after fifteen years, I still didn't know the answer.

Thirteen

～～

The Saks storefront beckoned to me like a beacon of light in the distance. I strode up to the window and let my gaze linger on the statement wool coats, over-the-knee leather boots, and bold maxi skirts that I could only dream of pulling off. Celeste had sent me here to put a look together for one of the models, but all I'd done so far was mentally place myself inside every outfit.

I stepped into the store and studied the new arrivals with the eye of a trained fashion director. But I'd barely made a dent in the trench coats when I found myself longing for Jeanette's presence. When we were younger, Jeanette had a hidden talent for singling out the most extravagant pieces in the store. I always joked that she needed to find a way to become wildly successful if she planned to support her expensive taste. A sigh escaped me as I ran my fingers along a price tag. Little did I know that my own words would come true one day.

I moved on to the boots, telling myself I didn't need training wheels anymore. Jeanette had given me her job because I was fully capable of putting together a look that would make Celeste proud. Besides, I'd been in New York long enough to have an intuitive sense of what worked and what didn't.

With an armful of clothes that mirrored the items I'd

sketched out for Celeste, I headed over to the cashier and placed them on the counter. Seeing the array of fabrics and patterns sent a jolt of excitement through me, and I realized this was the closest I'd come to bringing my vision to life. For once, I had a concrete, tangible version of what had been an abstract concept in my mind not too long ago.

After the clothes were tucked away in Saks's signature black-and-white bag, I hailed a cab and headed back to the office. The entire way there, I eyed the clothes in the bag, trying to picture each combination on the fashion pages of *Couture*. Putting them in that spotlight made me aware of all their flaws, as if the muted lighting of the store had softened their edges. By the time the cab stopped in front of the Trade Center, I was convinced that nothing I'd picked out was worthy of fashion magazine stardom.

I ran into Vanessa on my way back to my office. She raised an eyebrow at the bag in my hand. "I didn't know today was retail therapy day."

The sting of her betrayal was still fresh, and it was my instinct to turn my back on her. But I knew that the same mind that had so artfully stolen my idea knew what would fit on the pages of the September issue better than I did.

I held up the two outfits I'd picked out. "Which do you think is better for the photo shoot?"

Vanessa closely examined the clothes in my hand. "I like what you were thinking with the dress. But I also think that top would look perfect with the new Stuart Weitzman boots that came in."

"That's what I was thinking too. It's impossible to decide."

"Personally, I prefer the dress."

I whirled around to see who had spoken and nearly ran into Shannon Reyes. The chart-topping, Grammy-winning pop superstar flashed me a smile that was even more luminous in person. I stared blankly at her, trying to process the fact that the same face I'd seen on stage at Madison Square Garden and plastered on countless billboards was standing in my workplace.

Vanessa cleared her throat. "This is her first time seeing a celebrity in the office. She just started here a couple weeks ago."

Shannon laughed. "Oh, don't worry. I was the same way when I ran into J. Lo in the studio while I was recording my first album. Although probably a lot worse, to be honest."

Her friendly, relaxed demeanor helped put me at ease, and I finally found my voice. "It's just that I'm a huge fan. My friend and I both skipped class to see you perform on *Jimmy Fallon* when we were in high school. You definitely didn't disappoint."

"I appreciate it," she said with that thousand-watt smile. "And I appreciate being chosen as the September cover girl. You guys have no idea how much this is helping my career."

Vanessa gave a short chuckle. "*Helping* your career? You're only one of the biggest stars in the music industry today."

Shannon shrugged. "It might seem like that to you guys, but my fan base is changing pretty quickly. Years ago, it was mostly teens who cared about my music. Like you and your friend," she said, gesturing toward me. "But now those teens have grown up and moved on. It can happen to anyone, really. That's why I need this exposure so much."

It struck me how open she was with us, how honest. I couldn't help but feel inspired by the way she maintained a sense of confidence, even when all the odds were against her.

Before I could decide what to say, she smiled at both of us again. "You might not realize it, but what you all do here at *Couture* is so important. It's one of the reasons I love what I do. Ever since my album sales started dropping, my agent insisted on making me feel like I wasn't good enough. But as soon as I walk into the *Couture* office, I feel beautiful again. Like I'm already accepted the way I am."

Up until that moment, I'd held on to the hope that my work would make a difference for everyone who read our magazine. It had been a fragile, nebulous hope, like a bubble that would pop at the slightest prick. But Shannon's words had solidified that bubble into firm concrete, letting me grasp it like my dream that was slowly becoming real. I was here to change lives. And if I could make one person feel the way Shannon Reyes felt, I knew my work had value.

Shannon glanced down at her phone, which had just lit up with a text. "Well, I have to go try on some clothes for the shoot." With a cursory glance at the stack of clothes on my arm, she said, "But seriously, go with the dress."

I watched her in a starstruck daze as she headed toward the fashion closet.

Vanessa sighed. "Don't you wish you could hang out with her? She's so chill. Unlike some of the stars we've had in the past."

"Do you really see celebrities that often? I feel like I just landed in L.A."

"Every now and then. Mostly when we're staging a photo shoot. We've had models, singers, actors, you name it."

"It feels surreal." After thinking for a moment, I looked up at Vanessa. "It's crazy to think that this is what I was missing out on all these years. I can't believe Jeanette willingly gave this job to me."

"Yeah, well, don't get too complacent." Her expression turned hard, and I was coldly reminded of the way she'd snatched my idea from under me when I least expected it. "I know it's easy to think you have it all figured out, but you'll start falling behind as soon as you get comfortable. Trust me. I've seen it happen plenty of times in my ten years here."

Her words weighed down on me, but I refused to let her know it. "If there's one thing I learned from farming, it's how to work hard day in and day out. Complacent doesn't exist in my book." I threw her a saccharine smile as I turned back toward my office. "But thanks for the advice."

I thought I saw a flash of anger in her eyes, but it evaporated before I could be sure. I still didn't understand what Vanessa had against me, and trying to figure it out was a waste of time. All I could do was focus on myself and my goals if I wanted my work to have an impact on *Couture*. Celeste's words from our last meeting rang through my thoughts, somehow louder this time: *Think hard about the type of mark you want to leave on this magazine.*

The mark I would leave was mine alone. It wasn't one that Vanessa or Chloe could leave. And if I wanted my mark to be authentic, I couldn't let anyone else's fingerprints taint the pen.

When I was back in my office, I messaged Anna in the wardrobe department to have her pick up my clothes. I took a moment to scan my to-do list before rummaging inside my purse for a pen. Instead of the hard edge of my favorite ballpoint, my fingers grazed the smooth, laminated paper of the open house flyer.

I pulled the flyer out of my bag ever so gently, as if it would disintegrate at my touch. I examined the loud print and polished photos, remembering how they'd felt like a slap in the face the first time I laid my eyes upon them. But this time was different. Now, the staged shots of the apartment seemed to beckon to me, telling me it was okay to dip my toes in the water. After all, I'd already spent two weeks perched on the edge of the pool, gazing longingly at the world that was close enough to touch.

Before I could linger on the thoughts for a moment longer, I stuffed the flyer back into my bag. I noticed idly that the recycling bin was right next to me, ready to swallow up the evidence of my mom's plan to make me stay here. But no matter how hard I tried to separate myself from the life that was reeling me in, I found myself hopelessly returning to it, like a wave receding back to the ocean.

I glanced at my office door just in time to spot Anna there. As I handed my clothes to her, she gave me a compliment on my sense of style that I only partially registered. The spotlight in my mind was still turned toward the look on Shannon's face when she'd talked about how much our work at *Couture* meant to her. That look had given me hope and solidified my mission at this company. I'd already started to carve out my path, and others had begun to notice it.

But that wasn't the worst part. At the core of my pain was the knowledge that there were millions of other faces across the country just like Shannon's. Faces upturned in hope, waiting to see how the next issue of the magazine would change their lives. Arms outstretched toward me, Vanessa, and everyone else at this company, expecting us to lift them up and give them the freedom to be their true selves.

Before I started working here, my dream had been a selfish one. I'd been the only star in the fantasies I conjured up: my name on the masthead and my unique designs on display for all the world to see. But now, my goal was about far more than just me. It was about everything this magazine stood for and what it did for our audience. It was about the young girls out there who found refuge in the pages of *Couture* like I had when I was a teenager who didn't know where she belonged.

My purpose at this company was clearer than it had ever been. So why did it feel like I was walking down a darkened road without a single lamppost to guide me?

***

The walk back to the hotel was a long and lonely one. The bitter wind cut straight through to the bone, making me wish I hadn't chosen style over comfort when I picked out my clothes that morning. Back on the farm, I wouldn't have even thought to sacrifice my warmth for the sake of making a fashion statement. I couldn't help but wonder if Tyler had been right in saying I was no longer the woman I used to be.

I nodded at the doorman once I reached the Four Seasons and headed to the elevator. During the ride up to the twenty-third floor, my last conversation with Tyler rolled through my mind. As much as I tried to brush it off, the way the call had ended still ate away at me. I didn't want to end on that kind of note. He had every right to be upset with me, but the least I could do was make an effort to patch things up between us.

The second I entered my room, I pulled out my phone and went straight to my contacts. Just before I hit Tyler's name, a call came in. The name on the screen gave me pause before I hit the accept button.

"Jeanette?" I sat hesitantly on the edge of the couch. "What's up?"

"Oh, you're about to find out. I have news with a capital *N*."

"Go on," I said, trying to ignore the unexplained anxiety that clawed at my chest.

"Remember when I told you that Derek and I were thinking about moving to the suburbs?"

"Yeah. At L'Artusi, right?"

"Exactly. Well, we looked around way before then. We started with New York and made it all the way to Colorado. It was quite the road trip. But out of all the places we visited, it was pretty much a consensus that Iowa had what we were looking for."

"And what is that, exactly?"

"Good schools, a tight-knit community, all that fun stuff," she said generically. "Anyway, we're officially proud owners of 16 Maple Drive in Riverville. I can't believe it's finally happening."

"Riverville? That's, like, ten miles away from me."

"I know, right? It's the perfect location. I have to admit, I never realized how nice Green Ridge County was until I stopped by your town three weeks ago."

I wanted to believe that her motives were purely about location, but I knew Jeanette too well to let myself be fooled by that fiction. The timing of the situation was too coincidental: as soon as I got comfortable in the city, she snatched up the first house she could find within a ten-mile radius of my farm. Just like she'd snatched up my spot at Grant the minute I gave it up.

"You're right—it is a nice place. But there are plenty of Rivervilles across the country." It took all the willpower inside me to stay calm and collected, even when I knew how this story was going to end. "There are some really nice small towns on the East Coast too. One of my friends from high school moved to Ramsey in New Jersey. Great school system, and it's close enough to the city that you can visit whenever you want."

"You know I wouldn't be caught dead in New Jersey, first of all. Second of all, I wanted to get away, Nora. I wanted to *escape*." Her voice suddenly grew intense, almost urgent. "Your story inspired me, you know. Just leaving everything behind and starting over. Not many people can do that."

The undercurrent of desperation in her voice was too familiar. It was like I was listening to myself fifteen years ago, itching for any opportunity to break free from the life I felt caged into. My fingers tightened around the phone. "No, they can't."

"So, where was I? Oh, right. There I was with Derek and my unborn baby, enjoying another afternoon in our new neighborhood, when I thought I might as well swing by your farm. And there was Tyler, who... How do I say this? Well, sorry, honey, but he looked like hell. So I offered to help out, being the friendly neighbor that I am. Turns out I actually have a natural talent for this farming business."

I laughed out loud before I could stop myself. "I'm sorry. That's a mental image that isn't coming together."

"Laugh all you want, but Tyler would back me up. Not to mention I might have just saved your farm by convincing him to buy this fancy robotic milking equipment. The salesman told me it can milk up to eighty cows, so it'll get the job done a lot faster than those run-of-the-mill machines you used to have."

The amused grin that had been dancing on my lips vanished just as quickly as it had appeared. I sank lower onto the couch. "No way. Tyler would never make such a big decision without consulting with me first."

"Well, he just did. I don't know if you've noticed, but you haven't been actively involved in the farm over the past couple of weeks. And there's only so much that one man can do." I could feel her picking up momentum in the short pause that followed. "You know, you should be thanking me. This job was killing Tyler before we bought the new equipment, especially without you around. Now that we have robots to do the work for him, he can finally have a life."

"Farming *is* his life." My heart was hammering so loudly, I could barely think straight. I hadn't forgotten about the bleak picture Tyler had painted when discussing our finances during our last conversation. He wasn't even sure if we would get our next loan approved, and now he was dropping money on robotic equipment like it was a new pair of shoes? "How did he pay for all this? Did you even factor in the cost of electricity and repairs?"

"First of all, I pitched in with the cost, and second, of course I did. Like I said, I have a knack for this business."

A small part of me was grateful that Jeanette had helped make Tyler's job easier, but hurt shrouded the kernel of gratitude inside me. I'd never imagined Tyler would exclude me from such a big undertaking. Or was it me who'd shut the door on him when he tried to let me in?

"Small farms like ours aren't conducive to robotics." I thought about Dave and all the work he'd had to do on his barn when he installed the robots. "We'll have to build a bigger barn to accommodate the new equipment. Not to mention our cows aren't used to these kinds of conditions. They might not adjust well, and who knows how much time that'll cost us?"

There was a beat of silence on the other end, then Jeanette exhaled slowly. "I was expecting you to be upset, but I didn't think you'd be this bad. It's sad, really. Tyler's the one who's been doing this all his life, and he was much more receptive to the change. Maybe you should think about keeping an open mind. It'll do you good."

"This isn't even you, Jeanette. You should be where I'm sitting right now, calling in fashion orders and sharing your brilliant ideas with the staff."

Her voice was surprisingly calm when she spoke. "I could say the same for you."

Before I could open my mouth, I heard an unmistakable voice in the background. My heart seized up in my chest. "Put him on."

"Who?"

"Tyler. I need to talk to him."

"Your call." There was a pause then some shuffling as she went to find him. When his voice came on, my breath stilled. It had only been a couple of days since I'd last spoken to him, but everything that had come between us made it feel like a year. It struck me how surreal it was to go from waking up next to someone every morning and spending the day working alongside them to living an entire life that they had no part in.

"I have to pick up Bridget from her friend's house soon,"

Tyler said. He sounded just as exhausted as the haggard man Jeanette had described.

"How could you do this?" I said, my voice breaking on the last word. Every ounce of bitterness inside me evaporated, and I found myself longing to connect with my husband like I used to. "This was a huge decision, and you didn't even talk to me about it. I'm just as much a part of the farm as you and the kids are."

"I'm not so sure about that anymore. I warned you about how bad things were getting, and you never came home."

"I've only been here for a couple of weeks. I'll be home as soon as I can." But even as the words came out, they sounded empty, devoid of meaning. If I wanted to see my ideas in print, I would have to stick around for longer than the two weeks I'd promised. And we both knew it.

I remembered with a sharp pang in my chest what I'd told Jeanette when I accepted her offer: *If I need to come back for any reason, I'm getting on the next flight to Des Moines. No questions.*

It had been so easy to say it then, to let the words slide off my tongue like honey. But that was before. Before I knew how much was riding on my job here. Before I knew the fear of tearing my dream out by the roots when it was just beginning to bloom.

"It was never two weeks. Face it. You're the type of person who always wants more. Yesterday, it was two weeks. Tomorrow, it'll be two months. Then I won't have a farm anymore."

His words stung more than I wanted to admit. The memory of the two of us lying side by side in the lush grass, sharing each other's hopes and dreams, flashed into my mind. That was the person I really was, the person Tyler had fallen in love with. Now he just saw me as another cliché. Someone who got a taste of success and continued to crave more and more, no matter the cost. *That's not me,* I wanted to scream, but I knew he wouldn't listen.

"What were you thinking with the new milking system? This isn't what you wanted." My voice dropped. "This isn't what your dad wanted."

"I had no choice. Our dairy is the only one in the neighborhood that hasn't switched to robotics yet. It won't be easy to adjust to the new equipment, but I can't do this on my own anymore." His voice grew quiet, as if he were afraid someone would hear him. "Caleb isn't helping out at all. I thought he was just going through a phase, but he's becoming more and more like my brother every day. He doesn't even bother milking the cows anymore. He goes straight up to his room after school and locks the door. I took away his video games yesterday, but that had no effect on him." He sighed. "I'm starting to think this is all because of you."

"Because of *me*?"

"You're setting a bad example for him. He saw the way you left the farm for the city. I wouldn't be surprised if he thinks it's okay for him to do the same thing."

"This isn't me. It's the new group of kids he's hanging out with. And if you'd waited for me instead of getting Jeanette to help, we could've worked things out."

"I've been waiting." His voice grew wearier with each word. "If I keep waiting, I'll be out of work."

"You replaced me." The words tasted bitter in my mouth.

"You did, Nora. You replaced all of us with your job. With New York City. All for a dream that doesn't exist anymore."

His words sent an ache through me that I couldn't brush off. "You always understood how I felt about seeing my work published in *Couture*. You believed in my goal even when I doubted it."

"Well, that's not what your goal was two weeks ago. This was supposed to be your chance to take Jeanette's place temporarily, remember? Now Jeanette is the one helping out on the farm, and you're setting these goals for *Couture* like it's a long-term career." There was silence for a moment before he said, "I gotta go."

I was about to tell him to wait, to hear me out, but I decided against it. If he really thought I was the person he said I was, then nothing I could tell him would change his mind.

I dropped my phone onto the couch and stared up at the ceiling, its stark whiteness exposing everything I was too afraid to admit myself. Even if I did go back home, I wouldn't be welcome there. Nothing would ever be the way it was before. Tyler had already found the help he needed, and I was officially useless.

I thought of Jeanette herding my cattle, of the new flannel top she'd surely bought flapping in the wind as she brought them into the barn. I pictured her greeting Tyler as he helped her put out the morning feed and saying hi to Caleb and Bridget as they hopped in the truck to go to school. Maybe she would even drive them there or pick them up later and ask them how their day was. After all, Tyler was so busy. *There's only so much that one man can do.*

I stopped as something registered in my brain with a deafening click. I sat up so fast I saw stars, realizing for the first time something I should've noticed weeks ago. Jeanette wasn't looking for someone else to replace her as fashion director. *I* was her permanent replacement. She acted like she'd just happened to find the perfect home in the suburbs, but she'd had her sights set on it all along. Now she was taking over my farm because she'd gotten me out of the way.

It was high school all over again. She'd waited until I'd given up my spot at Grant so she could take it for herself, and now she'd pushed me away from my farm and family so she could live out her own domestic fantasy.

Before I could think it through, I snatched my work bag from the coffee table. I fished out the open house flyer and scanned it for the phone number. My hands shaking, I picked up my phone and entered the digits. Tyler thought I'd made my decision by staying in the city, but he'd made his too. Jeanette was the perfect replacement for me: she had the same determination and same work ethic. But unlike me, she always found a way to summon whatever she wanted the second she decided she wanted it.

I swallowed the tears that were collecting in my eyes, refusing to feel the hurt that was threatening to overtake me. Let Jeanette stay there. Maybe her big robotics plan would pay off, and she would do more for the farm than I ever had. Let her have all the glory. That was what she'd always wanted, ever since the day we first spoke to each other.

The speaker on the other end jolted me out of my rumination. I cleared my throat, using up every last ounce of strength to steady my voice. "Hello, I'm calling about the open house at 351 West 57th." I turned my eyes to the window, the city lights studding the sky like lights on a runway. "Do you have any more room for interested renters?"

Fourteen

∽

When I stepped into Starbucks on Sunday afternoon, it only took me a few seconds to spot Chloe's cascading waves in the back corner of the café. I walked to her table and sat down across from her. As soon as she saw me, she smiled. "Liking your New York address?"

A couple of days had passed since I moved into my new apartment near the World Trade Center. I'd fallen in love with it during the open house last Saturday, and my feelings had only grown stronger once I settled in. The building was nestled into a corner of the street that was flanked by natural beauty. On one side was a lush, quiet park mostly frequented by families, and on the other was a majestic view of the Hudson River that looked like it'd been plucked from a magazine.

Everything about it was perfect. Too perfect, even. Maybe that was why I spent my first two hours there curled up on the couch, wanting nothing more than to be back in my cozy farmhouse with its weathered shingles and creaky floorboards. Even though the apartment was only a fraction of the size of the house, it felt cavernous. I longed to fill it with Bridget's carefree laughter, Caleb's fast-paced chatter that I could hardly keep up with, and Tyler's contented whistling as he made his coffee every morning. But all I received in response was silence that rang incessantly in my ears.

I didn't mention any of this to Chloe. Instead, I said, "The apartment is amazing. The views are more gorgeous than my hotel room, if that's even possible."

She took a long sip of her coffee, an unreadable look in her eyes. When she set her cup down, she studied me closely. "So, is this a permanent thing now?"

I hesitated. "I'm going to have to pack my bags eventually. But the more time I spend here, the harder it is to leave." I swirled the straw in my coffee, thinking about how much had changed since my first day at the company. "When I started working here, I thought I would get a feel for the job and help out Jeanette until she found a replacement. But it's so hard to walk away now that I know I'm capable of achieving so much more."

She tilted her head at me with a curious look. "You said you left the city in your twenties, right?"

I nodded.

"Why? I can tell you love it here. Plus, you've been at *Couture* for—what? About three weeks now? Even Celeste is impressed by what you've done so far. And believe me when I say impressing Celeste Moore is no easy task."

My fingers absently grazed the chain of my necklace as I wondered how much I felt comfortable sharing with her. "Things didn't go as planned when I was in college," I said. "Being in the city constantly reminded me of the mistakes I made, and I needed to get away from it all. I remember sitting in my room, staring out the window at the world that was outside New York. Then I discovered the farm, and I felt like I could breathe again. Like I was free." I shifted my gaze to the busy sidewalk outside the window. "But it's different now that I'm older. So much time has passed since college, and I feel like I have a second chance to live out my dream."

When I glanced back up at Chloe, I half expected her to react the way Jeanette had when I'd confided in her at the café—with a look of scorn or an amused smile that didn't take me seriously. Instead, her eyes rested on me with open curiosity, like a child exploring an unfamiliar place.

"Do you still feel that way about the farm?" she asked softly, as if she knew she was wading through sensitive waters.

"Of course I do." But when I looked at her again, I saw that she'd meant something different.

She didn't just mean to ask if I still enjoyed living on the farm. She was asking if I still felt the same magic in the air when I wandered through the fields. If I still wore the dirt on my hands like a badge of honor. If I still felt like I was a part of something bigger than myself. Or if I'd simply let the spark die out and was settling for a life that I'd learned to live with, just because it was comfortable. Familiar.

"It's not like that. I chose the farm all those years ago, and I..." I'd been about to say I still chose it every day, but that couldn't have been farther from the truth. Not when I sat in my high-rise apartment over a thousand miles away from home, wondering how the cows were adjusting to the new milking equipment. Not when I was chatting with one of my *Couture* colleagues in a warm coffee shop while Tyler was freezing in the frost-coated fields.

I could tell by Chloe's expression that she saw all of that in what I wasn't telling her. "Look, I know you haven't had the best start with some of the other staff members," she said. "Especially with Vanessa taking credit for your idea."

"You know about that?"

She shrugged. "It wasn't too hard to figure out. I overheard your idea about making your school uniform stand out, and Vanessa's pitch during the emergency meeting sounded pretty similar to that. I would've said something, but I figured it wasn't my place to do that." She sighed. "It was hard to find a reason to keep hanging out with Vanessa after that."

"It's not a big deal," I said, remembering how Celeste had praised my backup plan. "I came up with something much better, anyway."

"I'm sure you did," she said with a smile. "But what I'm trying to say is, we're not all out to get you. If you need someone to talk to, I'm here. And you can tell me what's really going on whenever you're ready."

I'd known before she said it that she wasn't like Vanessa or the others. Maybe it was the way she didn't get involved in the office drama or how she didn't seem to let the job go to her head. As much as I wanted to open up to her, though, this didn't feel like the time or place to do it. I needed time to sort out my thoughts before I put them on display for someone else to see.

"Thanks," I said instead, knowing it was enough. "I appreciate it."

After I took a sip of my mocha Frappuccino, Chloe glanced at me. "Any other plans for the weekend?"

"Nothing special," I said with a shrug. "I'm just getting to know my new neighborhood. I should fit in all my exploring before Monday, though, because Celeste has a penchant for unloading a month's worth of work on us during those editorial meetings."

She laughed. "Only two meetings, and you're already getting the hang of it." She took a sip of her coffee. "God only knows what Celeste has planned for tomorrow. Rumor has it she's going to test some crazy new idea and see what we do with it."

"That definitely sounds like Celeste," I said. "Well, I'm prepared this time. I won't be caught off guard like I was at the first meeting."

"I admire your optimism, but you can't truly be prepared when it comes to Celeste. Many have tried. Almost no one has succeeded."

Before I could respond, Chloe's phone buzzed. She glanced down at it. "Crap, that's my roommate. She got locked out again." With a sigh, she said, "I'd better head out now. We should do this again, though."

"Definitely."

As we made our way out of the coffee shop, I mulled over Chloe's warning about Celeste. I refused to let her words throw me, especially when I'd just begun to gather the confidence I'd craved for so long. If I was going to succeed as a fashion director, I needed to show the editor in chief that I deserved to be here. And that meant handling anything she threw at me with grace, no matter how much it tested me.

***

The stack of papers in Celeste's hands landed on the conference room table with a thud. Her hard gaze flicked over the room. "We have a lot of work to do."

I could feel the collective dread in the small space as palpably as the windchill outside. People exchanged nervous glances with each other, the same unspoken question in their eyes: who was in trouble this time?

"Thanks to Nora, we have many promising ideas to work with for the September issue. However, this is just the beginning. I need maximum focus and commitment from each of you if we're going to put those ideas into action."

I couldn't help but notice that she hadn't mentioned Vanessa's ideas at all. I felt Vanessa's eyes on me while Celeste spoke, but I didn't meet them. Making eye contact with her would mean acknowledging there was competition between us, when all I was interested in doing was focusing on my own path.

"Today, we're going to focus on the main theme of the issue. Changing lives. Making an impact." Her eyes flitted toward me. "Nora, I remember you mentioning that you wanted to incorporate success stories into the magazine. You suggested interviewing everyday people to inspire our readers, correct?"

I nodded. "That's right."

Celeste sat down at the head of the table, her posture relaxing ever so slightly. She steepled her fingers and studied the semicircle of writers and editors. Her head jerked suddenly toward Olivia, the fashion and style writer. "Olivia, what is the biggest risk you've ever taken?"

Celeste's plan dawned on me in that moment. *We* were the everyday people she wanted to profile in the feature article.

Chloe was right—she did have something unexpected up her sleeve.

Poor Olivia's face turned beet red. She hesitated, struggling ostensibly to come up with something worthy of Celeste's interest. "I tried out for cheerleading one time in high school," she said, her timid voice hardly selling the idea. "I didn't make the squad, but I'm glad I put myself out there and took a chance."

Celeste looked unimpressed, if not a bit bored. She turned to the next victim, whom I recognized as Adrianna, the beauty editor. "Adrianna? What do you have to share with us?"

She brightened at once. "I studied abroad in Italy during my junior year of college. It was my first time flying outside of the US, and I was a nervous wreck. But I do have some family over in Florence, so that helped me feel more at home. I wouldn't have had any of the amazing experiences I had if I stayed in South Carolina."

Celeste was beginning to look impatient. "I can find a thousand other stories exactly like yours, Adrianna. Perhaps you can pitch your idea to the editor at *People* magazine instead."

Adrianna was visibly deflated, but our boss had already moved on to her next subject. Each story followed the same template: various attempts people made at going against the grain, but without causing considerable disruption. It was like they'd dived headfirst into the water but grasped onto a life preserver as soon as they landed. I listened intently, trying to picture each anecdote plastered on the pages of the September issue, but every story fell flat.

After half a dozen people had spoken, Celeste turned to face me. It was my turn. I didn't even have to think about my answer to her question. It was already etched into my heart, its ridges deepened and solidified through the years. But for some reason, opening my mouth and articulating it in front of all these people gave me pause.

As I met the eyes of my colleagues, I felt like I'd just taken off all my clothes in front of them. Other than the time I met Jeanette at the Bluebird Café, there were only two times in my life where I'd spoken so candidly about my escape. The first had been in my poorly lit hotel room, tears streaming down my cheeks as I fielded my parents' frantic calls about where I was. And the second time was in Tyler's truck as we rode down the expressway one night, the tranquil darkness of the empty road masking my insecurities as I opened up to him about everything that brought me to Fairlane.

Both were private moments that I'd shared with the people I loved, and it had been a challenge even then to speak so openly about my deepest hopes and fears. The thought of laying all of that bare before the stark, judgmental eyes of my coworkers made my stomach twist with dread.

I pushed away the doubts, telling myself they were just trying to throw me off track. This was exactly what I wanted to say. It was the reason for the vision I'd come up with for the new issue, the reason why I believed in it with such fierceness.

I took a shaky breath and turned to face my audience. As I told the story that had become a part of me, my coworkers' expressions changed from shock to horror to awe. It was like they were living it right alongside me, from the moment I hopped in my car and set off on my trip to the moment I arrived at my new home. Seeing how my colleagues were hanging on to my every word made me think of how our readers would react if I put my story out there.

When I was finished, Celeste turned to address the rest of the group. "This is exactly what I was looking for. Someone who took a risk with no safety net. A risk that changed her life for the better."

She glanced at me, and her eyes were bright. I'd never seen her so excited about anything in the three weeks I'd spent here. "We have a lot to think about now. I expect you all to look at Nora's story as an example of how you should be improving this magazine."

Before I could stop myself, I looked in Vanessa's direction. I expected to see resentment in her eyes, or any trace of the bitterness she seemed to harbor toward me. Instead, I was taken aback to see that she looked hurt. Cheated. Like I'd stolen something that was rightfully hers. An unexplained sense of guilt welled up inside me, even though I wasn't sure what I'd done wrong.

When the meeting was over, everyone filed out and returned to their work as if it were just another day. For me, though, it was anything but. A visible shift in the atmosphere had taken place after I discussed my past, a shift that only I could feel. My role at the magazine had just become personal, and I had the feeling it would never be the same again.

"Nora. A word, please?"

I instinctively tensed up as I approached Celeste. Even though I'd safely landed on her good side, I still hadn't outgrown the dread I felt whenever she wanted to speak to me one-on-one.

"I know you wanted the feature article to be focused on

156 - Elena Goudelias

others who have changed their lives. But I no longer see the need to turn the spotlight outward." She gave me a knowing smile. "Your story will resonate with many of our readers, especially because it came from a *Couture* staff member herself. Empathy is essential to effective storytelling. And it's hard not to empathize with a young woman who left everything behind because she believed in something greater than herself."

Tears rose to the surface, but I blinked them back before they could fall. I *had* believed that there was a better life for me out there, and I'd molded it entirely on my own. Once that life had come into focus, I'd poured my soul into it, dedicating every last drop to nurturing the farm and starting a family. But now, as I stood in the city I'd wanted to escape so badly while watching the life I'd built wither away, I wasn't sure what I believed in anymore.

"So, you want me to reproduce the story I just told for the magazine?" I asked, making a concentrated effort to steady my voice. As I thought back to my last meeting with Celeste, I realized the woman had a knack for unearthing the emotions I'd worked hard to bury.

She gave me a thoughtful look. "Yes and no. The story itself is wonderful, but I can tell you're a bit removed from it. After all, it's been years since you left home." Her eyes bore directly into mine. "I need you to place yourself in that period of your life again. Talk to your family. Ask them questions. Have them piece together any details that you may have forgotten about. You need to remember as much as you can about that day. The success of this issue depends on it."

My heartbeat picked up. "Things with my family are complicated, to say the least. I don't know if they'd be the best people to talk to."

"If anything, that makes it even better. People love tension. Your complications with your family will add more depth to your story." She tucked her files under her arm and turned toward the door. "If I were you, I'd get started as soon as possible."

I blinked as she strode out of the room. Even though I'd broken the ice with my parents during our lunch, getting them to reopen old wounds would put us right back to where we started. After all the work I'd put in to bring us closer, I couldn't risk losing them again.

At the same time, Celeste made a solid point. I remembered scrolling through the *Couture* website as a teen and clicking enthusiastically on articles that gave readers a glimpse into staff members' wardrobes, their lifestyles, and their daily routines. It was like I had the privilege to hang out with them as I would with a close friend. If I found the courage to open up about my past, our readers would cling to that just as I had.

I headed back to my office, trying to sort out my thoughts. Talking to my parents about the past was still out of the question. The sound of my mother's voice during that first phone call after I left home was burned into my mind, overclouding all the hope and freedom I'd felt that day. And then there was my dad, whose uncharacteristic anger had made me shrink back in fear like a small child.

I shook my head to block out the memory. Maybe I couldn't go down that road with my parents, but I knew someone else who would walk down it with me. It wouldn't be pretty, but it was the only option I had left. After all, my brother was the only one who'd been patient enough to hear me out when I first ran away. And he'd been the only one to talk some sense into my mother after our disastrous Thanksgiving dinner.

I took out my phone and drew in a breath. Our last phone call might not have ended well, but if I'd made any progress with my parents, there was a light at the end of the tunnel. Slowly, I began to type out a message:

Hey, Luke – hope everything's good on your end. I was thinking we could get together sometime this weekend for lunch. Let me know what works best for you.

I tucked my phone back into my bag, praying that I'd made the right decision. It *had* to be the right decision. Or else I would have this over my head, too, leaving me to wonder how I could have done things differently.

Fifteen

～

I lay in bed the next morning, hardly finding the strength to move a muscle. Questions had been swimming through my mind all night, robbing me of the sleep I desperately needed. How was Tyler handling the new farm setup? Had the cows adjusted to the robotic equipment yet? Were the kids doing okay in school?

The last question weighed on my chest like an anvil. I hadn't forgotten about how excited Bridget was to start the new semester in January. On her first day back, she'd dived headfirst into the building like she'd been waiting all her life for that day to come. Was she still working toward her ambitious goals? Or had she lost sight of them because of everything going on at home?

Then there was Caleb. Every time he crossed my mind, I worried about the kids he was hanging out with and how they were influencing him. Rejecting the farm had probably only been the tip of the iceberg.

When I found it in me to face the day ahead, I did my best at putting together a fashion-director-worthy outfit and made my way toward the Trade Center. At one point during the short walk, I scrolled through my contacts and let my finger hover momentarily over Tyler's name. But I couldn't bring myself to call him. Now that he was convinced I'd permanently chosen the magazine over the farm, there wasn't a single word left to say.

The moment I stepped into my office, I started to tackle the rough draft of my personal experience essay, but my mind wouldn't stop wandering. Thinking about Caleb and Bridget that morning had caused past hurts to resurface after I'd managed to stifle them under my workload for the past few weeks. Now, as I brought the open wound to the light, I saw how deep it really was. It wasn't the kind of wound that needed time to heal. I had to do something about it.

I turned on my computer and logged into my email account. The only way I could find out how my kids were really doing was by reaching out to their principal, Mrs. Saunders. She was something of a legend at Fairlane Public School. She'd been the principal when Tyler attended the school, and she was still going strong thirty years later. All her years of experience meant nothing got past her when it came to her students. I knew she would be honest with me if something was going on.

After I sent the email, I returned to my work while stealing the occasional glance at my inbox. Her reply came at a quarter past three, when all the students had already left school. I clicked on the message the second it arrived:

Hello, Nora:

Are you available to call me? I think it would be best if we discussed this over the phone. My number is 712-568-9443.

I look forward to hearing from you.

-Patricia

I typed out a quick message to Zoe, one of the fashion assistants, to let her know I was putting her in charge of the photo shoot prep. Any of the assistants would be thrilled to be a part of anything that didn't involve answering phones or sending emails.

I rose from my chair and snuck out of the office, careful not to draw attention to myself. As I passed Chloe's desk, I nudged her and said, "If anyone asks where I am, tell them I had to check on an order at Saks."

She nodded without asking questions. "You got it."

"Thanks." I continued my walk to the elevators while trying to look as casual as possible. Saks was a good subway ride away from the office, plus a bit of walking, so that gave me plenty of time to dedicate my full attention to the phone call.

Once I was a good half mile away from the Trade Center, I found a bench in a quiet green space and sat down. I pulled up Mrs. Saunders's email and called the number she'd listed. I crossed and uncrossed my legs as I waited for her to answer, growing more uneasy with every passing second.

"Hello?" Her voice sounded older since the last time I'd heard it, and I suddenly felt like I'd been away from home for a year rather than a few weeks.

"Hi, Mrs. Saunders. It's Nora. I got your email about discussing Caleb and Bridget."

"Oh, please. Call me Patricia." I could almost picture her waving off my formality. "Nora, how are you? Your husband informed me that you're in New York now, correct?"

Heat rushed to my cheeks as I realized I'd never mentioned in my email that I was out of town. "Yes, that's correct. My friend is on maternity leave, and she offered me a job at *Couture*. It's just temporary, though," I added quickly, feeling the woman's judgmental eyes on me from over a thousand miles away.

"I see. And when do you plan on coming back to Fairlane?"

I watched a pigeon swoop in to claim an abandoned french fry by my feet. "Well, I'm working toward an important deadline, so I can't leave just yet. But my friend promised me that she'd find someone else to take my place soon." I decided against telling her that Jeanette never actually promised to fill my place after I left.

A long pause followed my fabricated response. "Listen, Nora. I'm sure your husband has already told you about your children's struggles at school, so I won't take up too much of your time. But I will tell you, as both an educator and a parent, that this is a poor arrangement for your children. They're confused. They don't understand why you're not coming home. Both of them are dealing with it differently, but neither of them is handling it very well."

I ignored the sharp pain in my chest and fought the urge to tell her the truth: that I wasn't welcome in my home anymore. That even if I hopped on a plane right that minute and showed up at the farmhouse, I would be a stranger to both Tyler and the kids. And that I was afraid I'd changed to the point where I could never be the same person I was before all of this happened.

In a voice that was caught somewhere between a whisper and a normal speaking voice, I said, "How are they coping with it?"

"I've spoken to their teachers about this, and they expressed concerns about both children. As far as your oldest is concerned, he's become rather uncooperative. He shows no signs of caring about his schoolwork or grades. In fact, I believe his teacher has three missing assignments from him at the moment. As for your daughter... Well, she's extremely quiet. When her teacher calls on her during class to get her involved, she's almost never paying attention. Sad to see, especially considering how bright she is."

I held the phone closer to my ear, as if that would make everything she was saying turn out to be false. "Maybe they need some more time to make friends. The first couple months of the new semester are always an adjustment. I know they'll find their way soon."

"Nora." Her calm and friendly voice took on a stern tone, and it startled me. "Do you know who's been showing up at the PTA meetings?"

My heart hammered in my chest like it knew the answer before I did. "Tyler?" I asked in a small voice.

"No. This other woman I've never seen before. I believe her name is Jeanette. She claims to be Caleb and Bridget's guardian." Mrs. Saunders paused. "May I ask why this stranger has the responsibility of caring for your children?"

I felt lightheaded and feared the bench would collapse from under me. "She doesn't. There's been some sort of misunderstanding." I swallowed, afraid to ask the question that was weighing on my mind. "Have you seen her anywhere else?"

"Outside of the PTA meetings? Why, no. But I would think she plays a big role in your children's lives if she took the time to discuss their education."

I held on to the side of the bench as if to steady myself. "Mrs. Sau—I mean, Patricia. I... I have to go now. My boss needs me for something. Thanks for taking the time to talk, though."

There was a beat of silence on the other end before she replied. "Certainly, Nora. Good luck with everything."

Once the conversation was over, I went to my contacts and hit Jeanette's new home number without thinking twice. I didn't know why I'd allowed things to get this far. All I knew was that letting Jeanette confront me at Daryl's had been one of my biggest mistakes. All she'd needed was an open door, and I'd swung it all the way open for her.

"Hello?" The male voice threw me off guard at first, but I put a name to it a moment later.

"Hey, Derek. It's Nora. Is Jeanette there?"

"No, she's over at the farm. I think she's supposed to come back soon, though. Can I take a message?"

I tightened my grip on the phone. "You mean *my* farm?"

"Yup, that's the one. She seems to be taking a liking to country life. I hope you're okay with it, by the way. We both thought having Jeanette on the farm would be a big help to you while you do your job."

"Actually, I'm not okay with it. I never was. Taking care of the cows was already crossing the line, and now I hear from my kids' principal that she's attending the PTA meetings? What else is she doing? Driving them to school? Cooking dinner for them?" A bitter taste filled my mouth as I pictured Jeanette asking the kids how their day was while pulling a steaming roast out of the oven.

"Relax, Nora. She's only attending the meetings so your husband can stay on the farm to watch the animals. She doesn't eat dinner with them or anything. It's just something to keep her busy during the day." He was silent for a moment before letting out a sigh. "You know, I thought since you've been friends for so long, this wouldn't be such a big deal. But apparently, I was wrong."

"Don't you see what she's doing?" I sounded hysterical compared to Derek's calm, rational tone, and I hated myself for it. "She's taking my family away from me. How can you not see that?"

"I don't see it, because it's not there. This is nothing more than a friend helping out a friend."

"A friend doesn't sabotage their friend's life." I paused as something else occurred to me. "What about the baby she's carrying? Isn't that enough for her? Not to mention she shouldn't be doing farmwork while she's pregnant."

"It's nothing strenuous. Your husband takes care of all the hard labor. Besides, Jeanette's been feeling a lot better lately. No morning sickness at all. I always knew she was resilient." After a beat, he said, "And to answer your other question, this is great practice for her. She's already proving how great of a mom she'll be when the baby is born. This is her first time raising a child, you know. It helps not to go into it blindfolded."

"Most people do. I know I did. Before I realized my dream wouldn't work out, the only child I intended to have was my career. But after I changed my mind, I figured it all out on my own. And I survived, just like she can."

Neither of us spoke for a long moment, and I watched a young father push a baby carriage past the bench I was sitting on. I stifled a sob as Derek spoke again. "Jeanette always talks about how you two drifted apart over the years, and now I see why. You're being anything but supportive right now. And just when she needs you the most."

I used all my strength to keep my voice even. "I can't just let her keep doing this. How do you expect me to trust her when she's drowning my family in debt thanks to her brilliant robotics idea?"

He barked out a bitter, humorless laugh. "Is that what you think is happening? I thought you were a journalist. You should check your facts before making assumptions like that."

"What are you talking about?" I demanded, even though a part of me already knew the answer.

"The farm is doing better than it ever has. At least, that's what Jeanette told me when she came home last night. Sure, it was a big investment, but it paid off. With the way milk production has been skyrocketing over the past month, the money that went into the new equipment hardly registers anymore."

The pain of hearing the one thing I didn't want to hear reached its gnarled fingers inside me. "She's lying," I croaked, but I knew deep down that it was the truth. Jeanette hadn't been successful at *Couture* because of her passion for the field—she'd never been as interested in fashion as I was. The reason for her success was a deadly combination of drive and business skills. She knew how to bring in a profit, and she'd changed the entire landscape of the magazine so that it attracted more readers than ever before.

To her, my farm was just another project that she'd decided to take on. She didn't care one iota about the well-being of the cows or the land they lived on. She approached it all with the detachment of a businesswoman who only saw the animals for the money they were worth. And that was the worst part of it: Jeanette didn't have any emotional investment in the farm, which was why she was so good at solving its problems without worrying about the consequences.

"No, she isn't. And considering how immature you're acting right now, it's better off she's helping instead of you." With that, the line went dead.

I shoved my phone back into my bag and stared out at the happy families dotting the park. Feeling my throat tighten, I trekked back to the office before my face betrayed my internal state. Jeanette had gotten what she wanted. I shouldn't have been surprised, given her track record. But I'd still been holding on to the sliver of hope that she would give up before she even started. That she would realize she was in over her head.

As I turned the corner, I wondered if Tyler was relieved that Jeanette had taken charge of the farm. I remembered how weary he'd sounded on the phone. He'd barely resembled the calm, easygoing man I knew. Even if he was initially resistant to the changes Jeanette made to the farm, there was no doubt he embraced them now. And none of it was thanks to me. While I'd made him second-guess his job, Jeanette had given him a reason to have faith in it again.

When I reached my office, I shut the door behind me and collapsed into my chair. This was about more than Jeanette taking my place. This was about her bringing all of my flaws to light so Tyler could see them. So he could recognize his mistake in letting someone as naïve and inexperienced as me take on such a demanding job. I still remembered his words to me when I'd been adjusting to country life: "The only farmers who survive are the ones who are in it for the long haul."

He didn't think I was in it for the long haul. He didn't think

I was ever coming back. That was why he'd found someone far more capable than I ever was. And the part that hurt the most was knowing that his thriving in my absence meant my presence had never really mattered in the first place.

Sixteen

～

"What's this?" Luke asked, pointing to the list of designers at the bottom of my outline.

"Those are some of the looks we're going to feature in the September issue. I picked all of them out." I looked up at my brother, letting my enthusiasm flow freely from my expression. "I know it's still early, but the issue is coming together exactly how I want it to."

We were seated at a booth in The Smith, one of my favorite hangouts from my high school days. Just sitting down for a quick lunch there felt like I'd been invited to an exclusive party. Even after all these years, stepping back into the high-energy atmosphere was like coming home again.

"That's great, Nora," Luke said. "I can tell you put a lot of work into this."

"I did." I slid the sheet of paper back into my folder. I'd brought along a copy of the feature outline I'd shared with Celeste. I wanted to give my brother a concrete example of the work I'd been doing since I joined *Couture,* and I could tell he was impressed.

"Remember when you had to come up with a new product idea for your fifth-grade art class?" Luke reminisced. "You'd make your rounds in the hall between classes and pitch your idea to anyone who would listen. In a way, you were already a budding saleswoman back then."

"I completely forgot about that," I admitted, laughing. "I guess that was before puberty hit and I realized I should've been too self-conscious to do that."

"Looks like you've come full circle with the way you're out-doing your coworkers." He gave me a knowing smile. "Jeanette told me how you're finding your place at the company, and I think it's awesome."

I froze. "You talked to Jeanette?"

"Yeah. I just wanted to catch up with your family to see how everyone was doing, and I got Jeanette on the phone instead. I hear she's helping out with the farmwork now." He paused to wipe his mouth. "Anyway, she told me it's like you were born for this. The job comes so naturally to you."

One of the most frustrating things about Jeanette was that she made it impossible to stay angry with her. Her genuine praise of my work was an echo of the close friend I'd held on to for so many years, not the traitor who claimed everything I had as her own before it fully escaped my grasp. And even though I knew what she'd said to Luke barely scratched the surface of who she was, I still wanted a reason to believe in the caring, supportive person I'd once known.

"Thanks," I said. "That means a lot." Feeling the urge to take the attention off myself, I glanced at my brother. "So, how are things going at Citigroup?"

"Everything's great. I'm planning on moving closer to the office, so it'll be a lot easier to get to work every day. My boss even told me about some great opportunities he has in store for me. I feel like I'm really going places now."

I recognized the fire in his eyes when he spoke, because it was the same spark I felt when I talked about my job. It seemed that the farther I grew apart from my life on the farm, the closer I bonded with my New York family. I'd always known that my parents and brother didn't understand why I'd chosen an unassuming life of farming over everything New York had to offer me. But as Luke and I discussed our jobs, it struck me that I was back on the same wavelength with my family. It was as if they'd breathed a sigh of relief when I took the job at *Couture* and thought, *This is the real Nora. This is who we've been waiting for her to become all this time.*

I forked a bite of pasta into my mouth and gingerly set my utensils to the side. We were already halfway through our meals, and I still hadn't gotten to the crux of why I'd arranged for us to meet. Knowing I couldn't put it off forever, I took a deep breath and met Luke's eyes.

"When I texted you, I was thinking about how much has changed since we last saw each other. We both were so different back then. But especially me." My eyes traveled back down to my plate as I summoned the strength to continue. "To this day, I still think about the morning I left home. Not just what led me to do it, but also how it affected Mom and Dad. And you."

I had his full attention now. He looked at me cautiously, as if he were tiptoeing through uncharted territory. Fighting the urge to change the subject, I forged on, despite the niggling feeling of dread in the pit of my stomach.

"Anyway, what I mean to ask is... Do you remember what happened after I left? When Mom and Dad found my note? I've gone over that memory again and again, and that's always been the one missing piece."

He set down his fork and looked at me head-on. "You're sure you want to know?"

His voice took on such a foreboding tone that I recoiled ever so slightly. Still, I maintained my resolve to get the answers I needed. "Yes. I do. Tell me everything."

I observed my brother as he returned to that place in his mind, the same place I'd worked tirelessly to leave behind me. It was painful to watch him revisit a part of our past that had torn our entire family apart, and just when I'd started to mend our fissured relationship. I stared at my lap, telling myself this was for the success of my piece. Nothing good would come out of it if I didn't extract the raw pain of my memories.

"Before they found the note, Mom and Dad thought you went for a walk to get some air. It made sense that you needed space after the huge argument you guys had about the probation letter."

I nodded, remembering that argument like it'd happened the other day. Luke, who was a high school senior when I was a college sophomore, had still been living with our parents then. Not only was he around to hear Mom and Dad warn me about letting my future pass me by, but he'd also woken up the next morning to see that my bedroom was already empty at six o'clock.

"It was Dad's idea to check the park. He knew you liked to go there when you were upset." He paused, and I wondered if he had the same image in his mind's eye—the image of me wandering through the canopy of trees in Central Park as a child, designating it as my secret hideout. Even as I grew up, I still escaped to there when I needed some time away from the chaos of the city.

"When they didn't see you there, they started searching the whole apartment. That's when they found the note."

I closed my eyes, trying to block out the memory that was rising to the surface more quickly than I could contain it. "What did they do?"

He let out a long breath. "They almost saw their lives flash before their eyes. I've never seen them so terrified before." His voice grew quiet, almost somber. "They started looking through your things for any hint of where you went. They called all your friends from school, but they didn't know anything. The worst part was that you didn't leave any footprints behind. Until you actually left, you never said anything about wanting to leave."

Because if I said something, I never would've done it, I answered silently. I stared at the table, steeling myself to ask the question I'd been waiting to ask since we sat down. With a cautious glance at Luke, I asked, "After they figured out where I was, did they just... give up?"

A thin veil of sadness cloaked his eyes. "That's not fair to them. You didn't give them a choice. Besides, you were an adult then. Adults make their own decisions, and it's clear you made yours."

"I know." I bit down on my lip, scrambling to think of something else to say, when Luke furrowed his brow.

"Why are you asking me all this? You've spent your entire life running away from your past, and now you're suddenly interested in every last detail? Come on, Nora. Tell me what's going on."

I leaned back against my chair, deflated. There was no use in coming up with excuses anymore. "My boss asked my whole team about the biggest risk we've ever taken, and she was most interested in my story. Now she wants me to publish it in the September issue."

Luke looked away, his lips set into a thin line. "I can't believe this." When he turned to face me again, he looked at me like I was a stranger. "Have you become completely numb to everything that happened? Did you forget about what Mom and Dad sounded like on the phone when they called you? Because if you remembered, you wouldn't be reproducing it for a fashion magazine." He practically spat out the last two words, as if they were contaminated.

I straightened. "It's not just for a *fashion magazine.* It's for people who need a reason to change their lives the way I did."

"The way you did? Face it, Nora. You don't care about any of that anymore. You don't remember what it was like to feel stuck in a life you hated. I can tell by the way you're asking these questions without flinching that they're meaningless to you. You're just using your 'story' to get more readers," he said, adding air quotes to the word *story.*

As I listened to Luke, I remembered how Celeste had called me out for being too far removed from my past after I shared my story. She'd been right all along, even if I wasn't ready to admit it.

"That might have been a long time ago, but I haven't forgotten about what it was like. I remember why I left home every time you or Mom or Dad don't give me the support I need. Just like you're doing right now." The words were loaded with vitriol, and I wanted to take them back as soon as they escaped my mouth.

Luke studied me closely. "You've changed, Nora. I thought

I'd get my sister back when you took this job, but you're not her anymore. And whoever you are, I don't think I want to get to know her." He stood up from his chair and grabbed his coat.

"Luke, wait." I looked at him, my eyes pleading. "I didn't mean it like that. It's just hard to be doing this on my own. And it's even harder when you don't support my work."

He gave me a long, hard look. "It sounds like you have all the support you need at *Couture*. Isn't that enough for you?" Without another word, he turned and made his way to the door.

As I watched him leave, I tried to ignore the hollow feeling in my stomach. Between Tyler telling me I wasn't the same person anymore and Luke looking at me like he didn't recognize me, it was hard to deny that something about me had changed over the past few weeks. Something that had turned me into the kind of person who let her family get hurt for the sake of her own success.

I glanced around at the young adults who populated the restaurant, thinking about the younger version of myself who'd wanted this life more than anything else. I still felt her inside me, especially during quiet moments when there was no one around to drown out her voice. Thinking of her made me want to believe in something I couldn't anymore: that I could excel as a fashion director while keeping the peace with my family. I now knew that was a fantasy, not the cruel reality that was unfolding before my eyes.

If I wanted to climb the heights I'd always dreamed of reaching, I would have to let everything close to my heart slip away little by little. I could choose to salvage my old life instead, but that would mean letting my achievements shrivel away before they bloomed into success.

The hole I'd dug myself into seemed to grow more confining during the subway ride home. In a weak attempt to keep my mind occupied, I sorted through my unread messages. There were a few texts from my colleagues and a voicemail. The number attached to the voicemail looked vaguely familiar, and I racked my brain to identify it. After scrolling through my old emails, I recognized it as Mrs. Saunders's. A knot sprouted in my stomach and tightened with every possible scenario I imagined. When it came to Mrs. Saunders, no news was ever good news.

The minute I was back in my hotel room, I opened my voicemails and played the message. I perched on the edge of the couch as the principal began explaining what I didn't want to hear.

"Hello, Nora. This is Patricia. I normally don't make calls like this, but I am simply stunned at the progress your children are making. Since the last time we spoke, both children have showed signs of growth both academically and personally. Their grades are going up in all their classes, and they even seem to be bonding with their peers. I'm particularly impressed with your youngest, Bridget. She's always struggled with her multiplication tables, but her teacher informed me that she nearly aced her last quiz. Caleb's teacher also noticed that he has become more cooperative in class and with his fellow students.

"I must say, this much improvement in such a short span of time is rather unusual. Perhaps your husband has hired a tutor for your kids? Whatever the reason is, I wanted to let you know that I'm seeing a real difference. Keep up whatever it is you're doing, Nora."

I stared at the wall as Mrs. Saunders's report filled me with every emotion from relief to dread. Relief had been my initial reaction to learning that my kids were doing better, but dread had taken its place when I understood why they were improving so quickly. It definitely wasn't Tyler's doing. He didn't have the time to tutor them for hours on end, and one would be hard-pressed to find such a skilled tutor in our one-horse town.

The answer was waiting right in front of my eyes, but I wasn't ready to peel them open just yet. I'd known all along that the PTA meetings were just the beginning of Jeanette's quest to claim my life as her own. An image of her helping Bridget master her multiplication tables flashed through my mind before I could block it out. I pictured Jeanette patiently lending an ear to my son and offering him the golden advice she'd extracted from one of her parenting books.

A pang of anxiety sliced through me as reality sank in. There was a reason Jeanette had earned that coveted acceptance letter from Grant. With so much untapped knowledge inside her, she probably knew about some secret teaching method that I was in the dark about. Whatever it was, it must have been a miracle if it kept Bridget from giving up after two problems like she did with me.

I put down my phone and walked to the desk in the corner of the living room. I knew Jeanette well, and she wouldn't be able to keep up her role of the down-to-earth farmer for much longer. She would eventually abandon the country roads that snaked toward my farm when she realized the only road that took her home was the West Side Highway.

I sat down at the desk and unzipped my work bag before pulling out my laptop. I didn't need Luke's help anymore. The story I needed to tell was at the forefront of my mind, and seeing Jeanette live the way I'd once lived helped me remember what it was like to start over in a new town, to build a new life without anyone's help.

I wrote with a renewed sense of purpose, focusing solely on the work I needed to do. Over the past thirty-five years, I'd come to understand that most things had a way of working themselves out. As long as I carried out my mission here, life would take care of the rest for me.

How it would do that was still a mystery, but I knew that it would. I believed it with the same reckless abandon of a carefree child who had nothing to lose. At the end of the day, it was that child inside me who reminded me not to give up on the dream that only I could see.

Seventeen

I raced toward the blinking light at the end of the crosswalk, reaching the curb just as the red hand turned solid. I was running late to my meeting with Melanie Sykes, the fashion trendsetter I was set to interview for the September issue. After I delivered my personal anecdote to Celeste, she'd loved it so much that she'd scrapped the story on eyeliner trends in favor of another personal-experience essay. Given the lack of inspiration from my coworkers during the last editorial meeting, though, Celeste preferred that we interview a celebrity our readers could relate to instead.

I reached the covered patio outside of Melanie's Gothic-style townhouse, where she'd agreed to do the interview. A major social media influencer, Melanie was most women's go-to for style advice. Getting an interview with her was the best way to show Celeste that I was serious about my job.

When I approached Melanie, she was seated at her patio table, her legs stretched out on the chair in front of her like she was lounging at the beach. She was scrolling mindlessly through her phone, tapping away every now and then at an invisible Instagram or Twitter post. It wasn't until I was standing a foot away from her that she finally registered that she had a visitor.

"Oh, hey." She slid her sunglasses to the top of her head and gave me a quick once-over. "Are you from *Couture*?"

"Sure am."

She patted the seat next to her. "Well, don't be shy."

I lowered myself onto the seat and fished around in my bag for my moleskin notebook, where I'd jotted down a few questions I wanted to ask her. I set it onto the table and offered her a smile. "Thanks for agreeing to meet me. I was hoping to give our readers a better idea of who you are and what you do."

She sat back in her chair. "I'm all yours."

"Great." I switched on my tape recorder and opened up to my first page of notes. "So, we'll start by talking about your career. You've obviously been a huge inspiration to young girls and women across the country. What risks did you take to get to where you are now?"

"I know it's hard to believe, but I had my heart set on becoming a marine biologist ever since my first trip to the aquarium when I was six. Then I took bio in high school, and that was the end of that dream."

I laughed, and Melanie went on with her story. "A few years later, I discovered the influencing industry, and I knew right away that it was perfect for me. I wanted my work to reach a global audience, and social media gave me the platform to do that. So I set up my Instagram account and never looked back. Naturally, I didn't know what the hell I was doing at nineteen, but I've never shied away from a challenge. It was something I knew I had to do, even if I didn't know exactly how I was going to get there."

I looked at her with admiration, wanting to tell her that we had more in common than she knew. But I remained professional and moved on to the next question. "Do you have a mantra that you follow? What does it mean to you?"

She thought for a second. "Not necessarily a mantra, per se, but I've always believed that it's your job to show life that you can take a few hits. Ninety-nine percent of the time, shit gets you down because you give it permission to get you down. But when you decide to rise above it, it eventually stops having power over you."

I looked up from my notes and studied her. "You mean nothing ever gets you down?"

"Of course it does. But whenever I'm tempted to wallow, I tell myself, 'Dammit, I'm not going to let it steal another second of my peace.' Even if I have to listen to 'Survivor' by Destiny's Child on repeat."

With a laugh, I said, "I really respect that. Not many people can do that."

She shrugged. "Anyone can, really. It might not be an easy choice, but it's still a choice at the end of the day."

I gave a nod of assent and glanced at the next question. "If you could change a part of your past or see into the future, which would you choose?"

"We're getting deep now, aren't we?" With a smile, she said, "I'm just kidding. That one's easy. Trying to change the past is a waste of time, so I'd have to go with seeing the future. If it turns out to be better than I expected, that's great. If it doesn't, then I would work my ass off to make sure I get exactly what I want."

When she finished speaking, I shut off the tape recorder. "Off the record, how do you have such a relaxed attitude toward life? You seem like you've gotten everything you want, and if there were any obstacles, you weren't too bothered by them."

"Trust me, this attitude was hard-earned. I used to obsess over every detail of my life. Sometimes it was the way I phrased my answer on a test. Other times, it was the way someone looked at me in the hall. I would dissect it all until it drove me crazy. It took me a while to realize how miserable I was, and when I did, I thought, 'This isn't even living anymore.' So I started accepting whatever came my way. It was the most liberating day of my life."

"It definitely sounds like it was."

She studied me for a moment. "Between you and me, though, you look like you care too much about something, and it's holding you back. There's something you want to do, but you're afraid of what will happen if you do it. I can see it in you."

I set down my notebook and met her eyes in genuine surprise. "You're not that far off," I said, thinking about how my life as a fashion director was always trying to take up more real estate in my heart. How Tyler still didn't fully understand how I felt about my job here, because I'd never been completely open with him about it.

"Well, if I were you, I'd go take care of that. If there's one thing I've learned in my twenty-eight years on this earth, it's that the things you don't do always haunt you more than the ones you do."

"I know a thing or two about that," I muttered. After a moment, I glanced up at her. "Thanks again for the interview. And your advice."

"Anytime, girl."

As she resumed scrolling through her phone, I made my way back to the office. I could only hope that the interview was enough to please my boss. Even though she'd approved of my ideas in the past, that didn't mean she wouldn't tear me apart if she felt the need to. My first editorial meeting was an ever-present reminder that I could never get too comfortable as long as I worked for Celeste.

When I stepped out of the elevator, I caught a glimpse of Vanessa talking to someone in the hallway. Because of all the aggressive layers of makeup and bold fashion choices, it was nearly impossible to tell who she was. Not until the woman slunk right past me did I recognize her as Hannah Walsh.

I did a double take as she headed over to the elevator. I turned around to face Vanessa, who wasn't even trying to hide the victorious smile on her face. Somehow, I found it in me to bite my tongue and offer her a courteous grin in response.

After Vanessa was safely out of the way, I planted myself next to Chloe's desk. She looked up from her computer and smiled. "Hey. What's up?"

"Did you see who just walked out of our office, or do I need another cup of coffee?"

"Nope, that was definitely Hannah Walsh." She eyed me for a moment. "And I'm gonna have to say no to the coffee. You're already jittery enough."

"How did Vanessa get an interview with her?"

She shrugged. "When Vanessa decides she wants something, she finds a way to get it. Jeanette definitely rubbed off on her in that way."

I watched as Vanessa stepped into Celeste's office. She was probably poising herself to be the star of the September issue, starting with snagging an interview with a singer who was second only to Beyoncé. A surge of anxiety shot through me as I came to terms with what I was about to lose. I'd worked too hard to let her take this all away from me.

I turned toward my office. "See you at lunch, then?"

Chloe shot me an inquisitive look. "Why do I have the feeling you're up to something?"

"Because you're more perceptive than everyone else here," I said, thinking about the multiple times my façade had failed to fool her.

"Fair enough." With an impish grin, she said, "But whatever it is you're doing, just make sure you do it right."

I mirrored her expression as I reached my office door. "Is there any other way to do it?"

I sat down at my desk and scanned the papers strewn across the surface. As I sifted through them, I tried to unearth the answer I needed from underneath all the rough drafts and photo shoot proofs. There had to be something I could do that Vanessa hadn't thought of, something that would give Celeste no choice but to turn her attention to me. But my mind was hopelessly blank, stripped of the inspiration I needed.

I leaned back in my chair and sighed. I wouldn't be able to move forward until I followed Melanie's advice. Tyler deserved to know how I felt about my job. He deserved to know how my purpose here ran far deeper than I'd ever thought it would. At most, I could hope that he would do his best to understand, even though he never really would. Not when my entire job stood for something he thought was frivolous at best. Not when the work he believed in had a practical purpose, with visible results at the end of the day.

In that moment, I was acutely aware of where our similarities ended. Even though we both worked the same job and shared the same values, he would always be a farmer, and I would always be an outsider trying to fit into a world where I never fully belonged. After all the time I'd spent growing apart from my husband, the differences in our goals was just as tangible as the physical distance between us.

I dismissed the thoughts and made a point to put them behind me for the next five hours. Yet I still snuck periodic glances at my watch, counting down the minutes until I could head back home and tell him everything that was on my mind.

Once I'd wrapped up the workday, I walked back to my apartment, rehearsing what I wanted to say to him. By the time I turned the key, my doubts had begun to stifle the confidence Melanie had instilled in me. But the unrest in my soul told me this was necessary, if not long overdue.

I took a breath and called his number. The only way I would get through this was if I made the decision to do it, ready or not.

"Hello?" His voice sounded distant, as if the thousand miles that separated us were audible through the phone.

My breath wavered as I spoke. "I need to talk to you about something."

"Hold on." I heard a vaguely familiar voice in the background that mingled with Tyler's, their words an indecipherable tangle. After a moment, Tyler returned to the phone. "Sorry about that. Dave just wanted to say goodbye before he starts his new job in Madison."

"He's leaving?"

"He had to shut down his farm. There was too much pressure on him, with his equipment failing and milk prices going down. He's been having trouble for a while, but I guess this was it for him." He sighed heavily. "He does have some family over in Wisconsin, but it's not easy to start all over like this."

My spirits deflated as the one thing we weren't saying hung in the air. After a moment's hesitation, I spoke up. "What does that mean for us?"

"For now, we're doing pretty well. Jeanette keeps an eye on the equipment while I get the feed and check on the crops. We have a good system going." He paused for a second. "What did you want to tell me?"

My every muscle tensed up as I gripped the phone. "If you have such a great system going, then I guess it doesn't matter if I'm not there anymore." Tears teased my eyelashes, and I let them fall freely, not caring if they seeped through my voice. "I was never a good enough farmer to get through the hard times. Remember the last time a storm destroyed all our crops? I was just as helpless as the cows. But Jeanette—well, she knows everything, doesn't she? Of course she saves the day without having a lick of farming experience."

"Nora, that's..." His voice trailed off as he addressed another voice in the background. When I recognized who it was, my heart stilled in my chest.

"Is that Caleb?" My voice caught on my son's name, as if his presence would elude me as soon as I acknowledged it.

Instead of getting a response from Tyler, I heard Caleb speak urgently into the phone. "Mom?"

"Caleb. Oh, it's so nice to hear from you again. Is everything all right?"

"I want to leave."

My stomach twisted with dread. "Leave where?" I said softly, even though the fear in my heart already knew what he meant.

"This stupid town. And this boring state. I'm tired of looking at cows and fields. I want to come to New York with you."

I faltered, knowing I had to tell him he couldn't come with me, but not wanting to crush his spirits either. "Honey, you know I'd love nothing more than for you to come out here. But Dad needs your help on the farm. He can't do it all on his own."

"But the new machines do all the work for him now. He doesn't need me anymore."

It struck me in that moment how listening to my son was like listening to myself. Before I could stop them, Tyler's words from our last conversation echoed through my thoughts: *I'm starting to think this is all because of you.*

"There's nothing to do here," Caleb went on. "But the city has tons of cool stuff to do, right?"

"Yes, but—"

"This kid at school said he has an older sister who works near Times Square. She can give us a tour of the city and everything."

My voice grew stern at the flip of a switch. "Caleb, you can't just leave with your friend. It isn't safe."

"But you left."

I ignored the sharp pang that shot through my chest. "I'm an adult. You're still too young."

"So I can move to the city when I'm a grownup?"

"Is that really what you want?" I asked, sorrow creeping into my voice. "You don't like the farm anymore?"

"What's the point? Dad's job isn't that important, anyway."

"Caleb! You stop that right now. Your father works hard to feed you and your sister every day."

"But your job is so much cooler. Jeanette told us about all the famous people that come to her office. She even said they have movie stars sometimes."

I was fighting a losing battle and we both knew it. I drew in a sharp breath. "I'm not going to say this again. We all need you to be on the farm. We need everyone to help out."

"Then why aren't you here?"

I bit down on my lip. "I needed to help Jeanette. She trusted me to do a good job, so I couldn't let her down."

"But you like it there. If you didn't, you would've come back home."

Every word he spoke was true, and that was what hurt the most. My son had always shared Tyler's perceptiveness, especially when it came to the things I didn't say out loud.

"I just need some time to sort things out right now. But you can't leave. Please tell me you'll try to help Dad out with the farm. He's worried about you."

There was a weighted pause. For a moment, I thought I'd lost him, but then he spoke again. "Fine. But it's not like it matters if we lose our farm. There's plenty of other dairies around here, anyway."

The vitriol that leaked from his voice didn't belong to the Caleb I knew. It was a harsh, foul imitation of my son. I thought back to what Bridget had told me over FaceTime about Caleb's group of friends—how they'd mercilessly pushed a defenseless student into the lockers. I wanted to believe that those kids were to blame for Caleb's uncharacteristic behavior, but I knew that wasn't the whole story. His friends might have steered him in the wrong direction, but I'd driven him to this point by unintentionally showing him it was okay to give up on what mattered to him. That as long as he found something new and alluring, there was nothing wrong with abandoning the old and familiar.

"How dare you talk like that? It matters to all of us."

"Whatever. I have to go."

Silence promptly replaced his voice, and I sank onto the couch in defeat. In the stillness of my living room, I meditated on the possibility of returning home. I pictured myself taking the cows out to the pasture and breathing in the sweet country air again. I pictured waking up every morning to my peaceful farmhouse, the quiet punctuated by Bridget's and Caleb's chatter. Piecing together the fragments of my old life reminded me that it was time to move on. I'd done my part here. I'd gotten a taste of working my dream career, like I'd been longing to for years.

But I would have been lying to myself if I said that tiny sip had satisfied me. The young girl who lived inside me was still alive and well, and she wanted more than a preview. She wanted the whole film, from start to finish, no matter how messy it got. If she'd wanted a mere taste, she would've taken a tour of the office and moved on.

I couldn't let her down. I couldn't back out. If I backed out now, I wouldn't even be able to say I tried. In some ways, quitting was worse than never taking the opportunity in the first place. I owed it to myself to see the entire thing through. I knew that with a conviction that kept me in the city, even when I knew in a corner of my heart that this wasn't meant to last forever.

Eighteen

∽

I swung open the door of the fashion closet and shut it behind me before anyone noticed. Once the coast was clear, I scanned the room to make sure all the models were set up. Tina, the one with a frame so narrow that I worried she'd collapse on the runway, fiddled with the strap of the dress I'd outfitted her in. Krysta and Madeline took turns critiquing themselves in the full-length mirror, and Natasha was completely entranced by the clothes and shoes showcased throughout the closet. I noted with a pang of nostalgia that she looked the way I'd felt when Vanessa first showed me the *Couture* gem.

As I recounted the women, I realized that one model was still missing. I frowned. "Does anyone know where Shaina is?"

"Probably in the bathroom, puking up that lasagna her grandma made her eat," Tina said.

"I don't blame her," Madeline said, still at the mercy of her reflection. "That thing probably had more calories than I ate all week."

Natasha's manicured fingers grazed the delicate fabric of the Dolce & Gabbana dress I'd picked out for Shaina. "She's smart. Now she'll be able to fit into this without sucking in her stomach."

Shaina appeared right on cue, her flushed cheeks complementing the radiant smile on her face. She marched up to Natasha and claimed the dress she was still admiring. "I'll take that, thank you." She let out a satisfied sigh as she held the dress up to the light. "I feel so much lighter now."

Krysta shot her a withering look. "You bitch. Now I have to walk all the way home to catch up to you."

As the four models continued their banter, I felt like I was watching the scene unfold from behind a glass wall. I'd spent the past three weeks marveling at how well I fit into my new workplace. But now, standing in a room full of women who turned disordered eating into a competition, I'd never felt more out of place. Working in fashion was about more than knowing which colors and designs looked good together. It was about seeing the world through a distorted lens of flesh and bones. A lens that clouded the view of reality.

"So, are we going to walk the runway or what?" Madeline's voice tore me away from my thoughts.

"Sure. Just let me double check your outfits." I walked over to each model and examined her look, reminding myself that this event was too important for me to get wrapped up in my feelings. After Vanessa turned heads with her Hannah Walsh interview, I had to go back to the drawing board. I'd asked myself how I could showcase all my favorite looks for the September issue and concluded that a fashion show was the perfect vehicle for my plan. Considering how enthusiastic Celeste was when I sent her the clothes I picked out at Saks, this event was a surefire way to get her attention.

After confirming that everything was set, I arranged the models into a neat row. Anxiety pulsed through me as I gingerly opened the door. If this went well, I would be reaching new levels as a fashion director. But if it didn't, I would be wasting Celeste's precious time. And if there was one way to get on her bad side, it was to give her the impression that her time wasn't important.

I faced the models who were lined up in front of me. "Okay, everyone. I know this isn't the traditional fashion show you're used to, but this could make or break the September issue. Just pretend the office is the catwalk at Fashion Week. And follow the markers."

"You have no idea how hard I had to work to convince my agent this was a good idea," Krysta said. "This better work."

The other models nodded in agreement, and my stomach flipped as I processed how much was riding on this show. But I refused to put my nerves on display. "Don't worry. Celeste can't tear her eyes away from a fashion show, especially an impromptu one."

I walked out into the hall and turned around to face the models. "Hold on a second." I knocked on Celeste's door and opened it before she had the chance to respond. "I hope you're not too busy right now. There's something I need to show you."

She didn't look up from her computer. "I can't possibly imagine how your shenanigans could be more important than what I'm doing right now."

Not off to the best start. I cleared my throat and tried to stay professional. "It's for the September issue. Trust me, it's well worth your time."

She studied me for a moment, as if she were gauging the importance of the event based on my facial features. With a weighted sigh, she turned to her computer and took her time with closing all the windows. "Well, if you insist."

My heart soared at the progress I'd made, no matter how miniscule. "You won't regret it," I said as I headed back into the hallway.

When Celeste stepped out of her office, I tried to get everyone's attention. "Hey, everyone. I know you're all busy working on the next issue, but I put something together for you that I think you'll enjoy." I paused as my colleagues looked up from their work and shifted their attention to me. "I wanted to do something a little different today. We all have great ideas for the September issue, and we're all doing our part in putting them together. But I felt the need to go a step further and give my ideas a visual component. That's why I'm presenting this fashion show to you all today."

I popped my head back into the fashion closet, where the models were waiting for their moment in the spotlight. "Showtime, ladies."

One by one, the women strutted out of the room and followed the line I'd delineated across the office. As they paraded down the makeshift runway, I felt a surge of pride at seeing my outfits modeled by professionals. The way all five women owned their looks helped bring them to life, giving my work a sense of visibility that it'd never had before.

Celeste studied the models with an unreadable expression, leaving me to wonder what was running through her mind. I'd been right about one thing, though: I'd gotten her attention. She stood there with her arms folded across her chest, her trained editor's eye dissecting each outfit. Whatever work she'd been attending to in her office had clearly been forgotten altogether.

Natasha struck one final pose at the end of the catwalk before joining the other four models by the fashion closet. For a brief moment, an all-encompassing silence rang through my ears, carrying every uncertainty I'd harbored about the show. Before I let the feeling consume me, Celeste spoke.

"In my thirty years at this magazine, I have never seen anything like this." The click of her heels reverberated through the hushed room, as if a microphone were attached to them. "A fashion show right in the office? It's quite inappropriate. Absurd, even. We don't have any of the resources or supplies needed to pull off such an ordeal."

The way my heart dropped all the way down to the pit of my stomach made me feel like a schoolkid again, seeing a furious red "D" plastered on the test I'd stayed up all night studying for. I couldn't bring myself to meet the models' eyes as I remembered Krysta's warning from before the show: *This better work.*

I had only myself to blame, of course. I'd been naïve to believe Celeste would be swayed by a bare-bones fashion show that I'd put together entirely on my own. Instead of outdoing Vanessa, I'd just placed myself ten steps behind her.

Celeste stopped right in front of me, her eyes searching. "Nora, over the past few weeks, I've come to know you as a smart, talented, and—most of all—dedicated worker. I know you would never shy away from a challenge. And that you don't settle for anything that isn't your absolute best work." She looked over her shoulder at the dejected models then turned her attention back to me. "But this isn't you. I know it isn't, because you could have done a whole lot better than this. Between this show and your interview with a soon-to-be B-lister, I'm worried you're getting too comfortable with your role at this company."

I struggled to come up with the right words. But as long as I was talking to Celeste, there were no right words.

"I need to remind you of how essential your job is. And if that means making you a little uncomfortable, then so be it." Her lips twisted into a smile that faintly resembled Jeanette's when she was up to no good. "Tell me, Nora. How do you feel about this?"

She poked her head into her office and emerged with a sheet of paper adorned with an array of words and photos. Superlatives like "Most Issues Sold" and "Highest Google Rankings" jumped out at me. Beside each phrase was a cutout from a past *Couture* issue or a printout of an online article. As I examined the accolades, I noticed that they all had one thing in common: Jeanette's name was attached to them.

"Jeanette put this together before she left. It's all of the things she accomplished during her time here. Some of them are covers she designed that attracted a record number of readers, and some are articles she pitched that caused our Google rankings to skyrocket. I don't think I need to tell you that she's done quite a lot for this magazine."

I read and reread each snippet, unable to tear my eyes away. I'd always known Jeanette had excelled in her career, but I hadn't realized she'd set so many precedents. Every single issue since Jeanette's arrival had followed the same layout and design that she'd developed.

"If you want to keep your spot here, you're going to have to earn it. And I expect you to go above and beyond what Jeanette did to prove that you're worthy of your job."

The answer I was supposed to give was dancing behind my lips, waiting for its moment to see the light. It rested on my tongue as if I were about to say it aloud: *Thanks, but you should find someone else to fill that role. I've already done my part here, and it's time to head back home.*

That was what I should have said. After all, the chances of me surpassing Jeanette's status at the magazine were slim to none. But Celeste had said it herself: I never shied away from a challenge. And what challenge was greater than leaving a mark on *Couture* that lasted longer than anyone else's?

"I'd love to. In fact, I already have a few ideas in mind."

"I thought so." Celeste trained her eyes on me without blinking. "Just make sure those ideas put this so-called fashion show to shame."

As she turned back to her office, I made my way toward my own. Before I could get there, though, I noticed Vanessa looking at me. This time, nothing in her expression suggested any hostility toward me. Instead, I detected a tinge of sadness in her eyes, as if she'd lost something she'd never known she had in the first place.

"For the record," she said, "Celeste only gives her speech about 'getting too comfortable' to her top employees." She gave me a sideways glance. "So you should be proud."

I offered her a cautious smile in return. "Thanks, Vanessa."

She started to go, then she turned to face me again. "By the way, I thought the fashion show was pretty cool." Before I could respond, she made her way back to her desk without looking back.

I blinked as she woke up her monitor and started typing. Her amicable behavior almost made me feel like I'd imagined her taking credit for my idea. Maybe she'd finally decided to put it behind her and start on a clean slate. The thought gave me hope that the seed of friendship we'd planted on my first day at work hadn't been obliterated yet.

I stepped into my office and returned to my desk. As I stared at all the tasks I'd scrawled into my planner, dread wriggled its way through me. Promising Celeste to step up my game had been one thing, but putting my ideas in motion was quite another.

I flipped through my planner and reviewed the ideas I'd come up with over the past few weeks. My gaze lingered on each assignment as the wheels churned in my head. If I combined my personal experience essay with the celebrity interviews I'd conducted, it was sure to be a hit with our readers. *If only there were some way to help the content touch our audience on a deeper level...*

My head snapped up as inspiration took root inside me. There *was* a way. There had been a way all along, and I was the only one to see it.

I practically darted over to Megan, the visual editor. Her computer screen displayed a blown-up version of the tentative September cover. "Hold off on that layout for a bit," I said almost breathlessly. "You'll end up changing it, anyway."

She shot me a curious look. "Are you sure?"

"Yup. I just need Celeste's official approval."

With a shrug, she said, "I'm not even sure if this is *Couture*-worthy yet, so that works for me."

It would be soon enough. But I kept the thought to myself

as I slunk back into my office. The last thing I wanted was to jinx the best idea I'd come up with so far.

Once I was seated at my desk again, I pulled up the *Couture* Twitter account and clicked on the list of followers. Nestled underneath the heading were the faces of over ten million people who cared enough about the magazine to keep up with its every update. I scrolled through the endless list, thinking that somewhere among the names was a girl just like the younger version of me who'd eagerly awaited the arrival of her monthly issue. She was hiding there somewhere, and it was up to me to find her.

I didn't stop scrolling until I stumbled upon a user whose profile picture was a designer-clad selfie. I studied the girl, who couldn't have been older than sixteen, and gave her mental props for pairing a black-and-white collar dress with maroon combat boots. It looked exactly like the kind of outfit I would have put together at her age.

I had the pressing feeling that this girl needed to hear what I was about to tell her. Before I could second-guess myself, I clicked on the Direct Message icon and typed out a quick note:

Hey, Dani! It's Nora, fashion director at Couture. How would you feel about being featured in a story about our readers' personal style? Let me know if you're interested!

I sent it then continued scrolling through the names to find another potential candidate. After copying the same message and inserting the names of several other followers, I sat back in my chair and waited. It was done now. All I could do was hope for the best.

My screen lit up barely two minutes later with a flabbergasted response from Dani. *Wait, me? Seriously?? This isn't a scam, is it?*

I replied to reassure her that it was completely legit, and I had barely sent out the message when a response from Nicole flew in: *100% here for it. When can I start?*

As I fought to keep up with the rapid-fire questions, I felt a stronger connection to my job than I'd ever felt before. It was like I'd come face-to-face with my purpose, like I could reach out and touch it. All this time, my readers had been sitting in the backseat of my mind, encouraging me to do the work they counted on me to do. But in that moment, they weren't just faceless figures I'd conjured up. They were living, breathing people who believed in the work I did. Who cared about what the magazine stood for as much as I did.

After collecting a response from everyone I'd messaged, I sent the webpage to the printer. I walked over to the copy room and gathered the sheet of paper as the machine spat it out. Once I was back in my office, I tucked it into a folder in my desk drawer. This was what I needed to look at whenever I lost faith in my mission. This was what I needed to remind myself of whenever I was tempted to forget why I'd come to New York.

It was what I needed to prove that people were listening, even when I was convinced that my voice didn't matter.

Nineteen

〰

Two days had passed since I emailed Celeste about featuring our readers' personal style in the September issue. The more I waited, the more I realized that waiting wasn't the hard part. The hard part was keeping my mind off my unanswered message and my boss's thoughts on it.

I eventually gave up on trying to distract myself and went to the only part of the building where I felt safe. The second I threw myself into the oasis of cashmere and leather, a sense of calm washed over me, drowning out the worries weighing on my mind. The fashion closet seemed to glimmer from within when it was stocked with new winter arrivals, just like the streets of Manhattan always shone a little more brightly during the Christmas season.

I was sifting idly through a stack of clothes when Chloe appeared, her phone pressed to her ear. She gave a little wave as she continued her conversation. "I already told you, Roy. We were supposed to have the Birkin bag returned last Thursday." She started pacing around the room, her forehead creased with concern. "Well, I guess you'll have to explain that to Celeste." After a brief pause, she said, "I don't know what to tell you, Roy. You should've thought of that before you lost track of a fifty-thousand-dollar handbag."

I gave Chloe a wan smile. "Sounds like Roy's going to be in for it."

She collapsed onto a stool beside the hats. "Sometimes I think about how much easier my job would be if people followed directions."

"Isn't Anna in charge of fashion closet orders?"

"She had a family emergency, so Celeste put me in charge temporarily." Chloe rolled her eyes. "You can see how well that's going."

"Don't worry. We'll make it through this crazy week somehow."

"How are you holding up, by the way? You know, with this being your first time working on the September issue."

I shrugged, wondering how well I was supposed to be handling it. "I emailed Celeste my pitch for one of the lifestyle articles, and I'm doing everything I can not to think about it. The waiting is pure torture."

"Trust me, I've been there. I thought I knew disappointment when my middle school crush chose my lab partner over me, but that didn't even compare to finding out that the essay I was most proud of wouldn't make it to print."

The thought of Celeste tossing my pitch into her trash folder made my stomach dip, but I forced a smile in spite of my unease. "I'll get through it no matter what happens. You did when you were new like me, right? And so did everyone else here."

"I like how you manage to stay positive through all this," she said with a small smile. "It's admirable."

Before I could offer a reply, Roy burst into the room, his already-pale face blanched with panic. "I can't find it anywhere. You gotta help me before Celeste finishes up her meeting."

Chloe let out a long sigh before turning to me. "Hey, I know how you can keep your mind off your assignment. Want to come to Bergdorf with me?"

I stared at her in disbelief. "You're *asking* if I want to go to Bergdorf?" I turned around and grinned at Roy. "Thanks for losing that bag."

"Don't encourage him." Chloe gathered her things and motioned for me to follow her. "Let's go before rush hour kicks in."

I walked out with her into the brisk day. The wind on my face was a welcome feeling after being cooped up with my thoughts for so long. As we trekked over to the subway station, I turned to her. "Do you really think the bag will still be there?"

She shrugged. "Maybe not, but at least I can say I tried. Besides, it isn't every day that you find an excuse to leave the office for a while."

"Let's make it quick, though," I said as we reached the platform. "I don't intend on turning this into a shopping trip."

"You have an incredible amount of willpower if you can spend a single minute in Bergdorf without trying on everything in your size."

"I never said I would succeed," I joked as we crammed into the packed train.

Once we reached our destination, I followed Chloe up the stairs of the subway station, blinking in the late afternoon sunlight. Midtown at this hour made Lower Manhattan look deserted. Between the congested streets and elaborate Fifth Avenue storefronts, I felt like I'd just walked into the middle of a movie set. It was hard not to feel like an awestruck tourist when I visited Midtown, even after twenty years of growing up a quick subway ride away from it.

My starry-eyed state reached its peak when I sauntered through the entrance of Bergdorf Goodman with Chloe. It was my very first step into the store ever since my return to the city, and the symphony of designer clothes most people could only dream of affording pulled me in just as the fashion closet had.

"Wait here. I'll go find someone to talk to."

"You don't have to tell me that twice," I said, already eyeing a pair of Aquatalia boots that looked like they were made for me.

I occupied myself for a good twenty minutes as I browsed my favorite sections of the store. But once I was knee-deep in the fur coats, I started to question the purpose of hunting down the perfect outfit. I didn't even know how much longer I was going to be in the city, and it seemed frivolous to update my wardrobe when my future at *Couture* was so uncertain. I eyed the stack of clothing on my arm and realized that none of it remotely fit into the farm life I'd left behind. That was, unless I was shopping for Jeanette.

I was deep in thought in the shoe section when Chloe strode up to me. "No luck on the Birkin. Roy better hope that Celeste doesn't fire him after this."

I fought back a shudder at the mere thought of it. "Poor guy. He looked like a deer in headlights when he told you what happened."

"Well, he should know better by now. He's been here longer than I have." She glanced at my empty hands. "Didn't find anything?"

"Trust me, I found plenty. But I'm not looking to do any more damage than I've already done since I got to the city."

"I admire your discipline." Chloe glanced back at the saleswoman she'd been chatting with about the missing bag. "You know, if Jeanette were here, she would have that bag in her hands in five minutes tops."

"She's definitely good at getting what she wants." An image of her helping Caleb and Bridget flashed into my mind, and I buried it before it could sour my mood.

"She always has been." Chloe let out a sigh. "But she's never been the same since the miscarriage."

Something cut deep into me as I looked at her. "Miscarriage?"

"You mean she didn't tell you?" When I didn't say anything, she studied me closely. "I thought you guys were close. It's hard to believe she didn't say anything about it."

I sat down on a chair by the boots, trying to absorb the news. A fresh wave of pain washed over me as I remembered Derek telling me that Jeanette's morning sickness had disappeared without explanation. I should have known that such a drastic improvement in such a small time frame meant something was wrong.

I glanced over at Chloe. "When did this happen?"

"About two weeks ago," she said as she sat down beside me. "I feel awful for her. She's in a really dark place."

Whenever I'd thought about Jeanette over the past few weeks, the spotlight of my thoughts had shone on her attempts to rob me of my Fairlane life. But now, I couldn't help but see my friend through the lens of everything she was going through. As I sat there surrounded by designer clothes that no longer had an effect on me, I set aside our messy past for just a moment. And in that moment, I saw her for who she really was. Someone in desperate pain. Someone who needed all the support she could get, regardless of how far she'd drifted from the close friend she used to have.

"She's a lot stronger than she thinks she is. I know she'll get through it." Chloe looked out the window for a moment before glancing at me. "You okay?"

"Yeah," I said, trying to steady my voice. "I... I should call her."

"Definitely. I'm sure she'd be happy to hear from you." She said it with such innocence that I couldn't help but wonder what she would think if she knew everything Jeanette had done to me.

We sat in silence for another long moment before Chloe finally stood up and checked her phone. "We'd better start heading back now. It's bad enough that Roy's going to be the reason for Celeste's next emergency meeting. We don't need to add to her rage by being no-shows at work."

"Fair enough." I did my best to keep up with her as she made her way out of the store, but my mind was still miles away.

We snaked through sidewalk traffic before descending the stairs of the Fifty-Ninth Street Station. After a failed attempt at distracting myself with a crossword app on my phone, I resorted to spending the rest of the train ride with my thoughts.

If there was one thing I knew about Jeanette that Chloe didn't, it was that the former fashion director would rather die than put her scars on display. I'd seen it in the tremendous effort it had taken her to admit she was pregnant. And even then, she'd hastily covered up the scandal by acting like it was her plan all along.

But what gnawed at me the most was that she'd told Chloe about the miscarriage. She'd let her former coworker see her wound in all its ugliness, even while it was still tender. I started to ask myself why she hadn't done the same for me, but the answer was as clear as ever. Jeanette had swapped our lives so masterfully, not leaving a single wrinkle in the fabric of her plan. If she admitted that anything had gone awry, she would be acknowledging that she'd messed up far worse than she'd ever thought she would.

As I stepped off the subway, I realized that her neglect to share the news with me only made me feel sorrier for her. She was crying out for help without letting me see her vulnerable enough to shed a tear.

I stopped walking and turned to Chloe. "You go on without me. I need to make a quick call."

She threw me a wary look. "Are you sure? Because as soon as Celeste finishes up her meeting, she'll want to know where you are."

"Don't worry. She'll probably be too busy fuming about Roy to care about that."

"Suit yourself." After a moment, she said, "I'll just tell her you're still looking for the bag if she does ask. That way, your absence will be for a good cause."

I smiled. "Thanks for having my back."

She gave me a thumbs-up and headed back toward the Trade Center.

Now that I was alone, I stared at the dim screen of my phone, wondering what I could possibly say to Jeanette in a time like this. I'd grown so accustomed to her effortless confidence, to her take-charge attitude that always enabled her to get what she wanted. Trying to comfort her after she'd been beaten down by failure was like trying to console a complete stranger.

I walked aimlessly up and down the sidewalk as I waited for her to pick up. When her voice came on, I stopped and sat on a bench near the office. "Jeanette, I'm so sorry. Chloe told me about the baby, and I can't imagine how much pain you're in right now."

"I'll be okay, Nora." Her voice was calm, a still river in the midst of a raging storm. "Life goes on. You can't let it get the best of you."

I stared at a piece of chipped paint on the bench and cleared my throat. "If you need anything, just let me know."

"You're already helping me. You took my place at *Couture*, and from what I heard, you're doing a pretty great job of it." She paused as the delighted squeals of young children peeked through the background. "I'm so glad I chose you to take over my job. You have no idea how much pressure you took off of me."

I held the phone closer to my ear. "Where are you?"

"Oh, I decided to take the kids to the aquarium. It's only about an hour away from the farm. Who knew, right? Once you get past all the corn fields, Iowa actually has some decent entertainment."

"*The* kids? You're saying it like they're your own." I stopped short as my own words sank in. The whole time she'd been taking care of Bridget and Caleb, she'd been doing it to fill the gaping hole in her heart where her own child was supposed to be. An overwhelming sense of sorrow swept over me, both for my hurting friend and for my kids who were lost and confused without me there.

"Your family has always been like my own family, Nora. You know that. Ever since the first day I visited your farm, Tyler and the kids have been so welcoming to me. You're really lucky to have them."

I remembered that day. It was the day Jeanette had changed my life as I knew it, when she'd offered me the job at *Couture*. An image flashed into my mind, and I closed my eyes, trying to put it into focus. Jeanette, leaning against the side of the barn, looking as if she owned it. Her relaxed posture, almost a little too relaxed for a city girl who had just wandered into cow country for the first time. And then there were Tyler's words when he alerted me of her arrival: *She's back.* She'd been there before, making herself comfortable on the farm so she could prepare for the job that was ahead of her.

I pictured her casually swinging by the farm while I was picking up the kids or driving to Daryl's, blissfully unaware of the plot she'd been weaving. I pictured Tyler's strong hands guiding her as she learned the ropes of the job, his arm brushing against hers as he helped her tend to the cows, and felt sick to my stomach.

"Anyway, I think my aquarium idea was genius," Jeanette said. "It's the perfect way for the kids to blow off some steam. Bridget hasn't stopped staring and pointing at the animals. Caleb seems to love it too, even though he insisted that this place is only for little kids."

The thought of everything I was missing out on burrowed a hole in my heart. "Put Bridget on the phone," I said.

"Bridget? Why?"

210 · Elena Goudelias

"Because I need to talk to her." Something had activated inside me, a protective instinct that I'd felt only a couple of times in my life with this level of ferocity. Once, when Bridget's teacher had called to tell me that she'd gotten lost on a field trip. And another time when I'd found out that Caleb's classmates were bullying him back in third grade.

Bridget's voice was breathless and ecstatic when it came through the speaker, and I had to pinch myself to stop the tears from falling. "Hi, Mommy! Guess where Jeanette took us today?"

Today. Like she'd already done this before. "Where, honey?" I played along.

"The aquarium! I saw a bunch of real-life sea animals, and it was awesome. Oh, and Jeanette just said she's going to get us jelly doughnuts!"

"Your favorite," I said, my voice barely audible. I drew in a shaky breath and asked the question that I was too afraid to know the answer to. "Has Jeanette taken you anywhere else over the last few weeks?"

"Oh, yeah. We went to Toy Town in the city, and she got me a brand-new doll. It looks just like me! And then we saw these stuffed animals at the supermarket, so Jeanette let me pick out whatever I wanted. I got a panda and a cow, just like Bluebell." Bluebell was Bridget's favorite cow on the farm, the one she'd formed an immediate bond with. She'd even named her. "And then we got to pick out whatever candy we wanted at the register."

"That sounds like a lot of fun." Tyler and I had gone to Dubuque with the kids a couple of times before, and we'd taken them to Toy Town as a special treat on both occasions. I didn't recall exactly what we'd let them bring home, but it was probably nothing more than a new shirt or pack of crayons. It definitely wasn't the Spoiled Kid Starter Kit, complete with toys, stuffed animals, candy, and everything in between.

"Are you going back home now?" I asked.

"Yeah. We stayed at Jeanette and Derek's house before we went to the aquarium. They let us watch TV and go on the computer. And we didn't even have to take a break to do homework!"

I rubbed my temples, wondering if this was what a midlife crisis felt like. "And is Daddy okay with this?"

"I think so. They're really nice to us."

I sighed inwardly. "Honey, can you put Jeanette back on the phone? I need to talk to her for a second."

"Okay. Bye, Mommy." Before I could respond, Jeanette's voice came on again. "Well, now you're updated. Can we move on?"

"Buying them everything you see at the store? Not making them do homework? How does any of that sound okay to you?"

"Look who's talking. Your kids were miserable before I came along, and now they're full of joy and Skittles. You should be thanking me."

"You can't give in to their every wish and call that parenting. You have to set rules and boundaries. Otherwise, they'll just run wild doing whatever they want."

"All I know is they're happy. Isn't that what you want?"

"Of course I want them to be happy. But not the way you're doing it. Because what you're doing is spoiling them so I look like the evil stepmother."

The faint sound of Caleb's voice trickled through the speaker, and Jeanette said something unintelligible to him. "I should go now," she told me. "We have to get to Dunkin' before the jelly doughnuts run out."

"Jeanette. Wait."

"Yeah?"

"How long have you been planning to move to Riverville and work on my farm? And don't give me any BS. I'm too tired for that."

There was complete silence on the other end, save for the lingering sounds of kids in the background. When she finally answered, her voice was barely above a murmur. "Since I realized you made the better choice in life."

Her honesty jarred me, rendering me speechless. As I mined for the right words, Jeanette went on. "And the worst part is that I almost had what you had. I almost had my own family and a cozy little yard and neighbors who cared enough to ask how I really was. But then the universe ripped it out of my womb before I got the chance to enjoy it."

She envied me. Jeanette Peterson envied what I had while she had everything I'd ever dreamed of. The irony was almost comical.

"I'm sorry, Jeanette. I didn't know you felt that way."

"Yes, you did. Why else would I take a maternity leave before I was even showing? I wanted to get out of there as soon as possible. And I know you figured out that my interview with you at the café was just an excuse to come out here. You might be a little naïve sometimes, but you're not an idiot."

"I don't get it. Celeste showed me all of your accolades the other day, and you can't tell me you didn't have a hell of a life."

She was quiet at first, and I sensed that she was about to expose another vulnerable side of her that I'd never seen before. "It's because you were *happy,* Nora. Whenever we talked on the phone during those fifteen years, I could practically see the glow on your face. The way you talked about life on the farm, you'd think you won the lottery or something. When I came here, I was almost expecting there to be some huge party that I didn't know about, but then I realized you just loved what you did." She paused, and her voice was delicate when she spoke again. "Plus, your whole family is perfect. I won't be surprised if Bridget ends up winning the Nobel Prize or something. And Tyler... I saw the way you two looked at each other before you left for the airport. What you have with him goes deeper than what most people have."

"Jeanette..." I started, but I didn't know what to say.

"It's funny, you know. You keep asking me how I could choose your life over mine, but I've always wondered the same thing about you." For a second, I thought she was going to cry, but she cloaked the sadness in her voice as swiftly as a magician hiding behind his cape. "Anyway, I really have to go now. Thanks for checking in."

I opened my mouth to speak, but the line went dead before I got the chance. I stared at my dark phone screen, thinking about how Jeanette hadn't been that open with me since high school. There was no doubt she was in a dark place if she'd been willing to let me see that much weakness.

Before I dropped my phone into my bag, I noticed the time and jumped up from the bench. Chloe was probably running out of excuses to give Celeste at this point.

I walked as quickly as I could toward the office, my shoulders heavy with the burden Jeanette had placed on them. The entire time I'd been dreaming about her life as a fashion director, she'd been longing to escape it. It contradicted everything I knew about Jeanette, making me wonder if I'd ever really known her at all.

As I reached the entrance of the office building, I flashed back to when Jeanette had sauntered into our third-period math class in seventh grade, proudly donning a shiny new pair of Steve Madden clogs. She'd confided to me in the locker room before PE that she'd spent all her allowance on those shoes. So when I saw the pride that emanated from her expression like a sunbeam, it was physically painful to see the light leave her eyes as the girl who sat across from her showed off her original Doc Martens.

I studied my friend's downtrodden expression and tried to offer the encouragement she desperately needed. But her eyes were glued to her classmate's combat boots, a fierce hunger etched into them that said, *I need that. Now.* I soon understood that Jeanette was never truly happy with her shoes in the first place. Instead, she'd been holding on to them with the loose, noncommittal grip of someone who was poised to snatch up the next best thing that crossed her path.

Back then, I'd wanted to help her see things differently, to show her that there was no need to compare herself to others. But what I hadn't realized at thirteen was that as long as she searched for something better than what she had, she would always find it.

Twenty

∽

A knock on my door greeted me early the next day. Expecting one of my usual morning visitors, I glanced up at the door, only to find Liz standing there with a folded sheet of paper in her hand. As I nodded and greeted her, she walked over and handed me the paper. "Celeste wanted me to give this to you. Congratulations." She added with a smile, "It's not every day I get to deliver great news like this."

I tried to mask my surprise as I thanked her. I'd never seen my stoic assistant express any degree of enthusiasm in all the time I'd known her. Even Celeste's indirect compliment on her new skirt had barely broken her brittle lips into a smile.

Once Liz was gone, I unfolded the sheet of paper and read a fuchsia sticky note attached to it:

Wonderful job on your pitch, Nora. I hope you'll be able to attend next Friday.

-Celeste

I removed the sticky note and read the paper it was attached to. It was an invitation to attend the exclusive unveiling event that *Couture* held every year for its September issue. As I let the words take effect, my breath caught in my throat. No one below Celeste Moore herself was ever allowed to make an appearance at events like this. Receiving a personal invitation was probably the closest I would ever come to getting promoted to editor in chief.

By the time I reached the end of the letter, my heart was pounding so loudly in my ears that I could hardly hear the buzz of the city outside. She wanted me to talk about my ideas in front of an audience of leading fashion icons and renowned journalists such as herself, all to tell the world about the inspired vision I had for the magazine.

This was everything I'd ever wanted summed up in two short paragraphs. It was the fantasy I'd nurtured when I passed by the *Couture* headquarters as a teenager, staring up at the towering building and dreaming about everything I could do if I gained access to the coveted office. And it was what I'd dared to hope would happen after I accepted Jeanette's offer and hopped on the plane to New York.

I glanced toward the door to see if anyone was waiting to speak with me. After confirming that the coast was clear, I grabbed my phone and scurried off to the ladies' room. I couldn't bear to keep the news to myself for another moment.

As I tapped my home number, I prayed that Tyler would forget about everything that had come between us and be as excited about my achievement as I was. I ached to reconnect with him in that effortless way that had gotten us through so much together, to slip back into the familiar bond we'd shared like a fuzzy, threadbare sweater. Most of all, though, I longed to believe that what we used to have could still be salvaged. That there was still a chance for us.

I waited a few moments, but no sound came through on the other end. Frowning, I called the number again and waited for someone to pick up. But there was no sign of life filtering through the speaker. The phone must have been disconnected. Did he think it was best if he didn't hear from me anymore?

With a sigh, I set my phone down and ran a hand through my hair. Tyler wasn't the type to go radio silent on me, no matter how badly I'd messed up. But even a patient, understanding man like him had his limits. Maybe, between Caleb going on a rebellious streak and his best friend closing down his farm, he'd finally given up waiting for me. And considering everything he'd had to deal with since I left, I couldn't blame him for not wanting to hear any more of my excuses.

I stifled a sob and put the sink on full blast, willing myself to keep it together. There was no proof that any of my fears were true. I was only listening to the doubts in my mind. Those baseless doubts didn't deserve another second of my energy.

I dabbed at my eyes with a paper towel and tossed it into the trash. I shot another glance at myself in the mirror, checking that my eyes held no traces of suppressed pain, and slid my phone into my pocket.

Just as I rounded the corner, my phone vibrated against my hip. When I pulled it out and saw Tyler's name, I turned back toward the restroom, almost giddy with relief.

"Hey," I said breathlessly after the door swung shut behind me. "I tried to call before, but it wouldn't go through."

"That's what I wanted to tell you. We just lost power, so the landline won't be working for a while."

"Oh." I tried to fight the disappointment that rose up inside me. He hadn't just been calling to ask how I was or how my job was going. "Well, I have great news, and it'll definitely make things better. My boss sent me an invite for this exclusive *Couture* event next week. Only the highest-ranking employees get to attend. Can you believe it? I've been hoping something like this would happen since my first day here, but I never really thought it would."

There was silence for a beat, and I worried that I'd said something wrong. Then he said, "That's great, Nora. You must've worked hard for that."

"I did," I said, pride ringing through my voice. "And it paid off. I wish you could come, but my boss made it clear that it's an exclusive event. I'll make sure to send plenty of pictures, though."

He was quiet for another moment. When he spoke, his voice had an accusatory edge to it that I'd never heard before. "Do you even know why the power went out?"

My heart plummeted as I realized I'd never asked about the outage. "Crap. I'm so sorry. I just... I was excited. And I know that's not an excuse, but I wanted to share the news with you so badly." I bit down on my lip, remembering Tyler's warning about February weather the night before I left Fairlane. "What happened? Another storm?"

"This is the worst one we've had in years. The new robotic equipment shut down completely, and I don't even want to work out how we're going to pay for repairs. Those prices have gone through the roof lately."

I leaned back against the wall and let out a long breath. "This is just a lot for me to think about right now." The second the words were out of my mouth, I wished I'd never said them. But it was too late.

"That's the thing, though. You're just thinking about it. You're not here to deal with any of it." He let a weighted pause follow. "It's been more than three weeks. How much longer are you going to keep doing this?"

Melanie's advice came to me again, and I grappled with the urge to get my feelings off my chest. I drew in a breath. "This job isn't what it was in the beginning. Back then, I thought I would get a feel for being a fashion director and move on. But I've already achieved so much more than I ever thought I would. My boss usually doesn't bat an eye at the new employees' ideas, but she's given me so much praise for what I've done so far. Even my coworkers have noticed. And now I got this invite... It's just so hard to walk away from all of it, you know?"

He let out a lungful of air. "Just admit it, Nora."

"Admit what?"

"You're getting comfortable there. That's what happens when you stay for too long. You see how much easier it is to work in an office with a roof over your head all day, where you don't have to get your hands dirty or fight off the cold. Then you wonder why anyone would choose such a hard life on the farm. Happens all the time. Just like it happened to my brother."

His words sat uncomfortably in my stomach, like a rich meal that I'd devoured too quickly. Everything we'd built together, all the dreams we'd tended to, all boiled down to him believing I didn't care anymore. That I'd given up.

I wasn't sure why I said what I said to him next. Maybe it was the stress of my demanding job, or maybe it was the worry that had taken root inside me from everything going on at home. Maybe it was because, deep down, I was afraid Tyler was right.

"Is that really what you think? That just because I wanted

to explore a different path, I don't care about the farm at all?" My voice trembled. "It's good to expose yourself to new things once in a while. But you wouldn't know, because you've lived in the same small town for thirty-eight years."

I felt the blow of my words as soon as they were out of my mouth. Pressing a hand to my lips, I remembered the last time the topic had come up. We'd been riding in his truck as he showed me around Fairlane, pointing out the spots that had defined his childhood and served as the backdrop of his memories. Being the restless wanderer that I was, I hadn't been able to wrap my head around the idea of being confined to the same small town for my entire life. That was when I'd asked him if he'd ever thought about living somewhere else.

I remembered his response, straightforward and simple: "I have everything I need here." His tone had been light and easy, and I knew he'd only heard the genuine curiosity in my question. But this time, he'd heard something different. He'd heard me say that I couldn't imagine spending the rest of my life living in the middle of nowhere, surrounded by cows and crops. That it was a waste of time to stay in the same place when there was an entire world to discover.

He was silent for so long that I was convinced he'd hung up. Then, quietly, he said, "I don't know, Nora. I don't even think I recognize you anymore."

When the line went dead, I caught a glimpse of my reflection in the bathroom mirror. The woman staring back at me was cloaked in makeup, and her modest dirty-blond bob had been sassed up with sharp, asymmetrical layers. Tyler's comment was true in more ways than one. If I showed up on the farm again, he wouldn't recognize me on the outside or the inside.

The door swung open, and Vanessa stepped into the bathroom, her features twisting into a questioning look when she saw me. "That's definitely not the face of someone who just got invited to *Couture*'s unveiling event."

I turned away before I let any other emotions leak through. "It's nothing."

She stood by the sink next to me, looking at me closely. After a moment, she sighed. "Look, I know I've kind of been a bitch to you lately. You know, with the way I took credit for your idea and tried to outdo you with that interview. It's just..." Her voice softened, and I caught a rare glimpse of vulnerability in her eyes. "When Jeanette left, I was ready to take her place as the new fashion director. I had it in the bag, more or less. I'd already known Celeste long enough to know exactly what she was looking for, and she seemed to think I had a bright future in that role." Her gaze drifted up to me. "Then I found out that this girl with no fashion experience was coming to take Jeanette's place, and I thought, 'She won't last more than a week.' Of course, I couldn't have been more wrong."

I struggled to summon up the right words. "Vanessa, I..."

"Face it. You've gotten everything you wanted since you started working here. With the way you're taking charge of the magazine, I never had the chance to show Celeste that I'm capable of being a great fashion director."

As she spoke, I couldn't help but see my actions as the sabotage that Vanessa had believed them to be. Looking at them in this new, darker light awoke me to the possibility that this dream was meant for my coworker and that I was never supposed to accept Jeanette's offer to begin with. After all, my life back home had been unraveling from the moment I wheeled my luggage out of the farmhouse.

Jeanette's words from our last phone call resounded in my mind, like an unheeded warning: *You made the better choice in life.*

To my absolute horror, the sob I'd stifled earlier escaped me without warning.

Vanessa's features sharpened with alarm, and she rested a gentle hand on my shoulder. "Hey, it's okay. Shit, I always ruin everything."

"It's not your fault." I waved a hand to dismiss the idea.

She studied me for a moment. "It was something that happened before I came in, right?" Taking my silence as a yes, she hopped up on the counter, her legs dangling off the side. "Well, I don't have the best track record in terms of being a friend to you, but I'm here to listen. If you're up to it."

I looked at her guardedly. Something had shifted in her since she'd told me she liked my fashion show. It was possible that she was just being insincere again, but with the way events were unfolding at home, I didn't have it in me to dissect her motives. The only thing I felt in that moment was an overwhelming desire to be heard.

I sat down next to her and let out a long breath. "I just got off the phone with my husband. A record-breaking storm hit earlier, and it did some serious damage to our equipment. This isn't the first time it's happened, so I want to believe he'll get through it. But with me not there... I don't know." I stared down at my boots, thinking about the news Liz had delivered to me barely twenty minutes ago. "It's like I'm stuck in this pattern. Every time something great happens at work, I find out that things are falling apart at home. And I want to enjoy my achievements, I really do. This is what I've been waiting for all my life. But it's getting so hard to juggle everything at once."

Her eyes glinted with understanding. "Kinda like you're being pulled in eight different directions?"

"Pretty much."

"A word of advice," she said, crossing her legs. "This job you're doing here? It's not the kind of job that can be juggled with another full-time commitment. And neither is farming, from what I can tell." She looked at me head-on. "So if you want a way out of this, you're going to have to let one of them go."

Her words shouldn't have crushed me the way they did, especially since I'd already known in a small part of me that they were the truth. But that didn't stop the hurt from suffusing my insides, obliterating any ounce of hope I'd managed to keep alive.

"How did I get caught in this mess?" I asked, mostly of myself.

But Vanessa heard it and threw me one of her no-nonsense looks. "It doesn't matter how you got here." She hopped off the counter and dusted herself off. "Just know that you have an exit. You just need to have the balls to walk through it."

She pulled out her makeup bag and applied a fresh coat of mascara.

I contemplated asking her which exit she was thinking of. But it was clear I had to figure that out for myself. As I headed back to my office, I stopped at my desk and picked up the invitation again. I turned it over in my hands, reading Celeste's note three more times. Her words glistened like a promise to me, a reminder that there was something bigger out there, waiting for me to seize it.

I opened my planner and penciled in the date of the event. One more week. This was it. There would be no excuses left after I attended the ceremony. What more could I want? I'd gotten personal recognition from the editor in chief, conquered every obstacle that should have knocked me down, and earned myself a slot at one of the magazine's most prestigious events. From every possible angle, I'd gotten everything I'd ever wanted and more. There was nothing left for me to desire.

At the same time, there was. There were countless days I hadn't yet lived. Days peppered with pleasant surprises and sparks of inspiration that made me come alive. Days where the pulse of the city became a part of me, urging me to dream bigger, to reach higher than I ever had before. Days that whispered a quiet sense of hope into me when I thought I couldn't go on any longer, reminding me why I'd come here in spite of all the reasons not to.

There was too much left. Too much that I hadn't fully experienced. Too much that I wasn't ready to abandon. And too much that wasn't worth giving up just yet.

Twenty-One

⌒⌒

The days passed by in a blur, sailing past me before I had the chance to live them. As the deadline for the September issue crept closer and closer, it anchored me to the city and the job I still had to finish. Seeing all the work that went into the publication process was like watching my creation come to life one step at a time. And, as I slowly came to understand, walking away from it now would mean letting it die a premature death.

But that didn't mean home was ever far from my mind. I put on my work outfit and thought of the way Bridget always laid out her clothes on her dresser the night before so she would be ready to go the next morning. As I grabbed my mocha Frappuccino from Starbucks, I remembered how Tyler used to tease me for not being able to tolerate coffee that wasn't masked with cloying syrups and heaps of sugar. Even my walk to the office made me think of the way Caleb always had his earbuds jammed into his ears when he walked out of school, making me wonder what kind of music he liked to listen to on his own.

I moved forward with the memories nipping at my heels, with all the pieces of what I'd left behind scattered across my path. The thought of returning home after all this was over failed to comfort me, because it was a point in time with no clear contour. All I could do was tiptoe cautiously around the fragments of my past, even as they continued to block my every move.

After another week of crossing off the days in my planner, the highlight of my time at *Couture* stood there in front of me, circled in scarlet ink. Tonight was the unveiling event that Celeste had invited me to last Wednesday. Seeing the words sent a thrill through me, with a bundle of nerves trailing closely behind. My most exciting night so far was also the one night I couldn't afford to mess up.

That evening after work, I combed through my closet in search of something worthy of the magazine's biggest event of the year. This wasn't the time to dwell on all the loose ends I'd left behind at home or on how much was riding on this one night. This was the time to put on my best outfit and smile like someone who had nothing to worry about besides being caught wearing last season's shoes.

I was pulling on my tights when my phone dinged in the living room. I hopped over to the coffee table and glanced at the screen, which displayed a text from Liz. *Celeste needs you to be there a half hour early. She said an NYT reporter wants to interview you.*

I reread the message two more times, just in case it forced me to wake up from the dream I was surely having. How did anyone at *The New York Times* even know who I was? Celeste must have put in a good word for me if they were bothered to speak to me at all.

I texted Liz a quick thanks and returned to my closet, suddenly noticing all my outfits' flaws under the scrutiny of the audience I would have. If Liz had told me about the reporter this close to the event, there was no telling who else would show up.

The stress of this night was starting to make my first day at *Couture* look like a stroll on the beach.

After looking up past *Couture* events and studiously scrolling through the company's mobile site, I was able to put together something respectable. Something that made me look like I had years of experience at the magazine, rather than the rollercoaster few weeks I'd been through.

I did my makeup in record time and fixed my hair just as quickly. Once everything was set, I paused in front of the door and set aside my concerns for a moment. This was the pinnacle of everything I'd hoped for since the sixth grade. I deserved to enjoy this night, no matter what I would have to face once it was over.

But as I slid into the backseat of a cab, the weight of everything I'd achieved pressed down on my shoulders, as if it were too much for me to bear alone. I had everything I'd ever wanted, every wish I'd kept tucked into a corner of my heart for all these years. I had everything I ever wanted, except someone to share the joy of my greatest success with.

I looked at the empty seat next to me and realized I already had that someone. Three of them, in fact. But they were over a thousand miles away, where I'd left them, waiting for me to let them through the only door of my life I'd shut them out of.

When I stepped out of the cab, I had the sense that a limo would have been more appropriate. The outside of the University Club looked like a red carpet premiere, with clusters of guests decked out in the most extravagant pieces they owned. In the few seconds it took me to scan the scene, I identified two Oscar de la Renta dresses, three pairs of Jimmy Choos, and a healthy smattering of Chanel bags. I glanced down at my comparatively modest outfit and wondered if I should've spent more time doing research.

I made my way toward the building and caught sight of Celeste standing in front of the entrance. Seeing that she was in the middle of a conversation, I started to turn elsewhere, but she met my eyes and motioned for me to come over. I approached her carefully, making a concentrated effort not to trip on my way up the steep steps.

"Everyone, this is Nora, my new fashion director," Celeste said to the small crowd that had gathered around her. "She had to step in after Jeanette took some time off, and she's already done quite a good job of filling her shoes. If it weren't for Nora, the whole magazine would've fallen apart after Jeanette left."

The eyes of Celeste's friends and colleagues bore a hole through me as they openly sized me up. I smiled at my boss, trying to look as relaxed as I could while my every word and move was being picked apart. "I'm part of a great team at *Couture*. It wouldn't be fair to take all the credit for what we've accomplished."

"Oh, don't be so self-effacing," said a rail-thin woman standing to Celeste's right. She glanced at the editor in chief. "Is she always this modest?"

"I'll tell you what she definitely is," Celeste said, looking directly at me. "She's tenacious. She doesn't take no for an answer, even when that's exactly what I tell her. Most of my employees would have walked away after I turned down their pitch, but she strode right into my office and gave me an entire presentation on why I should reconsider. Which is what I eventually did."

My cheeks flamed. "It's just that the idea was really important to me. I wanted to do what was best for the magazine."

"I can tell," piped in another woman standing across from me. "You certainly have the look of a dedicated *Couture* employee."

"Thank you," I said, just as a sharply dressed man leaned toward Celeste to whisper something in her ear. She nodded and gave me a bright smile. "Nora, this is Matthew from *The New York Times*. He wants to ask you a few questions before we begin the reception."

I started a little as Matthew extended his hand to me. I'd been so wrapped up in making a good impression that the interview had completely slipped my mind. "Of course," I said, giving the reporter a firm handshake. "I'd love to."

"Great." He found a spot away from all the activity and led me there. After a quick glance at the notepad in his hand, he turned to face me. "So, from what I've heard from Celeste, you're the new face of *Couture*. You've been working there for less than a month, but your story has already inspired millions of readers. Could you tell me more about the work you've been doing for the magazine?"

The smile on my face came naturally as I detailed my plan for the September issue. I touched on everything from the minimalist fashion photo shoot to the article featuring our readers' personal styles. I saw the layout in my mind just as clearly as I had while I penned my ideas, and the words flowed out of me with the same ease.

Matthew nodded as he scribbled down some notes. "I also hear you're a native New Yorker."

"Born and raised," I confirmed.

"But you took a bit of a detour a while back. Is it true that you moved all the way out to Iowa and married a farmer?"

The mention of home sent a sharp ache through my chest. "Yes, that's correct. I moved away about fifteen years ago."

"What led you to make such a drastic change? From what I understand, you've wanted to go into fashion ever since you were a kid. Can you talk about what inspired you to go in a completely different direction?"

I did my best to think quickly. Dodging the question altogether would be too obvious, but I couldn't tell the unfiltered truth either. I gave Matthew what I hoped was my most professional smile. "I'm a firm believer that life is meant to be explored. If you stay in the same place for too long, things start to stagnate. Moving to the country showed me an entirely new way of life that I never would've discovered if I stayed in the city. In the end, I'm glad I took such a big chance."

Matthew nodded without tearing his eyes away from his notes. "I take it that's why you came back to New York? It sounds like things started to 'stagnate' for you at home."

My heart plummeted. Now that he'd put my answer in that light, I realized it wasn't what I'd meant to say at all. "That's not true," I said, more forcefully than I intended. "Working at *Couture* was a wonderful experience that taught me a lot, but I can't stay here forever." Thinking back to what Jeanette had said to me on the phone, I added, "Life goes on."

I noticed he wasn't scribbling in his notepad anymore, and I looked at him expectantly. "Aren't you going to write that down?"

He gave me a satisfied smile. "I have all the answers I need."

"Wait," I called after him, but he was already heading back

toward the street. With an exasperated sigh, I turned back to the building that everyone had disappeared into. I rushed up the steps and found my way into the main hall of the University Club. Just as quickly as I'd fallen into a panic over my misconstrued words, I rose right out of it to absorb the scene before my eyes. All of the guests were gathered in a massive, wood-paneled room with stained-glass windows that reached up to the ceiling. An ornate chandelier was suspended in the center of the ceiling, illuminating the circular tables that guests were gathered around as they talked among themselves.

I scanned the room for Celeste and found her seated at a table in the center of the action. As I approached her, she gestured to the empty seat beside one of her colleagues. I recognized everyone from outside the club, except for a dark-haired woman sitting across from Celeste. She didn't look older than twenty-two.

"Nora, this is Stephanie," Celeste said. "She's going to be covering the event for *City Chic,* a publication that covers current events in the New York fashion scene." She leaned toward me, as if she were about to divulge a juicy secret. "But she told me that she has big aspirations for the future of her career. Perhaps you could share some words of wisdom with her, if it wouldn't be too much trouble."

"Of course not." As I turned to greet Stephanie, I wondered when I'd become the poster child for fashion magazine success. I had the feeling that Jeanette hadn't been too far from that title just under a month ago.

"How did you become successful so quickly?" she asked, her eyes filled with a mixture of awe and respect. "I mean, our readers are wondering," she backpedaled, but it was clear she was only asking the question for herself.

"Well, it might have come quickly, but it definitely didn't come easily. I can't tell you how many times I stayed in the office until only the janitors were left."

"It's true," Celeste said after taking a sip of wine. "She has quite the work ethic." Turning to me, she added, "In many ways, you remind me of Jeanette. She dedicated her entire life to her work at *Couture*. That is, until she decided it no longer suited her," she said, her voice thick with distaste.

Her compliment didn't sit right with me. Jeanette had dedicated her entire life to her work because that was the only life she had. If I was showing the same amount of devotion, then I was doing something terribly wrong.

"I don't think it's fair to compare her to Jeanette," said the thin woman I'd met outside the building. "Jeanette left as soon as she found a different path for herself. Nora has the commitment of someone who's in it for the long haul."

"Definitely," Stephanie agreed. "How could you ever walk away from all this? I know I would kill to be in your place right now."

Ever since Celeste introduced me to Stephanie, I'd had the nagging feeling that she reminded me of someone I couldn't identify. But now, as I watched her face light up with unabated enthusiasm, I realized it was me. Something about Stephanie's romanticized notion of the fashion industry made me feel like I was looking into the eyes of the hopeful girl I'd once been. And just like I couldn't crush the spirits of that fragile child, I couldn't bring myself to tell Stephanie the truth—that I would have to walk away from this life eventually.

"Maybe you will," I told her encouragingly. "I didn't think I'd be sitting here right now, but anything's possible."

Once the words were out of my mouth, I knew I was directing them to myself just as much as Stephanie. Anything *was* possible. I clutched that hope as if it would rectify everything in my life, as if it had the power to make me believe in my future as freely as I had when I'd still had my whole life ahead of me.

Before Stephanie could respond, Celeste rose from her seat. "It's time to get this evening started." She made her way to the front of the room as silence cloaked the entire hall. Meanwhile, Stephanie gazed up at my boss as if she were a goddess about to unleash her powers over the audience. If I were her age when I'd started working at *Couture,* I would have looked just as starry-eyed as she did.

"Good evening, everyone," Celeste began as she sifted through some papers. "We're all gathered here tonight to celebrate the release of the September issue of *Couture.* While it won't be officially coming out until later this year, we hold this event each February to give an exclusive preview of our most important issue.

"A monumental amount of effort goes into this issue on behalf of my editorial team. From the early stages of conception to the final proofing, our writers and editors give their all to make this publication happen." Her eyes met mine for a brief moment, then she went on. "However, while some have simply done their jobs, others have truly stepped up and demonstrated their dedication to the magazine. It's people like them who help make *Couture* what it is today.

"When Nora Evans took the place of Jeanette Peterson, my former fashion director, I wasn't expecting much more than a creative employee with a keen interest in fashion and beauty. That is, after all, the formula for nearly everyone I've hired over the course of my career. But Nora proved to be different from the very beginning. With her unrivaled work ethic and her determination to see every project through to the end, it's easy to see why Jeanette insisted that Nora fill her shoes." She looked directly at me again before continuing. "Without further ado, I'd like to invite Nora Evans to speak about the work she's done for the September issue of *Couture.*"

The guests applauded as I made my way toward the front of the room, praying no one could see my hands trembling. I'd planned out every last detail of my speech, but nowhere in my outline had I included advice on how not to look like a nervous wreck.

"Hi, everyone," I said, my voice sounding distant through the echo of the microphone. "You'll have to lower your standards after Celeste, because I'm not the best at public speaking."

A ripple of laughter spread across the room, and the sound helped put me at ease. I glanced down at my notes before raising my head toward the crowd. "If I asked each one of you what you'd like to change about your life, you all would probably have an answer ready. Maybe you want to change careers, move to a different state, or even start eating healthier. Regardless of how you'd answer the question, there's one thing that would unite every single response: the desire to better yourself. To reach for something higher than where you're currently standing, so you can improve not just your own life, but the lives of those around you. It was that universal desire for change and self-improvement that inspired my idea for the issue."

I segued into an outline of the layout I'd put together, growing steadily more relaxed as I went on. I reminded myself that Celeste had personally invited me to this event and that everyone was here because they cared about the magazine as much as I did. I belonged here just as much as every other person in this room.

After I wrapped up my speech, applause accompanied my walk back to my table like music at an award ceremony. A rush of adrenaline had electrified my system as soon as I finished speaking, and it was surging through me at top speed by the time I reached my seat. I'd never fantasized about what it would be like to be famous, but I had a pretty good idea that this feeling came close to it.

I'd barely sat down when Stephanie turned to me, her eyes wide. "You were amazing. And so was your idea for the magazine. I wish I had your creativity."

"Well done, Nora." Celeste's smile held more sincerity than I'd ever seen from her. "I knew I made the right choice by inviting you to speak."

I tried to respond to Stephanie or my boss, but I was choked up with a feeling I couldn't identify. It ran deeper than the pride I'd felt when my art teacher used my sketch as a prototype for the class project or when my mom and dad cheered me on at my high school graduation. This time, I'd made an impact that reached much farther than the neighborhood I'd grown up in or the people I knew. Seeing the pride on Celeste's face, I knew this was just the beginning. Once the issue reached the publication stage, it had the potential to change the lives of people I'd never met before.

A couple of Celeste's colleagues spoke next, and I picked at my plate of hors d'oeuvres, too excited to eat a single bite. In a small part of my mind, I was aware that I'd reached my goal of catching up to Jeanette's accomplishments at the magazine. And in that same area of my mind, I knew this was my ticket to go home. All I had to do was call up Jeanette and tell her where I was, maybe even put Celeste on the phone and have her repeat her introduction about what a dedicated employee I was. My friend would be physically unable to resist returning to her career after she understood everything she'd given up.

I knew precisely what I had to do, but as I mentally replayed my boss's words and the roar of applause that had followed my speech, I couldn't bring myself to do it. I pulled my phone out of my bag and stared at Jeanette's name in my contacts, as if willing myself to make the move. *Just a quick call,* I told myself. *You know you can't stay here forever.*

"Hey, do you think we could exchange contact info?" Stephanie's voice broke me out of my mental tug-of-war. "You know, just in case I need some career advice. I think you'd be a great mentor."

Her look of pure ambition pulled me back to the present and away from the blurry reality of my life at home. "Sure, of course." I typed my phone number and email address into my notes app and passed it over to her. "I can help with anything you need. Just let me know."

She smiled gratefully and gave me her own contact information. After I slipped my phone back into my bag, I returned to my plate and started nibbling on some bruschetta. I longed for time to stay suspended in this one night so I could fully live in the moment before it slipped away indefinitely. I knew too well that feelings like this never lasted long. It would only be a matter of time before I was back in my apartment, replaying the event in my head in the form of a memory.

But the night passed by before I had the chance to keep it enclosed in my hand. I watched as guests started to file out of the main hall and into the chill of the late-February night. The glow of the wood-paneled room flickered with each person who left until it finally died out, stripped of the warmth of joy and celebration.

I pulled myself up from my seat with effort, as though leaving the room would mean leaving behind everything I'd been recognized for between these walls. I let out a sigh and walked toward the exit. The only person left in the hall was the server who'd offered me hors d'oeuvres, and even he looked ready to pack up and leave.

As I headed down the steps of the University Club, I noticed Celeste standing at the foot of the steps, looking at her phone. When she heard me coming, she tore her gaze away from the screen and walked over to meet me. "There you are. I was beginning to wonder if you'd gotten lost."

"I was just trying to take it all in. It's not every day that I'm invited to an exclusive *Couture* event."

"Well, you'd better start getting used to it."

I threw her a questioning look. "What do you mean?"

"We need to start thinking about the next steps, Nora. I already told you that you did an incredible job on the upcoming issue. But that's not enough. Our readers are going to want more after they see what you've put together, and it's my job to make sure they get it."

"Next steps?" I repeated dumbly. I heard distant alarm bells going off in my head, but I was still too caught up in the enchantment of the night to figure out what they were trying to warn me about.

"I'm talking about building an online presence, of course. Millions of readers visit our website expecting content of the same caliber as our magazine, and with the ideas you've come up with, it only makes sense for you to start contributing to our website as well."

It was impossible to ignore the permanence in her words, the way she assumed I would be doing this for years to come. I opened my mouth, but all the words I wanted to say had dried up on my tongue.

"Anyway, I think it's wise to build on the story you wrote up about your escape to the country. Considering how well our fans responded to it when I previewed it on social media, there's a good chance they'll want more of it on our website." She looked at me expectantly. "Any thoughts?"

I looked into the eyes of the person who'd just exalted my achievements in a roomful of people and heard myself say, "That sounds great."

"Wonderful. I spoke about this with my colleagues earlier, and we all agree that your story needs a more personal angle for the website. Then I thought, what better way to capture someone's personal experiences than to get a firsthand account? So I'm sending the camera crew to your farm."

I stared at her, failing to grasp her words. She sighed and filled in the blanks for me. "It's just a few camera operators and reporters. They'll interview your family, snap some photos, get a feel for life in the country. Our readers will love it. I can already tell."

"But what about running the farm? My family has an important job to do, and they can't do it if you turn my home into a reality show. Not to mention that's an overt infringement of their privacy."

"Well, perhaps you should've thought of that before you agreed to becoming the new fashion director."

The ground started to split apart under my feet, the world suddenly too weak to hold me together. We would lose our farm if Celeste went through with her plan. With the way Tyler had been struggling since I left, there was no extra cushion that allowed him to dedicate any attention to the magazine.

"I didn't agree to this," I said, finally finding my voice. "I didn't agree to sending the media to my home. I'm sorry, but this can't happen."

Her patient expression froze over in the blink of an eye. The change was so swift, it made my blood run cold. "You don't know how lucky you are to have come this far," she said. "If you turn this down, there's someone just as talented as you waiting in the wings. And don't even count on seeing your name in the September issue if you don't agree to my terms. A few of your colleagues already shared their own thoughts with me, and I'll replace your ideas with theirs in a heartbeat if I need to."

All it took was a single thought of the work I'd put into that issue, and I felt a gaping hole in the ground where there had only been cracks moments earlier. She couldn't take that away from me. Inside that magazine were countless sleepless nights, hours and hours of revisions and reworkings, and more stress and self-doubt than I'd ever had to conquer for such a pro-longed period of time. All of that was about to be for absolutely nothing.

I ran a hand through my hair, my mind racing wildly with

suggestions. "But... there has to be another way. I'll do anything else you want me to do, but I can't let you intrude on my life back home."

Celeste eyed me for a long moment before she turned back toward the street. "There is no other way, Nora. Either you let your family be a part of this, or you can forget about seeing your ideas in the magazine." She paused at the curb and turned back to me, her icy gray eyes sending a shiver down my spine. "And I don't care what I said to everyone tonight. Never think for a second that you're irreplaceable."

Twenty-Two

~~

That Sunday night, sleep came in short, fitful bursts. Each time I drifted off, the thought of Celeste's ultimatum jolted me awake. Her threat echoed through my mind, its finality like a bloated period at the end of a sentence. *I'll replace your ideas with theirs in a heartbeat if I need to.* If someone were to nullify nearly a month of work with a single sentence, I couldn't imagine anyone more suited to the role than Celeste.

The first rays of sun poked through my blinds, feebly illuminating the walls with thin streaks of light. Even though I was lying completely still in bed, my heart wouldn't give up its insistent pounding. I knew my boss would be waiting in her office for me to approve or reject the filming on the farm. But even after having spent most of the night wide awake with my thoughts, I still hadn't come up with an answer.

I dragged myself out of the comfort of my bed and stumbled into the bathroom. The harsh light made my head throb, and I plucked my toothbrush from the edge of the sink, noticing that my fingers were trembling.

A camera crew. A full crew of operators and reporters descending on our small family farm. Such an ordeal would be enough to send anyone into a tizzy, but Tyler would be a different story. He'd even balked at the idea of sharing our personal photos on Facebook. Turning our farm into a Hollywood set would be asking far too much of him.

But as I brushed, I thought about the storm that had destroyed the new milking machines. The money from the filming could help us cover the cost of repairs. If that turned out to be true, Tyler would have to see the value in bringing the crew to the farm. After all, he'd approved of the robotic equipment once he'd seen how it would bring in more profit and make his job easier.

By the time I reached the elevator bank, I was clinging to the prospect of financial gain as if it were a life preserver. Underneath that precarious benefit was a slew of drawbacks that were far more certain. Just picturing the look on my husband's face when he saw the trailer pull into the farm made my skin prickle with unease.

Then there were the kids. Starting school hadn't been especially smooth for either of them. At the same time, Jeanette seemed to be doing a good job of helping them through the rough patches. As much as it hurt to see her occupy a growing role in my kids' lives, it was a relief to know that they were being taken care of for the time being.

I let out a sigh as I pushed open the door of my apartment building. For every excuse I thought of to send the crew to the farm, there was an equally valid excuse not to. Vanessa's advice returned to my thoughts, almost in response: *If you want a way out of this, you're going to have to let one of them go.*

The reminder sent a bite through the already-ferocious wind, and I jammed my hands into my fur-lined coat pockets. Making a decision then and there seemed too permanent, too irreversible. It was as if I preferred to remain in this state of limbo for as long as I could manage, balancing my conflicting interests with the grace of a skilled gymnast. But I was beginning to see that my attempts to balance it all were nothing more than an illusion. With every decision I made that nourished my magazine-related goals, I was starving my goals back on the farm.

I went straight to my office, as if avoiding Celeste would preclude me from having to give her my final answer. But I knew all too well that she would go out of her way to find me if I didn't show my face all day. Besides, I could feel my decision incubating inside me, and only then did I realize I'd been leaning toward it since Celeste presented her terms to me.

Before I could take a moment to think it through, there was a knock at the door. I turned toward Megan and gave her a welcoming smile, grateful for the distraction. "Hey, Megan. Do you have the photo layout for the lipliner story?"

"Just what I came here to give you." She handed me a set of glossy, high-def photos featuring assorted lipliner products. With a nervous look, she said, "Let me know what you think. The printer was having some issues yesterday, so I had to throw something together at the last minute."

"Don't worry. These already look amazing."

Reassured, she smiled and headed back to her desk. I started to give the photos a closer look but didn't get very far. The usual line of coworkers was already forming outside my office door.

As I assisted each one of them, I delved into their problems in an effort to drown out my own. I helped Chloe polish her draft, gave Jacob the SEO data for the *Couture* website, and fed Bianca ideas for her lifestyle article. The more I busied myself with my daily responsibilities, the more I found myself justifying the choice I'd made. It almost seemed natural to send the crew to the farm, like it was just another item on my to-do list. At the end of the day, that was what it was: a part of my role at the company—just like everything else I'd been doing since day one.

Once there was a lull in foot traffic outside my office, I rose from my chair and took measured steps into the hall. There was no sense in putting this off any longer. I already knew what I wanted, and it was time to own it.

Celeste had her phone cradled between her shoulder and ear when I reached her office. Meeting my eyes, she lowered the receiver and threw me an expectant look. "Yes?"

I stood up straight, one hand resting on the doorframe. "I've thought about your proposal, and I think it's best if we send in the crew. As long as they don't cause too much interference, of course."

Her smile was knowing, as if she'd been waiting for me to deliver that exact response. Turning back to the receiver, she said, "I just spoke to her now, actually. You can go ahead and unload the trailer."

I froze in the doorway. "You already flew them in?"

She waved a dismissive hand. "Of course I did. You weren't actually going to turn down this opportunity, were you?"

"Well, this isn't the type of thing you do without thinking it through first. I had to make sure it was what I really wanted."

She chuckled, as if the idea were preposterous. "Oh, Nora. Don't fool yourself. If you didn't want this, you wouldn't be standing here right now."

I tried to come up with a reply, but she was right. No one

came as far as I had without wanting success to her very core. But as I watched my boss chatter away with the unseen person on the other line, I couldn't help feeling like I'd become her puppet. It was as if I yielded to her every demand without putting my own needs into the picture, and she expected me to do just that.

Celeste set the phone back in its cradle and fished a manila folder out of her desk drawer. "Take this," she said as she handed it to me. "These are some of the questions our reporters plan on asking your family during the interviews. Look them over and make sure they cover everything of interest. You can feel free to add more if there's something else you have in mind."

I accepted the folder and tucked it under my arm as I headed back to my desk. Once I was alone, I opened it and examined its contents. The first sheet of paper showcased a list of topics to be covered, which ranged from an overview of daily life on the farm to a synopsis of the most common struggles today's dairy farmers contend with. I thumbed through the pages, not seeing anything out of line, until I reached the end of the packet.

Gingerly, I peeled it from the folder's backside and positioned it under the glow of my desk lamp. I was still for a moment as I absorbed each of the questions:

What is the best part about your job? The most challenging?
What does being a farmer mean to you?
Describe your main goals right now and how you plan to achieve them.
What motivates you to do what you do every day?

A vague sense of disappointment settled over me as I put down the paper. The reporters had covered all the ground I'd expected them to, and the answers would be enough to satisfy our inquisitive readers. But I couldn't fight the desire to dig a little deeper. It was as if these questions were my way of communicating with my family after so much time apart. If this was my only chance of telling them how I really felt, I had to make the most of it.

I grabbed a pen and poised it above the sheet of paper, my mind racing. For a moment, I removed the reporters from the picture and imagined I was the one asking the questions. I dug deep to find the precise words I needed to capture what I wanted to get out of this filming. Only then did I know exactly what I needed to ask.

I scribbled down my revised set of questions and delivered it to Celeste. I stood silently by her desk as she read through them without comment. Once she was done, she offered up a cunning smile. And I couldn't help but feel like I'd just sealed my fate.

***

A couple of days later, I was sitting at the tiny dining table I'd pushed into a corner of my cramped apartment, a soggy slice of pizza sitting untouched on my plate. I knew I'd been in New York for too long when all the pizza was starting to taste the same.

I pushed the plate away and unlocked my phone for the fifth time in less than ten minutes. I could blame the food all I wanted, but I hadn't had much of an appetite since I'd given Celeste the green light on the filming. Tyler had yet to call or text me about the crew, and his silence was far more painful than the anger I'd anticipated. Did he kick them out? Was he trying to reason with them somehow? The only thing I knew for certain was that he would get the crew off the farm one way or another.

I wandered into my bedroom and started tooling around in the desk beside my bed, itching for a distraction. But I'd caught up on all my work assignments, and my schedule was empty for the rest of the night. There was nothing left to do but wallow in the feelings I could no longer ignore.

I sat on the edge of my bed and cradled my head in my hands. Agreeing to the interview had been a mistake. Not only was I missing the answers I needed from my family, but I'd also slashed the last flimsy thread that our relationship had been hanging by.

The distant ding of my phone tore through my thoughts. Nerves stirred in my belly as I leapt up from my bed and bolted toward the dining room table. I grasped my phone, my spirits dipping when I saw that Chloe had texted me instead:

Look at the video section of the Couture site. Now.

Panic seized my chest as I opened my laptop and typed in the website address. My heart was racing before I even knew what I was going to find. With a trembling finger, I hit the video tab and scanned the selection of clips on the main page. But I didn't have to scroll far before the unmistakable clapboard siding of the farmhouse jumped out at me.

Moisture broke out across my forehead as I hit the play button. A woman with perfectly defined waves and lipstick a shade too bright appeared in the shot, her exuberant smile complementing the piercing blue sky that blanketed the farm.

"I'm here in Fairlane, Iowa, home of our very own fashion

director, Nora Evans. Nora agreed to give *Couture* readers an inside look into her life on the dairy farm that she lives on with her husband and kids. Right now, I'm with her family to speak to them about the ups and downs of farming."

She turned to an unseen interviewee and smiled. "Tyler, I hear this farm has been in your family for four generations. Can you talk to me about the importance of tradition and family values to you?"

The camera shifted to include Tyler in the shot, and all the breath left my lungs. His smile was bright, almost luminous. The sunlight highlighted the scruff on his face and lit up his already-sparkling eyes. He looked happy. Like I'd never left him behind in the first place. Like he hadn't been forced to shoulder the burden of the farm on his own while I pursued a dream he didn't believe in.

"Of course," he said, and explained how he'd inherited the farm and learned about the business. As he spoke, suspicion took hold of me. Why had he agreed to do the interview? There was nothing stopping him from telling the crew to have a nice day in his hospitable midwestern way and sending them off. I should've been relieved, but something didn't feel right about the sunny image in front of me.

"I can't imagine it was easy to take on such a big responsibility at a young age," the reporter said. "What's the most important lesson you learned from it?"

Hearing my own questions spill out of the reporter's mouth made them sound raw, unedited. I waited for him to respond, my breath trapped in my lungs.

"One of the main things every farmer learns early on is how you always need to be thinking about the future. You can't predict everything, but you'll have a much easier time at the start of the season if you're prepared for it." He cast his eyes downward and smiled. "That's something I've taught to my kids here."

The camera zoomed in on Caleb's elated face, and I pressed a hand over my mouth to contain the rising sob inside me. He looked happier than I'd seen him in months, with his mouth twisted into that goofy smile that he showed off when he was so excited he couldn't contain it. Knowing I wasn't there to witness his joy in real life sent a fresh wave of grief through me.

The reporter smiled encouragingly at my son. "How do you help out on the farm?"

"I do lots of stuff. I help Dad milk the cows and feed them every day. Sometimes, he even lets me ride in his tractor. It's a lot of fun."

I blinked, trying to reconcile the boy who'd rebelled against farming with the one speaking to the reporter. As the camera flashed back to Tyler's smiling face, it hit me. Having a crew straight from New York City visit my home made the hard, dirty business of farming look like material fit for a movie. The job that had once seemed like a chore to Caleb now seemed glamorous. Coveted. I could see it in the way his eyes danced with light, in the way he observed the land with a renewed sense of wonder. He looked the same way he had when I'd showed him the view from my hotel room during our FaceTime call.

"And what about you?"

I snapped back to attention as the reporter lowered her microphone toward Bridget's mouth. "I love helping the cows every day," she said, her grin infectious. "I named some of them too. Like Bluebell. And Pearl. I want to be a farmer one day. Or a vet!"

This revelation seemed to pique the reporter's interest, and she turned back to Caleb. "Do you want to become a farmer too? Like your sister?"

I could feel Tyler holding his breath as he waited for Caleb to answer. I was doing it too, my entire body suspended in anticipation. Caleb tilted his head, as if deeply considering the question, and said, "I think so. Maybe one day."

I was so overcome with emotion at the potential in his words that I failed to see the one thing jumping out at me. Tyler had noticed the shift in Caleb's attitude before I did. He'd seen it as soon as the crew stepped onto the farm, and he knew this was his only chance of getting the old Caleb back. Even if he had to entertain personal questions from a reporter, he would do it if it meant making his troubled son happy again.

Tears were already forming in my eyes when the reporter raised her eyebrows. "Oh. Looks like we have a special guest today."

Jeanette strode toward the camera, her usually tidy brown curls hanging loosely in a ponytail. She was wearing a green flannel top that was lightly spotted with dirt, and her skin had a faint sheen of moisture, as if she'd just finished toiling all morning long. Pride radiated from her expression, the look of someone who worked hard but relished every minute of it—the same way I imagined I'd looked during my first few weeks on the farm.

"I'm Jeanette." She beamed at the camera. "I was the fashion director at *Couture* just a month ago. My good friend Nora has taken my place since then, and I'm so grateful for it. If she didn't step in, I never would've had the chance to help out on her farm and see what her life was really like. Obviously, this isn't the type of work I'd normally do, and it took me a while to adjust to country life. But now I understand why this job means so much to my friend. It really changes you."

The woman nodded emphatically at Jeanette, as if she knew exactly what it was like to toil in the fields all day. "I know what you mean."

"No, you don't," I said out loud, a slight tremble in my voice. I wasn't even sure if I was directing the words to the reporter or Jeanette.

"I never would've gotten the hang of farming if it weren't for the people around me. Tyler was so patient with me when I learned how to do Nora's job. And Bridget and Caleb are always willing to help out when they can."

"Looks like the four of you make a great team," the reporter said.

Team. The four letters slithered through my veins, tainting my blood like venom. My breaths grew ragged as I observed the portrait in front of me. Caleb and Bridget were standing side by side, Bridget giggling as her brother whispered something in her ear. Jeanette had shifted her eyes from the camera to the children, her face illuminated by the joy of witnessing their wholesome exchange. Meanwhile, Tyler stood at the heart of it all, his hands planted on his hips and his eyes resting on the bucolic land that surrounded him. He looked calm. Contented. Miles away from the worn-down man who seemed to answer the phone every time I called.

"There you have it, *Couture* fans. A real-life representation of life on the farm from the perspective of an Iowa family. Stay tuned for more lifestyle videos right here on our website. Until next time, I'm Victoria Monroe reporting from Fairlane, Iowa."

As the screen went dark, I sat there, unmoving. I was vaguely aware of my heart beating and of my breathing, quick and shallow, like I'd just broken into a sprint.

Family.

Team.

I rose abruptly from my chair and stumbled toward the desk in the corner of the room. I searched for something I hadn't yet identified, my fingers groping blindly in the dark drawers. It wasn't until I retrieved the photo that I realized I'd been looking for it all along.

I stared at the image in my hands, the shadows and contours telling a story I knew by heart. Tyler and I were standing in front of the barn, our smiles tired but hopeful. I was cradling a baby Bridget in my arms while two-year-old Caleb stood at my feet. My clothing was splotched with the various stains of farmwork, and my face was bright with the hope of everything that was yet to come. The picture overlapped almost perfectly with the image of Jeanette and my family standing in front of the camera.

Something was rising inside me, inflating faster than I could stop it. I'd given up all of that. I'd been so preoccupied with living my unlived life in New York that I'd abandoned the life I actually had. The one that truly counted. And only after Jeanette took my place did I see that it was a better life than I ever could've asked for.

I shoved the photo back into the drawer, and my knees gave out, finally buckling under the weight of everything I'd just seen. I sank to the floor as my limbs grew weak with tears that escaped some dark, unguarded part of me. As I let out gasping breaths, my mind flooded with images that swam through my mind like a photo reel. Jeanette placing a tender hand on Bridget's shoulder. Tyler's face frozen in his ready smile as Caleb described his role on the farm. The reporter melting over the squeaky-clean portrait of a happy family.

That should have been me. Instead, I was on the floor of my darkened apartment, living a life that didn't make sense anymore.

I eyed my phone on the dresser and reached for it. I scrolled through my contacts until I found Chloe's name, remembering what she'd told me the day we met for coffee: *If you need someone to talk to, I'm here.*

I rested my head against the wall as I waited for her to pick up. With a fresh jolt of pain, it occurred to me how Tyler was the one I normally leaned on in times like this. He would still have filled that role if I hadn't splintered his last shard of trust in me.

"Hey," Chloe said. "Did you watch the video?"

I opened my mouth to answer, but the words were trapped in my throat. Gently, she said, "Are you okay?"

When I finally found my voice, it came out strangled. "I can't be here anymore." A hiccup broke through my words, and I fought to keep another round of tears from breaking free. "I can't do this. Working at *Couture*. Being in the city. I just... This isn't what I want anymore."

She didn't object. She didn't ask if I was crazy for even thinking about leaving this life behind. Instead, she spoke in a voice that was barely above a whisper. "I know." An hour seemed to pass before she said again, almost inaudibly, "Believe me, I know."

I wiped the moisture away from my eyes with my sweater sleeve. "I just wish there was a way out of all this."

"There is," she said, and I thought about what Vanessa had told me in the bathroom. "There always is. And as long as you look for it, you'll find it."

Twenty-Three

Every step I took down the long, empty hallway seemed to reverberate through the entire building. The staccato click of my heels bounced off the stark white walls as I turned the corner toward my office. I pulled my keys out of my bag and opened the door before settling into my desk chair.

I looked down at my phone: 8:02. I had a whole day ahead of me, and I could barely find the energy to turn on my computer.

A long breath escaped me as I flipped open my planner and scanned the tasks I'd enthusiastically written out just several days earlier. Reading the list now, I saw how empty and meaningless each item was. Anyone else could easily take on my responsibilities. A younger, less jaded fashion enthusiast with an eye for cutting-edge trends. A keen businesswoman with years of experience under her belt. A creative visionary with ideas that transformed the entire landscape of the magazine.

Never think for a second that you're irreplaceable.

Celeste may have taken a month to admit that I was just as disposable as everyone else, but I knew she'd always believed it. Even when she'd talked me up in front of her colleagues, when she'd told me I was different from everyone else, and when she'd listened to my ideas with a glint in her eyes. Jeanette had probably told her all about my lifelong dream to work in fashion, and Celeste had dangled the bait before my eyes. And I'd been foolish enough to take it.

I shut my planner and started sifting through emails. I'd barely read through two of them when there was a tangle of voices at my door. I glanced up and saw Bianca and Megan standing in the threshold, their eyes wide.

"Was that really your family in the video yesterday?" Bianca asked.

I forced a smile. "Yeah, it wa—"

"I had no idea you lived on a farm," Megan broke in. "It must be so weird for you to live in a big city now."

"Actually, I—"

"I'm only here to ask permission to kidnap Bridget, because I'm pretty sure she's the most adorable thing I've ever seen," another voice chimed in from the hallway.

The voices continued to blur together until I could no longer decipher them. When I caught sight of Chloe's white-blonde mane, I sent her a silent plea for help. She broke up the growing crowd like a concert security guard and stepped into my office before closing the door behind her.

She sat down in front of my desk, her eyebrows knitted together with concern. "Feeling okay?"

I shrugged. "As okay as I can feel, given the circumstances." With a weak smile, I said, "Thanks for not acting like a crazed fangirl."

She rolled her eyes. "People here will pounce on the smallest opportunity for entertainment." She offered up a smile. "But they were right about your kids being adorable."

"Thanks," I said, making a concentrated effort to cloak the

sadness in my eyes. Before I could worry about Chloe noticing, her phone gave off four subsequent dings, the screen filling up with notifications. She went to silence it, but I caught several more alerts flying in before she did.

I raised an eyebrow. "Did you become famous overnight or something?"

"You mean you haven't checked our Twitter recently?"

When I shook my head, she tapped the Twitter icon and handed her phone to me. I scrolled through the notification center and scanned the replies that had rapidly accumulated. Readers were commenting on the video in droves, a good number of them gushing over my seemingly perfect family and longing to be on the picturesque, sun-drenched pasture that the cameramen had ramped up with their professional effects. While a handful of fans questioned why I wasn't in the video, most of them noted that Jeanette had been a caring friend for stepping in and taking care of the animals while I was gone.

As I read through the comments, the saddest irony dawned on me. My life at home had been the subject of so much praise, envy, and awe since the video was released, and I wasn't even there to live it.

I handed the phone back to Chloe. "I just need some time to process all this."

"No, sure. I'll leave you alone." She checked my face once more before heading out the door. "But if you need anything else, just let me know."

I nodded, grateful for her help, but also tired of feeling like I needed to be constantly monitored. As a sudden wave of exhaustion swept over me, I realized I wanted nothing more than to be alone.

I opened my desk drawer and pulled out a draft from one of the writers, hoping that I could keep the visitors at bay if I looked busy. Before I shut the drawer, I caught sight of the Twitter webpage that I'd printed out after recruiting readers to be featured in the issue. I pulled it out of the drawer and read through every single comment again. The unrelenting enthusiasm of our fans leapt out at me, an enthusiasm that still hadn't lost its luster in all the time that had passed.

I couldn't deny that, at least for these loyal followers, my work here wasn't done. I owed it to them to finish what I'd started here. Our readers had occupied a corner of my mind since my first day here, and abandoning them would feel as if I were abandoning the young girl I'd once been, the one who still lived in a small part of me.

The buzz of my phone sliced through my thoughts. I stole a cautious glance at the screen, as if it would explode as soon as I picked it up. I held my breath and hit the accept button. "Jeanette? What's up?"

"I'm screwed, Nora. Like, royally screwed. You've got to help me."

The desperation in her voice filled me with dread. Jeanette never discarded her cool and collected front, even in the direst of situations. "What happened?"

"There's something wrong with Bluebell. She won't get up. I looked up her symptoms, and it sounds like she has some kind of infection. I'm scared we'll lose the rest of the cattle if it starts to spread." She paused for a moment. "Tyler's still dropping the kids off at school, but I don't want to be him when he finds out."

My mind was on full alert now, sending the rest of my

body into a dizzying panic. Bluebell was the cow I'd known the longest, and I had the kind of bond with her that I imagined I would have with a pet if I'd owned one. Once Bridget was old enough to start taking care of the cattle, she'd fallen in love with Bluebell too. She still visited her stall first when it was time for the afternoon milking.

"What kind of infection? How did this happen?"

"I don't know. It happened after the cows were milked." Her voice wavered with fear, and it unsettled me just as much as the news she'd delivered. "I must have forgotten to clean the machines after the last milking. Normally, the machines would do it automatically, but we had to switch back to the old equipment after the storm."

It was my instinct to scold her, to tell her she should've known better, but I could tell she was just as afraid as I was. I bit down on my lip. "Okay, maybe this isn't as bad as you think. I'm sure if you wait until Tyler gets back—"

"Nora, we need you here. Now."

The sternness in her tone startled me. As her demand sank in, I flashed back to the way she'd extolled farm life in the *Couture* video. She'd made even the most mundane parts of the job sound like a privilege to take part in. I sat up straighter. "Well, you didn't seem to need me in that video yesterday. Because to me and everyone else who watched it, it looked like you had everything figured out."

She laughed in disbelief. "Nora, I don't know what the *hell* I'm doing. Sure, I can figure out how to milk a cow and keep it fed. But in situations like this, where it really matters, I don't know any more than Vanessa or Liz."

"Then how come Derek told me the farm was thriving without me? If my job was so important, the place would've fallen apart as soon as I came to New York. Not to mention my kids became top students as soon as you started tutoring them."

"I never tutored them, Nora. I can't teach to save my life. I wrote all the multiplication tables on an index card and showed Bridget how to hide it from the teacher during exams. And the best I could come up with for Caleb was threatening to embarrass him in front of his friends if he didn't improve his grades." She let out a heavy sigh. "All of that showed me I was never cut out to be a mom. It took me a while to admit it, and it still hurts like hell, but I think the miscarriage happened for a reason."

The weight of her admission sat like a rock between us. She went on before I could reply. "As for the farm, the only reason we held it all together in the beginning is because there was nothing holding us back. But now that things are getting tough, it's obvious I'm not cut out for the job. That's why we need you here. You've never been the type to run away at the first sign of difficulty."

I eyed the open drawer of my desk, where Jeanette's list of accolades peeked out from the corner. "Well, I could say the same thing about you. There's no way you would've made it this far at *Couture* if you weren't good at handling adversity."

"*Couture* was one thing, and you know that. I don't love farming the same way you do. It was easy to think I loved it when the sun was shining and all the cows were healthy, but now I know that was an idealized version of it. You're not like that, though. You stuck around for all the ugly parts of it, even when it was easier to walk away."

I tried to speak past the lump in my throat, but the crack in my voice betrayed it. "Then why am I all the way in New York when I should be there?"

The pause that followed was so long, I wondered if she'd heard me. After a moment, she spoke, haltingly but clearly. "If you're going to blame someone for that, you should blame me."

"What are you talking about?"

"The whole reason you're there in the first place. I was miserable when I was at *Couture*, and all I could think about was how badly you wanted to work in fashion as a kid. A part of me hoped you still had that dream, even though you'd already built a new life that you loved. So instead of letting you move on, I dragged you back into the past so I could escape the shitty life I was living." She let out a weighted sigh. "And you can see how well that went. First, I lost my baby, and now I've ruined your entire farm."

I was quiet for a moment as I absorbed her words. Then, gently, I said, "Do you know how much time I wasted wondering how my life would've turned out if I went to Grant? I lost years, Jeanette. Years. All that time, I never felt like I was fully living my life. It was like a part of me was always trapped in the past." I paused as the past few years flashed through my mind like I was watching them on fast-forward. "So, in a way, you did me a favor. Because if you didn't give me this chance, I would still be wondering what could've been."

When Jeanette spoke, her voice was delicate. "I had no idea. You seemed so happy the past fifteen years, it's hard to believe you were still haunted by the past."

"I was happy. But not in the way I wanted to be." I glanced around the office, suddenly frantic. "I just don't know how I'm supposed to leave all this behind. What will everyone do without me?"

"They'll be fine. Was anyone crying over me leaving when you first got there?"

When I didn't respond, she said, "Exactly. Believe me, that's the last thing you should be worrying about."

I thought back to when I'd told Chloe I wished there was a way out, and her response echoed in my mind: *There always is. And as long as you look for it, you'll find it.*

I turned my gaze to the window, where the line of skyscrapers held an empty promise that I'd blindly held on to for weeks. As my eyes swept across the peaks for the last time, I realized I'd come full circle. I was once again the young woman who'd searched beyond the horizon for something bigger, something that she could hold on to without loosening her grip. But while that destination had been a nebulous one back then, I knew exactly where I was meant to go now.

"So. This is it, huh?"

"Don't say it like that," Jeanette said. "You have so much ahead of you. You never needed *Couture* to live the life you want, anyway."

The faintest shadow of a smile broke across my face. "I know."

"So, are you going to get your ass back to Fairlane, or what?"

I thought about the comments from our readers, how they'd reminded me of the reason I'd come here in the first place. I hesitated for a moment. "There's just one more thing I have to take care of. Can you keep an eye on Bluebell in the meantime?"

"I'll do my best. But I don't know how much longer I can manage."

"Don't worry. I'll be there as soon as I can."

After I set the phone down, I stepped out of my office and headed to the ladies' room. As the door swung shut behind me, I studied my face in the mirror. I'd never noticed how the pressure of living up to Celeste's expectations and filling Jeanette's shoes had sunk into the crevices of my features, fraying them down to the last thread. I looked and felt like I'd aged years after the whirlwind month at this company.

But somewhere beyond the burdened visage in the clouded glass was the youthful, carefree girl I still guarded in an unseen part of me. The one who'd silently cheered me on by the sidelines with every victory and shared my pain with every defeat. The one who'd been waiting patiently for me to bring my vision to life for the past fifteen years.

Letting her down would be the final nail in the coffin. It would mean closing the door on my dream indefinitely, without a single glance backward. The finality of that idea sent a flurry of nerves through my stomach, as if I were taking an exam that I didn't know any of the answers to.

Just as I turned back toward my office in defeat, I felt the gentlest tap in my soul, a wordless whisper from the depths of my heart. I froze in place, trying to listen to it before it slipped away just as stealthily as it had come. Only after a moment did I recognize the voice as that of the girl inside me. *Go,* she said. *You don't belong here anymore.*

My heart knocked against my chest as the words took effect, pulling me into an all-encompassing embrace. I expected to feel crushing disappointment from knowing that it was finally over.

Instead, as the burden inside me loosened its suffocating grip on my heart, my knees grew weak with relief. After so many years, I finally had it in my palm, where I could clasp it tightly without worrying about it slipping through my fingers.

Freedom. The word ran through my fingers and danced behind my eyes like the light I'd lost for too long. It was all behind me now. Every moment of grief. Every second of sorrow that had stolen my joy. For the first time, I was able to set it all down at my feet, where it couldn't haunt me anymore. For the first time, I felt as light as air, free of the weight I'd been needlessly carrying around with me.

For the first time, I was ready to move on.

Twenty-Four

The hallway was drenched in silence as I found my way to Celeste's office. The overpowering freedom that had lifted my spirits after my phone call with Jeanette had now simmered down into a mere flicker. While I traced the familiar paths of the office with my footsteps, the weight of everything I was about to leave behind burdened my stride. I saw every feature, every corner of the office for the memory it would soon become.

I turned to my left and caught a glimpse of the fashion closet, remembering how Vanessa had led me inside without explanation and watched as I drifted dreamily through the fashion haven. I passed the conference room and flashed back to when Celeste rejected my pitch in front of my colleagues. I rounded the corner by Vanessa's desk and recalled Shannon Reyes turning up out of thin air to tell me how my work made an impact that stretched far beyond the walls of this building.

And just as I stopped outside Celeste's office, I remembered the worst defeat of my short-lived fashion career. I could still see the models strutting down the makeshift runway, only to be shot down by the editor in chief. Even more vivid in my memory was the faintest glimmer in Celeste's eye when she'd challenged me to surpass Jeanette's achievements.

Somehow, I'd risen to the challenge. Somehow, I'd rounded up an army of *Couture* readers who believed in the magazine just as much as I did in hopes of leaving an indelible mark on the publication's history. And, somehow, the leap had earned me a spot at one of the magazine's most exclusive events.

I stopped walking for a second, soaking up each moment like the waning rays of sun on a summer evening. Even though I knew my time to move forward had arrived in earnest, the memories would be a part of me long after I stepped through these doors for the last time. It was my job to guard those memories as a reminder of everything I'd learned during my time here.

I stood at Celeste's door, willing myself to knock and deliver the words I'd repeated to myself ad nauseum, but my hands hung limp at my sides. Something was missing. The most vital piece of the puzzle I'd labored over for the past few hours.

I turned and walked over to Vanessa's desk, where the features editor was poring over a stack of papers, deep in thought. "Hey," I said gently. "Do you have a second? Celeste wanted to talk to us about something." It was technically a lie, but it was the only way I would get her to Celeste's office without letting her in on my plan.

Vanessa's eyes narrowed ever so slightly. "You sure about that? Because I've been here for years, and Liz is always the one to tell me when Celeste wants to see me."

"I'm just telling you what she said." With my most encouraging smile, I turned toward the editor's office. "Come on. It'll be worth it, I promise."

With her brow still furrowed, she rose from her seat and followed me down the hall. My heart slammed against my chest, and I feared my knees would buckle at any moment. Still, I didn't slow down. The second I relaxed my pace, I would talk myself out of what I was about to do.

As I reached the doorway, I was relieved to see that my boss was assuming her usual position at her computer, not busy with another employee, like I'd feared she would be. Even if miniscule, it was a small victory.

"Celeste," I began, my voice quivering. I cleared my throat and started again. "There's something I need to tell you."

She sighed without removing her eyes from the screen, as if my mere presence were an inconvenience. "Please make it quick. If I don't get this model for our next shoot, the editor at *Cosmo* will snatch her right from me."

I stood up straighter, feigning a confidence that had abandoned me a long time ago. "When I started working here, I didn't know what to expect. I'd spent years dreaming about what it would be like to have a successful fashion career, but that fantasy was miles away from reality." I paused and tried to find my voice again. "I should've figured out a long time ago that this job didn't align with who I was. But it's a good thing I got a call from my friend telling me that my farm is in danger, because otherwise, I still would've been trying to convince myself I could make my dream work."

Celeste had been staring disinterestedly at her monitor at the start of my monologue, but now she was looking at me head-on, her razor-sharp glare daring me to continue. With my hands trembling at my sides, I accepted the challenge.

"My family needs me. And it took me too long to realize that you don't need me at all. You said it yourself, didn't you? 'There's someone just as talented as you waiting in the wings.'

Well, you were right. We both know I'm not the first person to want this life. In fact, there are plenty of other qualified women out there who want this much more than I thought I did."

I glanced at Vanessa, who was too flustered to speak. As I met her eyes, I silently forgave the coworker who'd gone to such great lengths to sabotage my goals, and instead I saw her for the vulnerable woman who'd opened up to me in the bathroom, laying bare her hopes of filling the fashion director position. I flashed her a quick smile as I forged ahead. "It's a good thing I found someone like that right here at *Couture*. Now that I think about it, Vanessa should've taken Jeanette's place right from the start. I can tell she's capable of doing great things for this magazine. That's why she's the perfect choice for the new fashion director."

I stopped to let my words sink in and was met with the stunned silence of the two women around me. Celeste's glasses were perched on the corner of her gaping mouth, and Vanessa's eyes were wider than Bridget's were when I'd surprised her with her favorite doll for Christmas. If someone told me the world had stopped spinning on its axis in that moment, I would've believed it.

"What is this talk of a new fashion director?" Celeste asked, the first one to recover. "We have an entire issue in the works. You can't just leave."

"You're right," I said, levelly meeting her gaze. "I should have done this a long time ago."

She scrambled for a response like a fish flopping around helplessly on land, and it struck me that I'd never seen this woman speechless before. A vein protruded in her neck as her eyes flashed. "Don't expect to see any of your work in the September issue, then. I have no problem scrapping all of your ideas."

Her threat sent a sharp ache through me, but I refused to let it show. "That's fine," I said calmly. "I'm sure your employees have plenty of other ideas that they can't wait to share."

I turned to Vanessa, who still looked like she needed to be pinched. "Best of luck, Vanessa. I know you'll do great."

Without another word, I headed back down the hallway, which suddenly seemed smaller than I remembered it. I strode through the office with a lightness on my feet that I'd never felt before. For a fleeting moment, the consequence of not seeing my work in *Couture* faded into oblivion, and I let myself bathe in the quiet peace of knowing I'd made the right decision.

I didn't stop walking until I reached my apartment, where I stepped into the hall closet and brushed the dust off my suitcase. With a rising sense of urgency, I yanked my clothes off their hangers and dropped them into the luggage, my hands working at a speed I hadn't realized they were capable of. The walls of the apartment were beginning to close in on me, and I had the pressing feeling that I couldn't get out of there fast enough.

When I was done, I took one final look at my temporary home, my gaze lingering on the skyline outside the window. Seeing the chain of skyscrapers for the last time reminded me of the night I'd left home, a night so distant in time but never far away in my memory. It was the liminal space between home and the unknown that had terrified me the most. I'd been caught in the blink in time between letting go of what I'd always known and reaching for something new. Something that demanded I plunge into darkness before I could call it my own.

Now I understood why that moment of transition had shaken me to my core. My roots would always snake down into the concrete of New York, but my branches had grasped onto the sprawling fields and wide-open skies of Iowa. It was time to return to the new home I'd spread my wings toward, even though I would always keep the city and what it had done for me tucked away in my heart.

I turned away from the window and made my way toward the door, my booted footsteps echoing in the empty room. After crossing over the threshold, I closed the door behind me with a final click. I took a second to make sure I had everything I needed, then rushed to the elevator so quickly, I almost tripped over my suitcase. I needed to get back home as soon as I could. Before the damage that was quickly ensuing on the farm became irreversible. Before I lost out on the only chance I had left.

***

"Attention, passengers. Flight 163 to Des Moines has been delayed due to heavy airport congestion. The new departure time is two forty p.m. We apologize for the inconvenience."

I let out a frustrated sigh, echoing the passengers around me. This was the second time my flight had been delayed in the two hours I'd spent at JFK. My confidence slipping away, I sent another text to Jeanette, updating her on my flight status. I'd left Tyler just as many voicemails, but there was no sign he even remembered I existed. Still, I couldn't bring myself to surrender. If Celeste had been right about one thing, it was that I never backed down, even when it was the more sensible thing to do.

When I reached his voicemail again, I sighed and left another message. "Hey. I don't know if you're still busy helping Bluebell, but I really need to tell you something. I'm trying to get home as fast I can. My flight's been delayed twice, though. That's JFK for you." I paused, checking the departures board for the tenth time in the past two minutes. Still no luck. "Anyway, call me as soon as you get this. Please."

As I ended the message, a stab of disappointment pierced me. He wouldn't call back. Why would he? I'd chosen to stay in the city and allowed everything to unravel at home. I wouldn't be surprised if he didn't speak a word to me once I got back.

"Where's home for you?" asked an older man sitting across from me. He sported a Hawkeyes baseball cap and a warm smile that would have fit right on the faces of my neighbors back home.

"Fairlane. It's a really small town. You've probably never heard of it."

To my surprise, his eyes glistened with recognition. "I drive through there on my way to work every day. It's a beautiful town. A lot of caring folks have gone out of their way to help me there." He smiled. "I'm sure they'll be glad to have you back."

I looked down at my shoes, thinking about how much I wished that were true. How it would've been true if I hadn't pushed everyone's limits and forced them to turn their backs on me.

"I don't know. I messed up pretty badly." My cheeks flamed as the words left my mouth, and I wondered why I'd shared such a personal detail with a complete stranger. It was as if missing my family had peeled away the protective sheen that I wore around people I didn't trust.

He gave me a look that told me he understood something I didn't. "I wouldn't let that keep you down. If your heart is in the right place, everyone around you will notice it."

His words engulfed me, lifting the uncertainties that weighed on my chest. I wanted him to be right. I'd never wanted anything so badly in my life.

Twenty-Five

~

I couldn't get home fast enough. I was positive that if I'd ridden a horse-drawn carriage to the farm, I would've been there already.

I pressed down on the gas, forcing the clunky rental car to chug along the highway. Even as I increased my speed, the anxiety that clawed at my stomach made it feel like I was slackening my pace with every passing second.

I checked my phone for what might've been the hundredth time since I got off the plane. The three-hour flight had been excruciating, with each minute slogging away like molasses oozing out of a jar. The second my feet touched the ground, I'd turned my phone back on and checked for missed calls or texts. I was turning into the zombie-eyed teens who walked out of Caleb and Bridget's school every afternoon, their tiny screens robbing them of the pleasure of observing the world around them.

Giving up on the hope that Tyler would call me back, I called Jeanette. She hadn't given me any more updates on Bluebell, which I hoped was a good sign. But I couldn't be too sure about anything anymore.

"Hey," I said when she picked up. "I'm almost home."

"Thank God. Tyler just called the vet, but she won't be here for a while. She has to help another farmer who's having an early calf. I just hope Bluebell can hold on in the meantime."

I drew in a sharp breath as longing tugged at my heart. It felt like a lifetime had passed since I'd seen my family, and I was closer than ever to narrowing the space between us. But after everything that had torn us apart over the past month, I feared I wasn't about to have the joyful reunion I'd been hoping for.

"He must be so worried," I said.

"Actually, he's handling it better than I thought he would. I guess he's seen everything after living on a farm all his life."

"Does he know I'm coming back?"

There was a brief pause. "I told him, but I don't think he's convinced you're staying."

I tried to suppress the sinking feeling in my stomach, but it was no use. "I don't blame him. How can he believe anything I say anymore?"

"Forget about the past now. It's over. You just have to show him that you're serious about staying, and he'll come around again."

I stared out at the landscape that rolled by my window and turned her words over in my mind. "You know, I never thought of you as an optimist."

"Yeah, well. I have my moments." After a beat of silence, she said, "So, how badly did Celeste take it when you quit?"

"Honestly? I think she's still recovering."

She laughed. "I can only imagine. It's not every day that someone encroaches on her throne."

"It's still hard to imagine I stood up to her like that." The editor's affronted expression flashed through my mind again, right on the heels of Vanessa's look of raw shock. "It feels like a dream."

"You were a lot gutsier than I was. I was able to hide behind my maternity leave excuse until she figured out I was never coming back. But you just went in there and ripped off the Band-Aid."

"I did, didn't I?" As I replayed the confrontation in my mind, something occurred to me. "But the funny thing is, it wasn't even scary once the words were out of my mouth. I felt... I don't know..."

"About fifty pounds lighter?"

I smiled at my friend's uncanny ability to finish my sentences. "Exactly."

"That's how I felt too." She let out a wistful sigh. "I guess we both aren't cut out to work at *Couture*."

"It's better off that way." The confidence in my words filled me to the brim, obliterating the darkness with their warm pools of light.

My heart rose up in my chest as I signaled at my exit, a visceral response to the dread that was settling like a rock in my stomach. "I just got off the expressway." I swallowed. "I don't know if I'm ready to face all this."

"Please don't tell me this is the same person who just told off Celeste Moore." She was back to being the Jeanette I knew and loved, and the knot in my stomach loosened. "We both know now's not the time to give up. The only way you're guaranteed to lose him is if you stop trying."

In spite of myself, a small smile crept onto my face. "If I managed to turn you into a walking motivational poster, then I've done something right."

"Don't get used to it."

I was still smiling to myself after we said our goodbyes, my eyes fixed on the road that snaked toward the farm. I gazed out the window at the scenery, my every cell soaking in the landscape that was as much a part of me as the blood in my veins. The trees extended their limbs in my direction, as if welcoming me back with open arms. I watched the wind caress the grass on either side of the road, the tall blades letting out a collective sigh of relief at my return. For a second, I almost believed there wasn't any turmoil waiting for me just a few yards away on the farm. In that moment, all that existed was the tranquil, bucolic scenery that lay undisturbed in my mind's eye.

When I pulled up to the clearing, my breaths grew shallow. Reality was creeping up on me, and I didn't know how much longer I could keep it at arm's length. It wasn't until I stopped the car that I finally felt the weight of everything that lay ahead of me.

I got out of the car and stepped onto the dirt road that led to the barn. There was a stillness in the air that settled over the pasture, like a gentle whisper reassuring me that everything was fine. Other than the handful of weeds that had begun to poke their heads through the earth, there was no sign that anything had changed since my departure. It was like time had stood still over the past month, holding its breath until my feet touched Iowa soil again.

I crossed the pasture with slow, cautious steps, as if I were afraid of disrupting the untroubled land. I didn't slow down until I saw an unmistakable head of dark-brown curls leaning toward the ground. My pulse sped up as I hurried over to Jeanette by the fence.

I found her kneeling beside Bluebell, who was lying help-lessly on her side. Jeanette looked up at me as I approached. "There you are. Please don't tell me this is as bad as I think it is."

I knelt beside the cow, trying to summon everything Tyler had taught me over the years. My hands probed her carefully in search of anything that was amiss. She was still responding to my touch, which meant that all hope wasn't lost yet. But her udder had begun to swell, and the damage showed no signs of slowing down.

"She's still alert, which is a good sign. But if she stays like this for too long, she could be at risk of nerve damage."

"I'm no cow expert, but that doesn't sound good."

I glanced in the direction of the barn. "Where's Tyler?"

"He's checking on the rest of the cattle. The infection al-ready started to spread to the other cows, and things can get bad if we don't keep it under control."

Jeanette cast her eyes downward, searching Bluebell. I thought I glimpsed a hint of sadness in them, but it slid away before I could wrap my fingers around it.

I studied her, trying to discern what she wasn't saying out loud. When it hit me, a dull sorrow wormed its way into my gut. "You're going to miss all of this, aren't you?"

She nodded, a movement that barely registered. A sad smile spread across her face. "Do you remember when we adopted a baby chick in third grade?"

"Yeah. Mrs. Martino's class, right?" We hadn't known each other back then, but anyone who ended up in Mrs. Martino's class had the privilege of parenting a delicate baby chick.

"Yup. Before that class, I never thought about what it

278 - *Elena Goudelias*

would be like to have a pet. But once I held that chick for the first time, something changed. It was like I suddenly wanted to look after it for the rest of my life to make sure it was okay." She gazed down at Bluebell again. "That's how I felt when I took care of your animals."

"I know how you feel." In that moment, I was struck by the similarities between us that had shone through in the *Couture* clip. Everything from the wonder in her voice to her newfound compassion for the livestock was a complete parallel of the person I'd been when I moved to Fairlane.

Her smile faded as her expression grew serious. "But this isn't for me. As much as I loved getting a break from my old life for a while, I can't stay here. You belong here more than anyone else."

"New York is probably wondering what happened to you," I said, and the corners of her mouth turned up ever so slightly.

"I do miss walking those streets," she said, gazing out at an invisible skyline. "And putting together outfits that I felt good in. And not having to drive across three towns just to find decent food."

As she let out a sigh, something struck me. I studied her pale-brown vest, her faded jeans, and her unkempt curls crowning her makeup-free face. My eyes shifted to my own Saint Laurent boots and the Alice and Olivia leather jacket that hung loosely on my shoulders. With a wry smile, I looked back up at Jeanette. "Remember when we were kids and we wondered what it'd be like to trade lives?"

Confusion crossed her face for a brief moment, then she did a double take at my outfit. "Well, damn. Looks like we achieved our goal." She smirked. "Can I have my designer wardrobe back now?"

"Sure thing. Just as long as I get my comfortable clothes back."

She flashed me a grin, but a sudden darkness promptly stole it from her, as if someone had slapped her in the face. She kicked at a pebble beside her feet. "Look, I know this can't even begin to make up for what I did, but... I'm really sorry. For taking over your farm and interfering with your kids' lives. I should've considered how much it would hurt you, but I was too caught up in my own selfish feelings."

I waited, but she didn't try to justify her behavior. Her apology was pure, unadulterated, without any pretenses burying her true intentions. The frankness of her words helped me see why she'd truly done what she did: not to senselessly sabotage me, but to find joy in a life that had filled me to the brim with it.

"I know what it feels like to be trapped in a life you hate," I said, thinking about all the nights I'd lain awake in my childhood apartment, dreaming with abandon about all the possibilities that were just out of reach. "Believe me, I know. And I'm not saying that makes it okay to steal someone else's life, because it doesn't. But no one should have to settle for anything that's less than what they deserve."

She smiled hesitantly, as if awaiting permission to let her true feelings shine through. "Thanks, Nora."

I mirrored her smile as I turned back to Bluebell. Before I attended to the cow, I looked at my friend again. "And, Jeanette?"

"Yeah?"

"I hope you find a life that you don't need to escape from."

As I looked out at the stretch of land that surrounded us, land that felt more like home than anywhere else in the world, I knew I meant every word.

"So do I," she said, more of a wish than a declaration. But I knew that with her determination, she would get there if she set her mind to it.

Long after the country air swallowed up the sound of her footsteps, I found myself alone with Bluebell. The truth settled heavily on my shoulders as I took another look at her. This was all up to me. I was the only one who hadn't been around when everything fell apart, and now I was the only one here to piece it back together.

I headed toward the barn in search of fresh hay, knowing that Bluebell had to have clean, dry bedding before she could be treated. I'd just reached the entrance when I stopped in my tracks and blinked. The entire interior of the barn was covered in tarp, and a string of film lights wrapped around the ceiling, pointing down toward an invisible scene. My breath caught in my throat as I noticed the room was stripped of all its hay and feed. The camera crew must have transported the fodder elsewhere to facilitate their filming. Where it had been moved was anyone's guess.

I scanned the fields and tried to think quickly. Not too long after, it came to me. Three years ago, a drought had swept across Iowa, leaving us to cope with a severe hay shortage. Ever since then, Tyler kept the rice hulls in the shed by the barn for emergencies like this.

I rushed over to the shed and found the supplies before using them to cover the space underneath Bluebell. I watched her settle into her new bedding, knowing as I observed her that something wasn't right. She still looked weak, her eyes devoid of their usual vitality. As I reached out to touch her gently, she let out a whimper that went straight to my heart.

I paced back and forth, pulling my brain apart for the answers I needed. I returned to the shed and started searching its contents, as if my mind knew what I needed before I did. I'd just begun to survey the shelves when I spotted the disinfectant tucked away in a corner on the top shelf.

I snatched it victoriously and ran back over to Bluebell. Kneeling next to her, I gently applied the disinfectant to her udder, being careful not to hurt her. A chill ran through the air as I searched her eyes for any sign of relief. I pulled my coat closer to my body and did my best to ignore the frosty air, knowing I couldn't abandon Bluebell now.

Only one thing was missing. She needed fiber to keep her immune system strong, and we stored soy hulls in the barn for that purpose. But, just like the hay that had evacuated the barn, there was no telling where the soy hulls were now.

I stood up and started walking across the field again, wondering if I should visit a nearby farm and see if they had any leftover feed to spare. Despite the biting wind that gnawed at my bones, I pushed forward. Something told me I wasn't doing this only for Bluebell anymore. I was doing this to prove that my time at *Couture* hadn't changed me into someone I no longer recognized. That I was still the same woman who'd chosen this life because it was what she truly wanted. I needed to prove it to the ones I loved, but most of all, I needed to prove it to myself.

I continued walking, but my confidence dwindled with every step. Anyone else would have given up at this point. I may have quit *Couture*, but I couldn't undo the choices that had torn me apart from my home and family. After all, I wouldn't be trekking through frigid temperatures to find food for a down cow if I'd turned down Jeanette's job offer. Realizing everything I'd unwittingly given up, I glanced behind me at my home. A current of loss flooded through me.

The low hum of an engine tore me away from my thoughts. I looked up as a pair of headlights pierced the darkness. The vet shut off the engine and hopped out of her truck before greeting me. "I was told that one of your cows has an infection," she said.

"Yes. I'll bring you over to her." My steps felt heavy as I led her toward Bluebell, as if I were wading through the ocean at high tide. For the first time, I meditated on the possibility that she wouldn't make it, and a wave of grief clouded the joy of returning home.

When we reached the spot where Bluebell lay, I explained to the vet what I'd done to help the cow before she'd arrived. The doctor listened as she knelt beside the animal to inspect her carefully. I watched her take the cow's temperature and examine her udder, silently praying that it wasn't too late. In some cases, down cows just needed the right treatment and enough time to achieve a full recovery. But it was the other cases, when the cow was too far gone to get better, that gnawed away at me little by little.

I was so focused on Bluebell that I almost didn't hear the dull thump of footsteps coming from behind me. I spun around and saw Tyler making his way toward us. My heart rose to my throat as he stopped in front of Bluebell and greeted the vet. His eyes flicked over to me, making my breath go still. I followed his gaze as it assessed my designer outfit and Manhattan-style haircut. While I studied his expression, I wondered if he was seeing the woman behind all the makeup and Fifth Avenue clothes, or if he only saw the stranger he believed I'd become.

"She's still alert, which is good news," the vet broke in, echoing my thoughts when I'd first found Bluebell. "Make sure you move her to a safer area when she's ready." She turned to face me with a confident look in her eyes. "She's going to be okay, though, and it's all your doing. If you hadn't been here to help her before I came, it might have been too late."

I struggled to process the news. If I'd tried to stick it out at *Couture* for a little bit longer or convinced myself that everything would work itself out, there was a good chance that Bluebell would've been in more critical condition. That, in turn, could have jeopardized the entire herd.

I ached to look up at Tyler, to see his reaction to the good news, and—I could only hope—to find some sign of his restored faith in me. But I feared that saving Bluebell's life wouldn't be enough to convince him I was the same person I'd always been.

I buried the fear as the vet handed us some medicine, along with a bit of advice on keeping Bluebell strong and healthy. We both thanked her, and she headed back to her truck. The sound of the engine stirring to life was deafening, as if it were highlighting the mounting tension between Tyler and me.

He finally met my eyes, his lips drawn into a thin line. "So, when are you heading back?"

A sharp pain jabbed at my chest as Jeanette's warning reinvaded my thoughts: *I don't think he's convinced you're staying.*

My eyes dropped to my feet. All I had left to give him was the truth, and all I had left to do was hope that it was enough.

"I quit. It's over. My boss already found a new fashion director to take my place. And she'll be the one to take over the September issue, because my boss warned me that she wouldn't use any of my ideas if I left." A chill in the air leaked through my coat sleeves, sending a shiver down my spine. I crossed my arms and stared at the frost-coated earth beneath my boots. "I don't know why I'm telling you all this. I don't even know how you can look at me right now."

Silence cloaked the already-hushed pasture, stretching on for far too long. I finally gave in and lifted my eyes toward him. The shadows of night obfuscated his face, rendering his expression unreadable. But I still picked up on an intense focus in his eyes that told me he was thinking deeply about everything I'd said.

He turned toward the barn before I could say anything else. "Come here."

I followed him as my heart beat uncertainly. He reached the line of trees that guarded the outer edge of the farm and sat down under a drooping elm, its skeleton limbs offering little reprieve from the rising windchill. I lowered myself onto the ground beside him and crossed my arms, wondering how his heat could feel so far away when we were sitting right beside each other.

Neither of us spoke for a moment that seemed to stretch out indefinitely. I tilted my head up at the impossibly large sky, a sky I'd only glimpsed in small doses back in New York. Looking at the vast, star-studded canopy made me want to believe I could move past everything that had happened. That I was free to begin on a blank slate, just like the white gems that newly spotted the inky blanket every night.

Tyler leaned back against the trunk and looked thoughtfully into the distance, as if he were lost in a memory. After a weighted moment, he said, "I had a friend in high school who went through a rough patch during our senior year. His grades started slipping, and he never seemed like himself. Then he found out one day that he was going to lose his MIT scholarship. That was when it really sank in for him. After that, he pulled himself up by his bootstraps and did what he had to do to get ahead. No one else was there to help him turn things around. It was all up to him."

He gave me a look that reached deep inside me. "My point is that it's what you do when you're under pressure that really matters, because that's when you know what you're going to lose. I know how hard it was to give up all your success, but you did it because you knew what was at stake."

My hand rested absently upon a tuft of cold grass, as if I were reaching out an invisible hand toward him. My skin burned with the desire to touch him again, to take shelter in his arms like I'd done so naturally in the past. But doing so still felt like a transgression, as if I were invading territory that was no longer mine.

"I messed up so badly," I said. "I came up with an excuse every time you asked me to come home. I complained about my problems when you tried to tell me about yours. And then I sent a camera crew to the farm for my own selfish reasons. How can you ever forgive me for all that?"

My words had an all-too-familiar ring to them. Before I could put my finger on it, I was coldly reminded of the way

Jeanette had sabotaged my farm out of a blind desire for happiness and success. I couldn't help but notice that we had more in common than I'd ever thought.

"Look, Nora." He looked at me head-on now, his expression not withholding a single truth. "You know what you did and how it affected us. You saw how it worried the kids. You saw how it put the entire farm in danger. And you know that it put a lot of strain on every single one of us, not just me."

"I know," I whispered. Hearing him say it out loud made the truth that much more difficult to digest.

"But you know something? Before you went to the city, you weren't fully yourself. I would always catch you looking distracted, like you were living in a memory. I knew you didn't sleep well some nights, because you barely found the energy to make breakfast for the kids. It showed in your face, too, even when you thought you were hiding it. Like you were only smiling to make yourself happy, not because you already were."

My stomach dipped as he dissected the pain I thought I'd successfully hid from sight the past few years. All this time I'd been deceiving myself, he'd witnessed me become a mere shadow of who I was.

"Even though you just got back, I already see a difference. Your eyes are brighter. You stand up straighter. And I saw the way you smiled when the vet told you that Bluebell was okay. I haven't seen you smile like that in years."

Tears pricked my eyelids as he went on. "I finally have you back, Nora. And if everything you went through over the past month helped you move on from the past, then I know it happened for a reason."

I felt my tears reaching a crescendo and knew they would

spill out at any moment. Before he could say anything else, I buried my head in his chest, breathing in the familiar scent of his worn flannel. All the confusion, loneliness, and fear that had been steadily bubbling to the surface during the past month had finally gushed out. But there was something else there too: relief. It wasn't too late. I hadn't whittled away at his final thread of hope in me. I didn't have to waste another second drifting aimlessly through the city, chasing a goal that didn't belong to me anymore.

He rubbed my back and kissed my hair as tears saturated my cheeks, cleansing me of the past and its tangled web of hurts. As I filled my lungs with the smell of him, of *home*, I found inside him the strength I couldn't find in myself. My time in New York had been tenuous at best, constantly teetering on the unsteady foundation it had been built on. And as I found my place in his arms again, I knew I'd let go of one of the few certainties in my life.

When I pulled away, my eyelashes still moist with tears, it was as if all the cold had been sucked out of the winter air. I searched his eyes, which gleamed in spite of the encroaching darkness, and felt a familiar pain worm its way through me. I knew where I'd last seen his eyes smile like that.

That five-minute video on the *Couture* website was the only bridge I had left to cross, the only thing still separating me from the untethered joy I longed to share with my family. Yet it somehow felt insurmountable, even as I sat beside the man who had just gifted me a new beginning.

He frowned and lifted my chin with his thumb. "What's wrong?"

I shook my head. "Nothing. It's just... you looked so happy in that video. The four of you together like that..."

His face grew serious as understanding dawned on him. "I was happy because I got Caleb back. You should have seen the look on his face when the crew showed up. It was like he was a completely different kid."

I sniffed. "But he was just starstruck. It doesn't mean he changed his mind about becoming a farmer."

"It wasn't just the cameras. Before they started filming, the reporter asked me a few questions about the farm as a warmup. And I saw it in his eyes—it was like a light bulb. He looked like he finally understood. Not just what our job means, but why we do it. Why we go out to the fields every morning, no matter what's on our minds. And why it's so important for us to keep up that tradition." He peered into my face, as if searching for something I couldn't see. "Sometimes, when you do the same thing day in and day out, you forget about why you're doing it. That's what happened with Caleb. He needed to remember what our job really means to us to come around to it again."

Caleb's transformation wasn't unlike my own. Long after I'd settled into my new home on the outskirts of Fairlane, I still couldn't shake the feeling that I didn't fit in with the rest of the town. Even though my job was more fulfilling than I'd ever imagined and I was surrounded by more love than I could fathom, reminders of my misfit status were never far away. Sometimes it was the looks I got in the grocery store when I wore a studded leather jacket. Other times, it was the way the cattle seemed to look past me at Tyler, waiting for someone more competent to take care of them.

But *Couture* made me remember why I'd left New York

in the first place. Whether it was the models comparing their skeletal frames or the cutthroat way my coworkers competed against each other, I'd grown more disconnected from my environment as time went on. It wasn't until I started longing for the dusty roads and kind, gentle people of Fairlane that I knew I was longing for home.

Tyler looked at me intently. "And there is no 'four of us.' Jeanette was only here to help out until you came back. But she didn't do your job anywhere near as well as you." A shadow passed over his eyes. "That's why I hated to hear you say on the phone that you weren't a good enough farmer to get through the hard times. With the way you saved Bluebell just now, I hope you know that isn't true. You handled that like any seasoned farmer would."

I smiled at the way he'd read my mind. "Well, I learned from the best."

A chill came over me then, and I crossed my arms against the cold. "We should head back inside now." I glanced behind me at the farmhouse. "I hope the kids are still up. I need to see them."

"They should be." He started to walk with me toward the house. "Come on, let's go before you freeze."

I followed him inside, thinking about everything I wanted to ask the kids about. I longed to know about their goals, their dreams, and even all the little ways they'd changed since I'd last seen them. It had taken me a month away from home to realize that all those little things added up in the long run and that they helped to build the young adults they would one day become.

When I opened the front door, I was greeted by an eerie silence that permeated the house. I stepped quietly into the living room and flipped on a lamp to chase away the shapeless dark. The house looked the same as I'd left it back in January, almost as if the world had hit the pause button once I went to New York. The familiarity enveloped me like a hug when I needed it most, and I let myself savor the feeling as much as I could.

"I don't want to wake them," I said quietly. "They're probably already asleep."

"Mommy!"

I turned my head toward the stairs, where the sound of little feet pattering on the steps lifted my spirits. Bridget appeared at the foot of the stairs and ran over before wrapping me in a suffocating hug. "You came back!"

"I sure did." I held her close, feeling tears spring to my eyes. "I missed you so much."

"Me too." She looked up at me, her eyes wide and eager. "What was it like in New York?"

"It was amazing. I'll tell you all about it tomorrow. You should get some rest now." Just as I leaned down to give her a kiss, I noticed Caleb walking up behind us. I let go of Bridget and enveloped my son into a hug. "Caleb, I missed you so much too."

I expected him to pull away from me, but to my surprise, he stayed right where he was. I clasped the moment like it would fly out of my hands at any second, knowing that times like these were either cherished or forgotten forever.

"Mom?" Caleb said as I took a step back to look at him.

"What is it, sweetie?" I tousled his hair as I tried to read his expression.

His eyes shifted nervously to the floor. "When are you going back to New York?"

I looked into his eyes, biting my lip to stop more tears from breaking free. I found myself thinking back to when the *New York Times* reporter had insinuated that my life back home had grown stagnant and when my mom had assumed I was beginning on a clean slate in the city. Both scars were still tender to the touch, but I knew that was all they were. Scars. Marks of a time that belonged to the past.

If I'd truly been dedicated to my dream of working in fashion, I would've chosen to attend Grant. For so long, I'd let myself believe that I'd turned down my dream school out of fear and that choosing to live on a farm was just my backup plan. But now I knew that I was running toward something, not away from it. The whole time I'd thought I was escaping, I was really coming home.

"I'm not," I said, looking back down at Caleb.

He glanced up at me with a face full of hope, and I felt a wave of relief in knowing I wasn't about to let him down this time.

"I'm not leaving," I said again, just to give the words the certainty they deserved. "I'm here to stay."

Twenty-Six

The sky was an unblemished blue as I took the cows out of the barn to graze on the pasture. The earth had been stripped of its bitter cold over the past few days, and I'd been taking advantage of the unseasonably warm weather by letting the cows spend more time outdoors. I peered over at the sweep of land stretching out in front of me, letting the fresh air brush against my face.

Two weeks after I'd returned home, signs of regrowth were already scattered across the farm. The robotic equipment was up and running again, and the cows had taken a liking to the new milking procedure. The cattle and farm equipment had safely returned to the barn, the filming crew having packed up their bags a long time ago. Even the farm itself boasted a bright-green hue that hadn't existed before, as if all the turmoil it endured in my absence had paved the way for new life.

I wiped my hands on my jeans, drying the beads of sweat that had accumulated over the long day. Seeing my home slowly come back to life was a rewarding process, but I would have been lying if I said the added work of restoration didn't make a grueling day of farming even more draining.

I sighed and glanced over at the cows that roamed freely across the field. I may have been exhausted, but it was a good kind of exhausted. The kind I felt when I knew I was working hard toward something I cared about.

Tyler emerged from the barn and stood beside me, admiring the landscape. "It's days like this that make me love what I do." After a thoughtful moment, he turned to face me. "You don't get days like this in New York, do you?"

I shrugged. "We do, but by the time you get a glimpse of the sky, a skyscraper blocks your view of it." I paused for a second and thought of the constant rush of people on the city streets, always zigzagging from one place to the next. "But the saddest thing is that no one really notices the color of the sky or the way the trees bloom in the spring. Everyone's either glued to their phones or rushing to the closest subway station."

His lips curled into a smile. "You sound just like you did when you first left New York. I guess some things never change."

"That's all right. I like it that way." I rested my head on his shoulder and soaked in the fruits of our labor. "We worked our butts off, didn't we?"

"Sure did. And it's already paying off."

I raised my head to smile at him. "Your dad would be proud."

His eyes twinkled, and I knew we both felt his father's pride as palpably as the soft breeze in the air.

"Mommy, we're out of Froot Loops!" I turned and saw Bridget racing toward us. "Can we get more?"

"What's the magic word?" Tyler prompted her.

"Please!" she exclaimed, as if it were the million-dollar answer on a game show. "Pretty, pretty please!"

I grinned at her unbridled enthusiasm. "Of course I'll go, sweetie. But you should stay and help Daddy feed the cows."

"You're the best!" She wrapped me in a tight hug before darting toward the pasture. "I need to see if Bluebell's okay!" she called back to us as she disappeared into the herd.

My gaze lingered on Bridget while she greeted her favorite cow. After the vet had stopped by to examine her, Bluebell had embarked on the path to recovery sooner than we'd expected. Her infection had nearly cleared up, and she was already showing signs of returning to the vibrant animal she'd once been. Now, as I watched my daughter make her rounds through the herd, I knew Bluebell's revival was one of the many things that had fueled my relief to be home again.

I turned away from the field and glanced at Tyler. "I guess I'm going to Daryl's, then. Do you need anything?"

"I could always use some more coffee," he said after thinking for a moment.

I gave him a teasing smile. "I guess some things never change."

After ducking into the house to grab my bag, I hopped into the truck and started the engine. I'd missed my long drives down I-80, and Bridget's cereal request was the perfect opportunity to indulge in the simple pleasure of a long, scenic road and the right music.

I turned onto the main road and flipped through the radio stations. As John Mellencamp sang his ode to small towns, I turned up the volume and rolled down the window. There was a bit of a chill in the air, but I didn't mind. It felt good to welcome the breeze on my face again, to fill my lungs with the familiar air of home.

As I merged onto the highway, my phone rang next to me. I glanced at it and saw my mom's name on the screen. My forehead creased into a frown as I put the phone on speaker. "Hi, Mom. Is everything okay?"

"I'm doing just fine, Nora. I was calling to ask about you. How's everything going at *Couture*?"

I sucked in a breath. "I'm back home now. I quit *Couture* a couple weeks ago."

I explained everything that had happened, wondering how she would react. I had the uneasy feeling that my decision to return to Fairlane would put us right back to where we started after I ran away from home. As my heart sank, I knew it was only a matter of time until we went our separate ways again.

In the silence that followed, my mind ran wild with all the possibilities of what she would say. I thought I was prepared for anything, which was why her next words threw me off guard. "I'm proud of you, Nora."

I stared at my phone, wondering if the reception was failing again. "But I told you, Celeste isn't including any of my work in the magazine."

"I'm not talking about what you did at *Couture*. I'm talking about how you chose to leave when your job forced you to sacrifice who you are. You found something you believed in, Nora, and you fought for it. That's more important than seeing your name printed in a magazine."

"Thanks, Mom." I tried to hide the emotion threatening to take over my voice. I'd been waiting my entire adult life to hear her say she was proud of me.

"I admit I'll never understand why you chose the life you have now, but I can tell it means a lot to you. It's so refreshing to hear you found something you care about this much. Few people do."

I smiled to myself, thinking about the way I'd saved Bluebell. "Yeah. I guess I am pretty lucky."

"Your brother will be proud too. He was worried you'd veered onto the wrong path. I'm sure he'll be glad to hear you've found your way again."

The memory of my lunch date with Luke floated back to the forefront of my mind. My stomach dipped as I remembered with painful clarity the way he'd accused me of manipulating my past for the magazine. I wondered if it would make a difference if I told him I'd given all that up, that I'd woken up from the lie I'd been living. On any other day, I might not have held out hope, but hearing my mom say the one thing I never thought she would say gave me a reason to have faith.

"I hope you're right."

"Trust me, I am. We all see how far you've come in just a few short weeks."

I peered out over the long road ahead of me and caught myself thinking about the day I left home. A lump formed in my throat as I remembered all the trauma my family had endured after I'd escaped. In the quiet of the truck and the stillness of the empty road, I understood the magnitude of what I'd put everyone through. Maybe it was because I wasn't thinking of myself anymore. I was thinking of Bridget and Caleb, and how there had been an empty space inside me while I'd been apart from them.

"Mom?" I took a deep breath, not even knowing how to begin. "I'm sorry for what I did. For leaving home without looking back. I know you didn't agree with my choices, but...

I shouldn't have just run away like that. I didn't even give us the chance to talk about what I planned to do." My voice was unsteady, but I went on anyway. "I can't imagine how you and Dad felt."

She didn't speak right away, and the silence tightened its grip on me with every passing second. When her voice finally came through the speaker, it was so quiet, I almost didn't hear it. "Fifteen years," she said. "That's how long I waited for you to understand."

My eyes pooled with tears, blurring my view of the road. "I was angry and confused, and I felt like I needed to get away from the city as soon as possible. And I would never change what I did, because I love the life I have now. But what I did to you was wrong. After being away from my own family for so long..." I stopped, unable to find the strength to continue.

"I know, honey. I know." In that moment, I knew I didn't have to say anything more.

As the landscape blurred past me, an idea peeked into the corner of my mind. I hesitated for a moment, then said, "You should come by the farm one day. The kids would love to see you and Dad."

She paused again, and I knew she was just as taken aback by my suggestion as I was. "But Thanksgiving is months away."

"I know. I just thought you'd come visit and see what my workday is like."

"You know what? I'd love that. I'm sure your father would too."

"Great. I'll talk to Tyler about it."

I saw my exit coming up and flipped on my turn signal. "Well, I have to run into the grocery store now. Shopping trips are never quick around here." I turned into the parking lot and glanced at my phone. "Thanks for calling."

"It's nothing, sweetie. Good luck with everything."

I smiled, knowing her words meant more than she thought they did. "Thanks, Mom."

I pulled into a parking spot and grabbed my bag. When the bell above the door chimed to announce my arrival, Kathleen glanced up from the cash register. "Oh, you're back! It's great to see you again, Nora. How was life in the big city?"

"It was great, but I'm glad to be home." I smiled.

"Well, I know what'll make your homecoming even better. Your friend Jeanette told me you were coming back, so I made sure my dad restocked the mocha blend for you. I know you can't go a day without that stuff."

"Thanks, Kathleen." The words barely squeezed past the lump in my throat. All the time I'd spent in New York had almost made me forget about how everyone in this town was always looking out for me.

After picking up a bag of my sweetened coffee, I swiped Tyler's unflavored brand from the shelf. I headed down the cereal aisle to pick up Bridget's Froot Loops and dropped it into my cart. Before I could double-check my shopping list, my phone dinged in my pocket.

I pulled it out and was met with a text from Chloe: *Celeste just approved the layout for the Sep. issue. Enjoy.* Below the message was a row of pictures, each one featuring a different part of the magazine. I studied the first one, which displayed the front cover of the issue. Emblazoned across the center was the heading: "Turning Over a New Leaf: Fashion and Inspiration for a Fresh Start." Beside the words sat a polished shot of Shannon

Reyes, who wore the same infectious smile that had illuminated the office during her visit.

I swiped through the photos, my throat tightening with every missed opportunity that passed me by. After scanning a few ads, I came across the famed masthead. The place where my teenage self had dreamed of having her name plastered at the top for the world to see. I scanned the names I'd gotten to know during my time at *Couture,* purposely avoiding the top of the page. I still couldn't bring myself to look at Vanessa's name nestled under the fashion director title. But as I started to swipe to the next picture, I saw what was actually written underneath the heading: *Stephanie Giordano.*

I stared at the name as if it would vanish the second I tore my eyes away from it. An image of Stephanie sitting across from me at the unveiling event flashed into my mind, her wide eyes and eager smile a mirror image of the young woman I'd once been. I remembered her words to me when we'd met at the reception: *How can you walk away from all this? I know I would kill to be in your place right now.*

I looked up from my phone, feeling a wave of relief wash over me. From the moment I met Stephanie, I'd seen inside of her the person I could've been. Celeste handing her the fashion director role was the closest I'd ever come to giving my younger self the life she'd been too afraid to live. But the biggest relief of all was knowing that the magazine was in good hands. I found myself breathing easier now that I knew someone as determined and passionate as Stephanie would be steering the ship.

I opened my notes app and found the number Stephanie had given me during the reception. I tapped out a text to her congratulating her on the position, while assuring her that I knew she'd had it in her all along. I knew those were the words I would need to hear if I were in my twenties again, when uncertainty and doubt were never far behind me. When even the smallest words of encouragement lifted me and carried me all the way over to the finish line.

As I glanced back down at the masthead, questions floated through my mind. Had Celeste fired Vanessa after she fell short of her expectations? Or had my boss known from the start that she wasn't the right fit for the fashion director position?

I sent a quick text to Chloe, knowing she would give me all the answers I needed. After I sent the message, I returned to the photo reel she'd sent me. My first instinct was to delete all the pictures and put an end to that period of my life. But as I scanned the headings that baited me into reading the full articles, my curiosity got the best of me. Maybe I wasn't a part of *Couture* anymore, but that didn't mean I didn't want to see what direction the magazine was going in.

Without a second thought, I saved every image to my camera roll. Only then did I realize that moving on from something didn't mean pretending it didn't exist. It meant looking it in the eye and staring it down without flinching.

After I paid and walked out of the store, I felt lighter, despite the bags that were weighing me down. I stuffed my groceries into the backseat and slid into the front of the cab. As I pulled out my phone, I saw a response from Chloe sitting at the top of the display: *Call me. There's too much to tell you over text.*

I called her right away. It felt like years had passed since I'd been caught up in the glamorous world of *Couture.* While it was a relief to be five states away from all the office drama, I secretly wondered how everyone had been holding up since I left.

"Where should I begin?" Chloe said when she picked up.

I thought for a moment. "After my dramatic exit would be perfect."

"Well, that's quite the starting point." She paused for effect before speaking again. "I don't think I've ever seen Celeste in a state of shock before, but you managed to pull that off."

"What about after she recovered?"

"Then she went back to being the Celeste we all know and love. Barking orders at everyone all day, turning down our suggestions, all that good stuff. Which brings me to why she chose Stephanie as the new fashion director."

I leaned forward in my seat. "What happened? Did Vanessa turn down the position?"

"Nope, but almost. She lasted maybe three hours before she started crying to Celeste about how *stressful* her job was. How it was destroying her *inner peace.* She hasn't made a peep about not getting promoted since then."

I laughed, imagining Vanessa's face twisting into panic as the usual mob of workers formed outside her door. "Why did Celeste replace me with Stephanie?"

"I heard she found out that Stephanie had all these great ideas for *City Chic,* and she couldn't let one of *Couture*'s biggest competitors have all the glory. So she basically stole Stephanie and brought her over to us. The best part was that Celeste barely had to convince her to leave her old job. That girl looked like she'd been waiting her whole life to sit at the fashion director's desk."

"I'm glad she's there," I said, meaning every word. "When I

met Stephanie at the reception, she seemed like the perfect person to take my place."

"Speaking of which, I give you major props for standing up to Celeste like that. I think we've all secretly wanted to do that at some point."

I smiled to myself as I turned onto the gravel road leading to the farm. After a thoughtful pause, I said, "Sometimes I think she was testing me to see how far I would go. It was like she was waiting for me to figure out that the magazine wasn't right for me and run back to my life at home. She knew my position was temporary, and she was just waiting to see how long I would last."

"Well, I think you did all you could. And don't worry about what Celeste thinks. You quit, but you didn't give up. You were just smart enough to know when it was time to move on."

A sense of calm spread through me as I realized Chloe seemed to understand me more than anyone else at the office had. "Thanks for always having my back, by the way. I think you might be the only one left at *Couture* who hasn't let the job go to their head."

"Same to you. Which is probably why you didn't last very long."

"I'll take that as a compliment," I said with a smile.

I pulled up in front of the barn and shut off the engine. As I looked out at the stretch of land in front of me, I let out a long breath. "I should get going now. Thanks for keeping me posted. And tell me if anything else happens that I should know about."

"Don't worry. I'll be the first to let you know if it does."

I looked around the farm after we said goodbye, knowing

this was just the beginning. There was an entire journey waiting for me once I accepted the fresh start that life was presenting me with.

I stole another glance at the *Couture* cover in my photo library and knew I was ready to start over. And for the first time, I could do it with both feet facing forward.

***

While Bridget was busy demolishing her Froot Loops, I stepped outside to refill the water troughs for the cows. I was halfway to the barn when I spotted Jeanette's car pulling into the driveway. She cut the engine and stepped out of the car. "Hey. Long time, no see."

I gave her a teasing smile. "Miss milking the cows already?"

"Hell no. After what happened to Bluebell, I'm swearing off farming for the rest of my life. How is she, by the way?"

"A lot better. Her infection is pretty much gone. And the other cows will be okay too, thank God."

"That's great to hear. I was so worried I screwed everything up."

"You didn't. If anything, you helped keep the place together while I was gone."

She glanced down at my shoes. "Nice boots."

I grinned. "Hey, just because I left *Couture* doesn't mean I have to give up my favorite brands. I just switch to my old boots if I'm doing any heavy work."

"I like it. Kind of like the best of both worlds."

"Exactly." I noticed the luggage in the backseat of her car and looked up at her. "You're leaving?"

A tranquil expression rested on her face, as if she'd gathered the past in her arms and set it behind her. "You know I never belonged here, Nora. I was just too stubborn to believe it when it was right in front of my face." A weighted sigh escaped her lungs. "Anyway, Derek and I sold the house last week, and we're headed back to New York tonight. I just came by to let you know."

"You're not going back to *Couture*, are you?"

"Back to that soul-sucking fashion factory? No, thank you." A hint of a smile played at the corners of her mouth. "But I did find a few marketing positions that interested me."

My face lit up at the news. "Jeanette, that's perfect. I always pictured you working in marketing. It was how you got so far at *Couture* to begin with."

"Yeah, well, don't get your hopes up. It's possible that my boss will be another Celeste who'll suck all the joy out of my work."

"Don't worry. If you survived Celeste, you can survive anything."

"Ain't that the truth." A thoughtful look passed over her eyes. "I guess we're right back where we started, huh?"

"I guess we are." As I gazed into the distance, I thought about everything I'd gone through during my time in the city, about everything it had taught me. "But, at the same time, we're not. There was so much we didn't know just a few months ago."

"You're right about that. It's funny to think how badly we wanted each other's lives, when really, we were just seeing what we wanted to see." A smirk spread across her face. "I lost track of how many times I'd be cooped up in my office, fantasizing about prancing through your fields and belting out songs from *The Sound of Music*."

The mental image made me burst out laughing. When I caught my breath, I said, "I always pictured you starring in your own fashion show. Like the models in that Barbie computer game we played when we were little."

She threw her head back and laughed like she had as a kid, which made me laugh right along with her. We went on for longer than the joke warranted, as if we were finding refuge from the pain that had stolen our present. As if we were seeking a lit path out of the darkness that we'd been groping our way around for too long.

She looked lighter, happier when our laughter died down. But as a private understanding seemed to descend on her, her face fell right along with it. She drew a line in the dirt with her boot. "This sucks."

I didn't have to ask her what she meant. After more than a decade of awkward, one-worded texts and infinite silences, our friendship was finally on the mend. Yet just as we fell back into the rhythm of our bond, our paths were about to diverge again.

"I'll visit the city more often than you think," I said. "Now that I'm closer with my family, it'll be nice to stop by every now and then."

A smile spread across her face. "That would be great." She jerked her head toward the barn. "Maybe you can even get Country Boy on board."

I laughed. "No way. Every time I bring Tyler to the city for the holidays, he looks like he can't get out of there fast enough."

"Well, I gave it a shot." She opened the door to the driver's seat and turned to me. "I guess this is goodbye, then. But only for now."

"Definitely. For now."

We were quiet as the air grew heavy around us. Then, wordlessly, we wrapped each other in a hug, grasping tightly onto the new growth we'd unearthed from the rubble of our past. Even though the gesture was a sign of a departure, the burgeoning hope inside me told me this ending would give way to newer and better beginnings.

"Safe travels," I said after we'd exchanged our final goodbyes.

She gave a little wave and turned on to the main road, her car shrinking into the horizon with each passing second.

When she was gone, I turned and headed into the farmhouse. Caleb's hunched figure came into view, his eyes glued to what looked like a worksheet. I walked over quietly to see what he was working on.

"Doing some homework?"

He started a little, as if he hadn't noticed me until I'd spoken. "Yeah. Mrs. Wilson told us to make a list of our goals for fifth grade."

"Do you know what yours are?" I sat down beside him and glanced at the sheet of paper. Printed across the page were half-finished sentences that Caleb had to complete, each one encouraging him to put a hazy future into focus. *I want to improve in _____. I want to learn more about _____. I hope to become _____.*

Frowning at the assignment, I couldn't help but think back to my own elementary school days, when the height of my existential contemplation was deciding what color pen to doodle in.

He shrugged. "Not yet."

My eyes lingered on the prompts, thinking about his change of heart in the *Couture* video. "What about this one?" I pointed to the line that followed *I hope to become.* "Do you still want to be a farmer one day?"

He looked directly at me then, his face open and honest. "I think I do. But Jake said he wants to be a doctor, and Michael wants to be a teacher. And maybe I want to be one of those things too. I don't know how to choose."

My heart soared with hope as I smiled at him. "Jake and Michael? Are those your new friends?"

"Yeah. They told the other kids to back off, and they listened because they're sixth graders." He tried not to show it, but I could see the gratitude in his eyes. I suddenly felt the urge to find Jake and Michael and give them a hug for giving me my son back.

"That's great, Caleb. They sound like really nice friends."

He gave me a small smile before returning to his homework. I observed his meditative state, thinking about how there was always a part of him that was lost in another world. At times, I felt that his solemn nature had forced him to grow up too fast, robbing him of the carefree stage of childhood that Bridget still embraced.

"What did your teacher say about the assignment? Did she explain the questions to you?"

He shrugged. "I dunno. She just told us to follow our dreams."

His words struck me, and I flashed back to the young child

I'd once been, telling everyone I knew about my dream of working in fashion. Back then, "follow your dreams" had been a beacon of hope, an excuse to wander down a promising path and see where it led. But now I recognized the danger of setting my sights on a moving target, of directing all my hope toward a goal that could change at any moment.

Life wasn't meant to be set in stone. Sometimes, life surprised you by giving you a loving family and a beautiful home in a town full of people who cared about you. Sometimes, it gave you a barn and a tractor instead of a fashion closet filled with clothes fresh off the runway. And sometimes, it proved that it knew what you wanted better than you did.

I wouldn't have been able to appreciate the way everything had worked out if I'd still been stubbornly pursuing the dream I'd had as a child. I would've been lost in a city I'd outgrown long ago, soothing myself with the false narrative that a job at *Couture* was still everything I ever wanted.

The past was a wasteland that I'd spent months trying to turn into fertile soil, and I only realized it was a futile effort when nothing grew. But now that I was home, I had an endless amount of time to plant the seeds for everything that was to come.

"That's nice, honey," I said carefully. "But you don't need to do that."

Caleb frowned. "Why not?"

"Trust me," I said, looking into the eyes of the man he would someday become. "You already know where you're going."

Acknowledgments

In the spring of 2020, when the world went into lockdown, my family and I fled New York City and sought refuge in the countryside. I found a deep sense of peace and belonging among the open air and verdant landscapes, much like Nora did after moving to Iowa. Her story came to me as I grappled with questions of identity, purpose, and what the true meaning of home is. If it weren't for my invaluable support system, that story wouldn't have evolved into the book you're reading now.

My heartfelt gratitude goes out to my mom and my sister, Christina, who generously read every chapter of my (very) rough draft and helped me shape it into a much more polished second draft. I also want to give a special thanks to my mom for all of her fashion advice that helped bring Nora's *Couture* journey to life. To both my mom and dad, thank you for supporting my art every step of the way and believing in me no matter what.

This book wouldn't have reached its full potential without the help of my editor, Stefanie. Thank you for empowering me to tell my best story and patiently working with me until I was satisfied with the end result. I'm deeply grateful for your insight into farming and the rural Midwest, which allowed me to depict Fairlane in a more authentic light.

Last but not least, thank you to each and every one of my readers. It means the world to me that you're holding my book in your hands right now. I hope it brings you as much joy as it brought me while writing it, and that you leave its pages better than you were before.

Elena Goudelias is a freelance writer and contemporary fiction author. Her work has been featured in *Bricolage,* Fordham University's comparative literature journal. A New Jersey native and current New York resident, she is no stranger to small town or big city life. *Beyond the Horizon* is her first novel.

CPSIA information can be obtained
at www.ICGtesting.com
Printed in the USA
BVHW041903210721
612567BV00014B/476